Lorna Cook is the author o
The Forgotten Village. It wa
recipient of the Romantic Novelists' Associati
Hessayon Award for New Writers as well as the winner of the Katie Fforde Debut Romantic Novel of the Year Award. Lorna lives in coastal South East England with her husband and two daughters.

Also by Lorna Cook

The Forgotten Village
The Forbidden Promise
The Girl from the Island
The Dressmaker's Secret

The Hidden Letters

LORNA COOK

avon.

Published by AVON
A division of HarperCollins*Publishers*
1 London Bridge Street
London SE1 9GF

www.harpercollins.co.uk

HarperCollins*Publishers*
Macken House, 39/40 Mayor Street Upper,
Dublin 1, D01 C9W8, Ireland

A Paperback Original 2023
2
First published in Great Britain by HarperCollins*Publishers* 2023

A catalogue copy of this book is available from the British Library.

ISBN: 978-0-00-852759-4

Typeset in Sabon by Palimpsest Book Production Ltd, Falkirk, Stirlingshire

Printed and Bound in the UK using 100% Renewable Electricity
at CPI Group (UK) Ltd

For Emily & Alice.
And for Socks, who is no longer here.

Oh, all the comrades e'er I had,
They're sorry for my going away,
And all the sweethearts e'er I had,
They'd wish me one more day to stay,
But since it falls unto my lot,
That I should rise and you should not,
I gently rise and softly call,
Good night and joy be with you all.

'The Parting Glass'
Traditional ballad

PART ONE

CHAPTER 1

ISAAC
CORNWALL
BEGINNING OF SUMMER, 1914

It isn't just the speed at which she runs past him that startles him the most, it's the fact she's barefoot, her shoes grasped in her hand, her long, cream, satin evening gown whipping her legs as she moves. From his position by the glasshouse, he watches her until she disappears into the line of trees that separates the garden from the lake. She's fast. Silent. And then she's gone. As she lets the darkness of the tree line engulf her, Isaac blinks, as if woken from a dream or enchantment.

He looks back to the house to see if anyone's following her, if she's being chased in a late-night parlour game that has now detached itself from the house party – a party at which he had just been in attendance – and into the grounds. But the silence that was present in the garden only moments ago has now returned. All is still, as if she had never run past him, as if she had never been there at all.

Isaac inhales on his cigarette, allowing the breeze from the sea to reach him in the recesses of the garden. The smoke from his tobacco forms swirling circles, disappearing as the air takes it up and into the sky. The moonlight that shines into the garden – his garden as he has foolishly come to think of it – and down to the sea far below the cliffs is the only light in this part of the estate. But further up the sloping lawn the lights and sounds of the party drift out onto the stone terrace as a door to the outside opens and closes once again, letting the echoes of piano music briefly escape. Inside, people are singing.

Should he go after her? Just to check. He dislodges that thought, sending it far away on a cloud of smoke. It isn't his place to go running after young women he hardly knows and he shouldn't even be out here at this time of night. But in all the months he's been staying here no one has ever found him in the garden out of hours. No one ever comes. She, only moments ago, hadn't even seen him standing there.

Sometimes he returns to the garden in the late summer evenings to work his mind through his ever-evolving plans for it; to work the soil like a common gardener when no one can see him; and to think, to disappear until the light fades and he can see no more.

This is where he escapes to think, when he *needs* to think, when his day's work has ended and the gardeners under his command have returned home to their families and beds. In the evening he often walks back here from his cottage gifted to him for the duration of his employment and stands just off the stone path on the peripheries of the formal gardens, where the clipped yew and box hedges hold the flowers in so very tightly and then just beyond, ash trees hide the ornamental lake – far out of sight of the house. Here, in this exact position, all around him is quiet, wide and open, the ink-black starry sky so very high above him, provides the breathing space he finds he needs even after a day full of wide open space.

The garden is different at night. The scents of the flowers are different. Evening primrose, jasmine – it all smells better at this time of night as the garden gives up the best of its nocturnal perfume. But he drowns it out regretfully now with his cigarette, inhaling, exhaling and watching the smoke plume and furl skyward.

But he can't relax as the seed of doubt has now planted itself in his mind and grows as rapidly as dandelion. Cordelia, that's her name; he remembers being introduced to her when she arrived back from London a few weeks ago. She's hardly ever been here, at least not while Isaac has. He looks in the direction in which she ran, even though she's out of sight now. Why was she running? And towards the lake?

He bends down, grinds out his cigarette and then stands up with it so no one has to clear up after him, holding the end between his fingers as he toys with ignoring what he's just seen. But he can't. Annoyed at her, annoyed at himself, he pushes away from the glasshouse, the sleeves of his evening shirt a little muddier than they were an hour ago. A minute has passed. Possibly two?

Stalling for time while he thinks, he takes the pullover he keeps on a hook in the potting shed, placing his evening jacket on the hook instead.

Another moment passes and still she's not returned. He's not sure why he expects her to return now but it's a strange thing to do, run into the darkness, run towards the lake.

Now it will bother him all night and into the early hours of the morning when the light hasn't quite penetrated his room but the birds herald the incoming dawn all the same. He'll wake up, if he sleeps at all, and he'll wonder if she's in the lake, that ornate evening dress billowing around her legs, as she lies dead. A cold finger of fear traces its way down the length of his spine and he knows he'll never forgive himself if he ignores that overwhelming feeling that really he should go and check.

He should already have been there by now.

The closer Isaac draws to the tree line, the quicker he moves, picking up pace until he too is running, his feet pounding as the clipped grass gives way to undergrowth and bracken. If he arrives to find her in a lovers' tryst he'll feel such a fool but at least he'll know she's safe. He pictures her just out of reach in the water and hurls himself the last few yards. He just has to know.

When he arrives at the boat jetty only faint ripples move across the water, slow and delicate, shimmering with silvery moonlight. He can't see bubbles of air. If she's gone in, it's happened some time ago when he was dallying by the glasshouse, pondering, wasting precious time.

Has she gone in? Has she fallen in or jumped on purpose? He looks around, wonders if she really did see him earlier or if he imagined her, then wonders if this is a trick at his expense.

Suddenly she surfaces, takes a breath and dives back under again. He's torn between calling out to her and moving away, out of sight, out of whatever this situation is but she's not seen him and now she's back into the depths.

He should leave. And yet he doesn't. Curiosity holds him with both hands and won't let go. Cordelia resurfaces again, hair smothered over her face. She's breathing deeply and lets out a wail of fear and frustration.

She's about to go under again and so he shouts, 'What are you doing?'

She turns suddenly and cries in fright at the sight of him standing there.

And then she rallies. 'He's gone in,' she cries. 'Help me.'

'Who has?' Isaac calls, his attention gripped. He bends down and promptly yanks off his shoes because he knows it doesn't really matter who's gone in there – regardless, Isaac's going in too.

'Clive,' is her simple reply. And then she's gone. Back under.

Clive. Her younger brother. Six if he's a day. How has he gone in? How does she know he's gone in? How can she have seen . . . But she's already under and Isaac reacts, moving swiftly, untying the pullover from around his neck, dropping it on the jetty as he takes a deep breath and dives into the water to find the boy.

Under the surface it's cold, dark and murky; silky pondweed stretches and slow-dances in time with the movement of water. Within seconds he's crossed paths with her. She's spinning almost wildly, pulling her hair from her face and propelling herself forward with pure determination.

Motivated, he swims in the other direction, searching for the boy, covering as much space as possible, heading down, down to the reeds that snake and wave where the sunlight never touches them. It doesn't take him long to reach the bottom, the weeds blurring his vision. His eyes partially adjust and he can only see as far as his arm, as far as his breaststroke will allow him to see at such a short distance. And then his chest constricts as he runs out of air and Isaac forces himself up and resurfaces.

She's nowhere to be seen and neither is the boy. He hopes in that time she's already swum to the surface, expelled dead air from her lungs, inhaled afresh and is trying again. He needs to find the child. He can't worry about her again too – not now. And then a laugh from the edge of the bank stills him. He knew it. He knew he was being played for a fool. He turns, expecting to see her laughing at him. He'll tell her what he thinks of her – to hell with whatever the consequences might be. He blinks water from his eyes, droplets from his lashes, and looks closer through the darkness. The figure laughing at him is short in stature and there's relief in Isaac's voice when he calls out, 'Clive?' If it's not Clive then it's his ghost and he's not sure he believes in them.

Clive laughs. 'Yes. I fooled both of you and I only meant to fool her.'

Some distance away, Cordelia resurfaces briefly, braces herself to go under again.

'Stop!' Isaac yells. 'Stop! Clive's here.'

She turns to look at him and then at her little brother on the bank. She cries with relief, tears freeing themselves and then she swims, choking back her emotions. Isaac swims too and the two of them climb the steep bank into the bracken and the darkness of the low-hanging weeping willow trees that swoop over the edge of the water. She's behind him and he turns back to her, wordlessly holding out his hand and she takes it, allowing him to help her, drag her upwards and away from the water.

Her ivory dress clings to her wet body and he doesn't know where to look or what to say. But he holds her as she climbs, one hand around her waist to help her along the last few feet of the bank.

'You're wet,' Clive says and his simple observation brings them both round.

She pulls at an overhanging branch to swing herself the final few feet towards the boy. Isaac winces. The tree is over two hundred years old or so he estimates. It doesn't need her doing that to it.

'What were you doing?' she shouts to Clive through chattering teeth.

'I told you I'd get you back for spilling hot cocoa all over my *Boy's Own Annual*,' he says, arms folded, smug.

Isaac closes the gap between them.

She screams at the child, her teeth gritted in a mix of cold and rage. 'I told you I didn't mean to. I told you it was an accident. I told you I'd buy you another one.'

Isaac doesn't mean to but he laughs. It slips out. He can't help it. She's twenty, if what he's heard is true. The child is six but it sounds as if the siblings are both still in the nursery arguing. Cordelia spins to look at him and their eyes meet properly for the first time. Isaac stops laughing but the smile is still on his face. It takes her a second and she looks back at Clive. 'You did this on purpose. You tricked me. You scared me.'

'And me,' Isaac mutters.

'Yes,' Clive proudly announces.

Before Isaac knows what's happening Cordelia reaches out and slaps the boy, the sound reverberating in the stillness of the night. The child turns his head automatically, looks away in shame and shock, his gaze connecting with Isaac's in a brief moment of solidarity.

'I thought you were dead! I thought you were dead!' Angry tears streak her still-damp face. She raises her hand again, anger has the better of her.

It reminds Isaac of the time when he was small and he ran out in front of a horse and cart. It was his late father who pulled him out the way and then in sheer relief he hadn't been hurt, gave Isaac the thrashing of his life. He darts forward, behind her and grabs her raised hand to stop her hurting Clive a second time.

'You've made your point,' he says into her ear, not quite realising the implications of what he's done until she lowers her arm and looks at him. She stares at him, dumbfounded. His hand is still on her wrist.

Slowly he unravels his fingers and she looks at the place where his grip had been.

'I'm sorry,' Isaac says quietly. 'I didn't want you to hit him again. Have I hurt you?'

She shakes her head, says stiffly, 'No.' Her brother is temporarily forgotten. 'Thank you,' she says. 'For your intervention.'

'I didn't do anything. The boy was standing there the whole time. Safe. Which is the main thing.'

'Yes,' she says, 'Yes, it is. I don't know what I'd have done if he hadn't been.'

Isaac has no answer. He wants to tell the boy he's an idiot. He wants to tell him that he really could have killed his sister – she could have been tangled in the reeds looking for him. If Isaac hadn't seen her, she'd have been completely alone in there. She could very possibly have drowned. Was she a strong swimmer?

She'd have been good enough for a few minutes more, he thinks. And then . . . he doesn't dare think anymore.

She's still rubbing the place where he'd held her.

'Are you sure I didn't hurt you?' he asks.

Her hand drops to her side and she looks at him. 'I'm sure.'

Neither of them speaks. She has blue eyes. He can see that now. He's never been close enough to see before and whenever she's entered the garden to stroll through since she returned from London, she's never once looked in his direction. Even at the party tonight, before he left early, their paths hadn't crossed. But in this pale moonlight he can see her fully now – this close. Her mouth is partially open and he looks at it, straight teeth behind lips turned pale from cold.

It's Clive who breaks the silence. 'Are you two going to kiss?' he asks, awestruck.

'No, of course not,' she snaps, turning away. 'He's a gardener.'

Isaac tries not to laugh. She does remember who he is then. And then he realises, damningly, that she's played down his job and then had the audacity to use it as a crime.

Then he notices the cold visibly prickling her skin. 'I've got a pullover on the jetty.' He looks down. 'Where are your shoes?'

She nods her head towards the water. 'In there I should imagine. I think I just threw them somewhere as I jumped in.'

Cordelia starts to walk gingerly over the mud and bracken. Isaac attempts to ignore her gasps of wincing pain as long as possible as he too picks his way carefully across the ground close behind her.

Clive trails behind, subdued, the game long since over. Isaac looks at him and offers him a sympathetic smile, putting his hand on Clive's shoulder as they walk. The boy knows he's in for another dose of wrath from his sister when Isaac's no longer nearby to shield him. Clive smiles dejectedly in return and rolls his eyes precociously, forcing Isaac to stifle a chuckle.

Ahead, the girl cries out in pain again as her bare foot finds something sharp. Isaac can stand it no longer.

'Enough of this,' he announces, picking her up in his arms. Without resistance she's almost limp, one arm around his neck. Her breath warms his cheek, the satin dress cold against him. Her fair hair has come down around her shoulders. Somewhere in that lake is probably a hundred of her hairpins gently sinking their way to rest on the soil for all eternity.

She shivers uncontrollably while he's circumnavigating the lake until he reaches the edge of the jetty, placing her on the wooden slats, holding her in case she might faint, although she seems hardier than that. But her teeth chatter and Isaac watches her carefully. Beside her, Clive has the good grace to look sheepish at the result of his own actions. Genuine concern for his sister slips onto his face as he watches her shake with cold.

'I'm sorry,' Clive says quietly, shamefully.

'Why did you do it?' Isaac asks. 'What possessed you?'

'She ruined my copy of *Boy's Own*,' Clive says, less forcefully than he had before.

'So you said,' Isaac replies.

Isaac lifts his pullover from the jetty and rolls it up, placing it over her head and pulling it down over the top of her damp clothes, helping her lift her arms into the sleeves.

'There we go,' he tells her reassuringly. She's unable to reply. Her teeth chatter harder. Isaac watches her carefully.

'It was only supposed to be a trick. She knows I can't swim properly yet. I'm still learning how,' Clive reveals. 'I waited up especially for her,' he continues. 'I told her where I was going and then I ran past her and out the door. She wasn't quick enough to catch me. I knew she wouldn't be. I only meant to scare her . . .' he attempts to justify. 'I didn't think she'd stay in the water for so long.'

There's no time for this. Isaac turns to Cordelia. 'I'm sure I don't need to tell you that you should get out of your wet things as soon as possible. Get your maid to run you a hot bath. I can run ahead to the house and ask her for you.'

'No,' she says as she shakes uncontrollably. She's not even got the words to reprimand her brother again. 'You've been . . . kind enough,' she stutters with cold. 'I can do it.'

'You haven't got any shoes. I can help you back or you can probably walk it all right from here,' he says. 'It's just lawn from here until the house.'

'Yes,' she says although to what, he's not sure. He turns to find his shoes and when he looks back, she's already walking towards the house.

'Will she be all right?' Clive asks. 'I only meant to scare her,' he repeats.

The boy is shame-faced and doesn't wait for Isaac's reply. Instead Clive runs after her, his hand slipping into hers. She clutches her brother's hand tightly as if she's considering the alternative outcome to tonight's events, one in which the boy really had drowned.

Isaac stands for a moment and watches them, ignoring his own shivering, and then decides to follow at a distance. He needs to make sure she really does make it back without issue. He pictures her swooning on the lawn and the boy having to summon help as she lies in wet clothes. She looks and sounds capable enough but his actions tonight will all have been for nothing if she dies of cold now.

Isaac follows them quietly back to the house and watches as Cordelia and her brother choose not to enter through the French doors, by which they'd no doubt shock the party-goers. She has the foresight to keep going, presumably to use the servants' entrance where she'll find her maid, order a hot bath, climb the servants' stairs and none of the guests or family will be any the wiser.

Satisfied, Isaac walks to the edge of the estate and to the cottage he's been loaned for the duration of his time here. He's aware of his cold wet shirt sticking uncomfortably to his skin. Above him the clouds gather together, conspiring with the Cornish sea breeze that smothers the moon. He shivers, his body reminding him that he too has been immersed in cold water. He needs to dry off, warm himself by the hearth, climb into bed. And not think about those blue eyes.

A sliver of moonlight appears, shining down on the lawn. On the ground in front of him something sparkles in the blades of grass. He walks towards it, stoops and picks it up, turning it over in his fingers. It's an ornate diamond hair clip. He watches the object sparkle and dance in the moonlight. It has to be hers.

He turns back and looks at the space by the house where she's disappeared. He won't follow her inside to give it to her now. She'll be long gone up the back stairs, slipping out of his pullover, out of her dress, out of calling distance, out of reach – as she always will be.

Isaac puts the jewellery in his pocket for safekeeping. He'll run it up to the house in the morning, say he found it in the grounds while assessing the landscaping progress. Half of that story is true. There need not be any further elaboration. He doubts very much Clive or Cordelia will tell their parents about the events of tonight. Why would they? It would reflect poorly on both of them, he imagines.

He wonders, after she's dressed will she return to the party? Will she forget about tonight so easily? She should. He's aware he occupies that halfway space between servant and 'one of them', although he's not one of them. Not really. Nor would he ever want to be. He's employed and with that comes a certain level and expectation of enforced distance. A distance he's happy to keep, despite the invitation to show him off, his progress and plans for the grounds at tonight's party.

On those rare occasions when he's reminded he's not one of them, when he enters the servants' hall after the kindly cook offers him something to eat, he hears stories; gossip from the upstairs staff who went to London with the family and returned to Cornwall with tales of Cordelia and her wildness in London. The men she was seen with. The men she wasn't seen with.

He wonders if she'll tell her lady's maid exactly what happened tonight, if Isaac will be mentioned or if his part in tonight's adventure will be conveniently discarded. Now he thinks about it, he hopes very much it's the latter. No good would come of him being mentioned.

To be forgotten entirely would be the best thing of all.

CHAPTER 2

CORDELIA

There is no chance of sleep, in that darkest of hours between night and day. Cordelia sits at her bedroom window and looks out towards the garden. She's still cold, despite the hot bath, despite wrapping herself in her blanket and her nightdress, despite the hot cocoa she's just drunk.

She told her maid, Ada, a fib as the bath was filled, as the salts were added, as she slipped into the heat of the water, scalding against her icy skin, her dress heavy, sopping on the floor.

'A silly game that got out of hand. A dare. I was the only one that went in. Is Father's birthday party still in full flow?'

Ada's frown was unmissable.

It wasn't, in the end, that she wanted to keep Clive from trouble; it was that she wanted to keep that gardener out of it. But why, she didn't know. None of them had done anything wrong. Perhaps when she'd slept on it, it would all make sense.

But at the window, she holds his pullover in her hands. It's dry now, all trace of the dampness from her shoulders shaken from it. She draped it in front of the fire and then dismissed her maid, saying that she could bathe and get herself into bed quite easily, 'but maybe another hot cocoa first?'

The cup sits empty on her dressing table, among her ivory brushes and what remains of her hairpins. The moon focuses its energy on the North Cornish coast, the fishing village of Pencallick, from which the house gets its name, is a short walk and where most of the outdoor staff travel in from, and in the distance the sea.

But closer, Cordelia can just about make out the tops of the ash trees that give way to the lake. Of course, he's not still there, down by the water. Not now. Why would he be? It's been hours. But she finds her eyes drawn to that spot, all the same.

Why was he there in the middle of the night, in the dark? Why wasn't he at the party? She'd not seen him slip out. But then, she reasons, she'd not been looking especially hard, or at all. Too busy with her brother Edwin's friends from university, due to return to their various homes tomorrow. Even now they're still revelling. They've left the French doors open and the few of them still awake at this hour are singing something by Irving Berlin. She yawns. She must try to rise when Ada brings her morning cup of tea, and wave the men off for the early train. Boys really, not quite men. Not yet.

She looks at her wrist where his fingers had held her. He'd not bruised or marked her. And she'd been honest when she'd told him he hadn't even hurt her. Nor had he intended to, she thinks. But she looks at the place where his hand had been all the same.

In the distance, a sliver of orange brightens the depths of the sky, a low coronet of gold to crown the Cornish horizon. Day is breaking. Soon a housemaid will slip quietly in to rebuild the fire and tea will be brought soon after, signalling silently that she must rise, dress for the day.

The same as she did yesterday.

The same as she will do tomorrow.

And every single day after that.

Cordelia decides not to tell anyone what happened at the lake, or the silly events that led up to it. She and Clive agreed it would not do to storm through the party, dripping wet with tales of japes and potential drownings. After having been caught in a tryst with the second son of an earl in the palm house during a ball, Cordelia needs to rebuild her reputation. One should only be considered *so* reckless in the space of a long summer.

She has bribed Clive for his silence with promises of using her allowance to send off to Fortnum & Mason for his favourite confectionery.

But now as the sun rises, glint by dazzling glint, she wonders how it is she is bribing Clive for his silence when it was he who'd started all the trouble off in the first place.

'Where did you creep off to during the party?'

Cordelia looks up from her breakfast in the dining room as her brother Edwin, older by nearly a year, enters the room. Until his arrival, she's been dining alone at the large table under the watchful gaze of the Duke of Wellington whose portrait graces the wall in oversized glory.

'You were missed,' Edwin continues, holding on to

the back of a walnut Chippendale dining chair and looking at her across the table.

Cordelia shakes her head, holds his gaze. 'Nowhere. Bed.' A slip of a fib. She had, at least, gone to bed eventually, although sleep had evaded her and her eyes now sting with tiredness. They're red. She can feel it.

'Snuck off?' Edwin queries.

'Not so as you'd notice.'

'I noticed,' he replies warmly and then lets it drop.

'Where are your friends?' Cordelia asks.

'They've gone,' Edwin says eyeing up the breakfast spread out in silver dishes on the sideboard. He begins lifting the lids, nosing inside. 'Ate in their rooms, or not at all. Then caught the early train. I don't even think Mungo went to sleep.'

'Which one was he?'

'The short one.'

'Oh yes.' She really must make more effort to learn people's names.

'It's going to be hot later today,' Edwin points out. 'Fancy a game of tennis before lunch while it's still a bit cooler?'

'Maybe,' she replies. 'How do you have the energy after last night? I might sleep a little first,' she says with a yawn. 'Or take a walk in the garden.'

'The new bit or the old bit?'

'The bit that's finished,' she replies.

'I'm pleased they installed the tennis court in time for this glorious weather,' Edwin continues. 'That was good timing.'

'Yes, it was. And the croquet lawn.' She had no idea what other plans were being put into practice outside and she'd been paying such little attention to the upheaval in the garden, her eyes glazing over when Father had shown her the plans for endless parkland, only lighting up at the formal gardens and the plans for abundant flowers.

But the tennis courts had been a pleasant surprise when they'd been unveiled. The Palladian-style Pencallick House had been in the family since Cordelia's grandfather had purchased it in 1835 but it had been built at some point in the 1700s. During the change in ownership, the formal gardens had never truly been 'formalised', as her father had put it. Now bits of it were new and bits of it were old and it seemed an arduous and, dare she say it, boring task to be in charge of.

Hence what that man was here to do: not only plan it and draw it all up, which she assumed had been done, but he actually seemed to be digging most of it himself too, with help from the various gardeners and apprentices. That was what had swung it for her father probably, having a man on site who wasn't too proud to carry out the hard tasks.

Also, presumably, he was cheap.

'You enjoy your garden walk then,' Edwin says, stretching like a cat before helping himself to eggs from the sideboard. He picks up some bread. Flicks it. 'Toast's cold. Any more coming do you know?'

'Probably,' she replies absently. 'Mother having a tray in her room?'

Edwin shrugs. 'Always.'

'No sign of Father?'

Her older brother turns from the sideboard and wiggles his hand near his mouth as a sign of too much drink – a gesture that Father might still be sleeping off the effects of the party. Cordelia laughs and pushes her plate away. For some reason she can't eat.

CHAPTER 3

ISAAC

He rises early, as usual. The cottage isn't big but it has two small bedrooms upstairs, in one of which his brother David, younger by eighteen months, sleeps. David pretends he's a keen and able landscaper and while he's good at the jobs he's tasked with, Isaac knows his heart isn't in it. But what else is David going to do? One day he'll find his calling and until then Isaac could do with the help.

'Get up,' he calls to David, knocking on his brother's door and entering when no reply is issued. 'You'll miss breakfast.'

A fundamental perk of employment is that they're given breakfast in the servants' hall – at least, when a house is already staffed and built. At the last gardens he'd landscaped, the house had been finished but remained eerily quiet, awaiting the arrival of both servants and masters.

'Not hungry,' David says groggily, turning in his state of sleepiness.

'If you were anyone else, I would fire you, because of your lateness.'

'Never,' David rally cries, punching his fist in the air. 'You love me far too much and besides, I'll be on site on time, shovel in hand, don't you worry.'

Isaac ignores this ridiculous comment. 'Can I borrow this?' He withdraws a pullover.

'Where's your one?'

'I lost it,' he says immediately. 'If I told you how, you'd never believe me.'

'Fair enough.' David rolls back over, closes his eyes. 'It's going to be hot today. You won't need it.'

But Isaac's already gone. From the bottom of the stairs he calls to David, 'Get up.' And then he leaves the cottage.

When he'd returned to their shared cottage last night, Isaac had found himself alone. He'd drawn himself a bath from the tap outside, heating the water and bathing in the tin tub while the flames crept up the chimney, and waited for the heat of both the fire and the water to withdraw the chill of the lake from his bones.

David had stumbled through the door an hour or two later, returned from the Fox and Moon public house, only a little intoxicated.

'What's that?' David had asked last night, ignoring Isaac wallowing in the tin tub. He'd seen the sparkle of the diamonds as the hair jewellery sat, safely, on the scrubbed kitchen table, placed there when Isaac had stripped his wet clothes from his body and hung them near the fire to dry.

'Nothing,' he'd said instinctively. 'I found it. It's one of theirs.' He gestured his head towards Pencallick House and then resumed soaking himself.

'Of course it's one of theirs,' David had scoffed. 'It's hardly yours, is it?' He'd stumbled over, picked it up and whistled at it with wide eyes. 'Mother used to have something very like this, do you remember? What do you think it costs?' he'd asked.

'I don't know,' Isaac had replied.

David had replaced it on the table, turning to open the doorway that led upstairs. 'I'll bet whoever owns it doesn't even know it's gone,' he'd called over his shoulder.

Isaac sat back in the bath, watching the steam rise from his arms as he'd rested them on either side of the tin bath. He didn't like to say he'd been thinking the same thing himself.

He'd found his gaze drawn to the item, looked at it sparkling in the firelight and then took it with him upstairs, placing it behind a book on his shelf for safekeeping. He'd meant to put it in his pocket and take it with him today but he'd forgotten it. He curses himself that he's not remembered to bring it as he walks across the parkland.

The way she'd spoken to him last night made it entirely obvious she considered him less than her. The thought makes him smile, laugh almost. Isaac is used to it, the divide is stark between those who own land and those who work it. Even if Isaac's education rivals hers – probably exceeds it, and his life experience too – them and us is just the way it is. Perhaps he should have chosen a profession that didn't involve holding a spade every now and again. He might look like one of them, he might sound like one of them, but they all considered him something else entirely.

CHAPTER 4

CORDELIA

On her walk she stumbles across him by accident in the newly constructed walled garden. There's still one wall left to be built on the far side and the gates have yet to be hung in the brick arch. She doesn't know whether to turn back or continue. Cowardice or bravery? She plumps for bravery and makes her way over to him.

He's on his knees and she watches him put a small tomato into his mouth, the action shocking her into pausing. And then she tries to forget she's just seen him eating the produce. 'Hello,' she says as she stops behind him. He turns abruptly, surprise evident.

'Hello,' he replies confidently, rising and looking at her. The sun is already focusing its intensity onto them and it isn't even late in the morning. He wipes his brow with the back of his arm, his movements unselfconscious. 'I found your ornament,' he begins.

'Ornament?' She's thrown off track at this.

He gestures to her fair hair. 'The diamonds.'

Instinctively she touches her hair, looks blank and then remembers what she was wearing last night. 'Did you?' she asks in wonder. 'Where?'

'In the grounds. Last night. I didn't bring it with me today. I forgot. I'm sorry. I'll bring it tomorrow, or later today if you're desperate for it.'

She gives him a quizzical look. 'I'm not desperate for a piece of jewellery. I didn't even realise it had fallen from my hair, neither did my maid. It was so late when I got in. And I was a little bit distracted.'

He offers no comment, just glances away from her as one of the younger apprentice gardeners appears, heading towards Isaac, clearly with a question. The boy thinks better of it on seeing her and turns the way he came. She watches as Isaac looks back to her with a frown on his face.

'Thank you,' she says. 'For last night. For trying to help.'

He looks down at the tomatoes as if he wants to get on with eating them and Cordelia stifles a laugh. Or perhaps it's because he's having trouble holding her gaze today, when he didn't seem to have a problem with it yesterday.

'I'm just glad the boy was safe,' Isaac says.

And then he smiles, as if to himself.

'Why are you smiling?' she asks.

He glances back at her. 'I don't think he'll do that again anytime soon.'

'Let's hope not,' she says knowingly. 'I didn't tell anyone and I don't think Clive will and I'd appreciate it if you wouldn't either.' She rushes out the words. 'It's complicated, I can't explain it but . . . well, it wouldn't do, really if people knew Clive and I had been in a silly spat and it had ended with me being in the lake in the middle of the night with a . . .' She stops herself just in time.

'A . . .?' Isaac queries his tone knowing. She can't tell if he's teasing her or not.

'Gardener. Landscaper. Whatever it is you are,' she says dismissively.

'I'm an architectural landscaper,' he replies.

'Yes. That,' she says in a hurry. And then, 'What are you doing? Other than eating the tomatoes,' she asks conversationally, looking at the vibrant, red fruit.

He smiles. 'Oh you saw that, did you? I'm pinching the side shoots from between the leaves.'

'Is that your job?'

'No,' he says. 'But I'm here and wondering where the bricklayer's got to. Thought I'd take a look at the vegetable beds while I'm at it and help out with what's actually a very quick task.'

'Do you know what you're doing?' she asks.

He laughs, far too loudly for her liking. It seemed a sensible question. 'With the vegetables or in general?'

He's teasing her. She knows he is. 'With the vegetables. With the . . . whatever it was you said, the pinching.'

'Yes,' he says. Is it her imagination or does he look a bit bored?

'May I ask why you're pinching the side shoots. What does it do?' She surprises herself by being interested in this. She'll only wonder why for the rest of the day if she doesn't find out now and she can't be bothered to go and look it up in a book.

'Pinching the side shoots between the leaves, allows these newly planted out tomatoes to grow one main stem so all the energy can be focused on that,' he says pointing to the healthy row of scarlet fruit.

She wants to ask, 'Why,' again but instead she replies, 'Oh.' She wasn't quite sure what he meant by all of that. 'Do you enjoy it?'

He frowns again. Cordelia's losing count of how often he does this. 'Yes.'

'You're not just doing it because you have to?'

'I don't have to,' he reminds her, the frown still in place.

'No, that's right.' He's put her on the back foot. How has he done that so swiftly? She knew she should have plumped for cowardice and kept walking.

His frown evens out and his eyebrows rise instead. She feels silly now, steps from one foot to the other.

'I mean . . .' she starts.

'I know what you mean,' he says, saving her. 'I do enjoy it, yes, bringing new life to something, tending the garden, encouraging growth. I've always enjoyed it. I've done it my whole life. And once you've learned how to do something, it's hard to simply forget it. Your father handed over most of the gardening team to help with landscaping and I can see they're thinly stretched. So, I may as well help where I can.'

'Why?'

'Why did he hand them over to me or why are they thinly stretched or why am I helping?'

She blinks, caught inside a world of confusion and it's all of her own doing.

'Cost effectiveness is probably the answer to all of those questions,' he says.

I didn't actually ask you any of those questions, she wants to reply.

'I'll bring your jewellery back tomorrow.' He brings their conversation to a close. 'It's currently safe behind a book in my bedroom.'

Cordelia wonders what sort of book her diamonds are behind. And what his bedroom might look like. And where is he staying? Is he on the estate or in the village?

'Thank you,' she says and then she realises that he's dismissed her. She turns to leave, unsure how the conversation had ended quite like that, unsure how the entire conversation had not gone the way she'd envisaged at all.

CHAPTER 5

ISAAC

At the end of his working day he's dripping with sweat, his clothes soaked. He doesn't know why but after Mr Carr-Lyon's daughter chanced upon him in the garden he found his energy had grown. Their conversation had been incredibly odd. He swirls it around in his mind as he would do ice in a glass. He lifts the fork to rotate some hardened soil, baked by the summer sun. He loves this, the menial jobs that look like nothing but do so much, the tiniest thing having so much effect.

His energy swells and forces an exit path through his hands as he works harder and harder, his hands moving faster and faster over the ground, digging until he thinks he must look half mad.

'Good man,' Gilbert, the sixty-year-old head gardener says in his warm West Country burr when he's seen what Isaac has done in the kitchen garden. 'That took you no time at all and saved me the job. I have to say, you're quite a surprise, mucking in like this. When Mr Carr-Lyon introduced you and you showed me your plans, you all done up in that suit and with that accent, I didn't think a few months later I'd catch you out here with us, doing most of the graft yourself.'

Isaac straightens his back out after a day's labour. 'I love it. My mother was an avid gardener and so I learned from her, although the grounds weren't a patch on this. I got a bit of a knack for it. And then landscaping and planning how to make things better came naturally. Assessing what was needed to make grounds and gardens look better, function better. Learning how to do that seemed like the next natural step. But the basics are built in, aren't they – once you've got a taste for it?' he reasons.

Gilbert agrees. 'I suppose they are, yes. I've never done anything else. Started as a gardener's apprentice at an estate near Polperro. I've lived and breathed it. The soil. The sea.' He sniffs the Cornish air. 'No better job,' he says proudly.

Isaac nods his agreement, doing as Gilbert does and inhaling the North Atlantic air deep into his lungs, feeling it land deeply. 'And it doesn't really do to tell people what to do and not actually understand the work you're asking of them,' he says.

Gilbert gives a knowing smile. 'There is that too. But really, you're out here putting your back into it because you enjoy it.'

Isaac laughs. 'That's probably the nub of it yes.'

He's been here too long, enjoying himself when really he should be down by the lake assessing the opportunity to extend it.

'I'm glad I helped. I do appreciate you and the outdoor staff aren't able to keep up with the amount of work now there's all this out here to contend with. And I am sorry I wasn't able to hire any extra hands.'

'All the work will be worth it,' Gilbert says. 'In the end, I'm sure. The place needed brightening up a bit.'

'I'm pleased you agree. Hopefully I'll leave here and the gardens and grounds will be easier for you to manage, now we've closed the gap between the formal gardens and the kitchen garden, brought the hot house out of disrepair and added the new conservatory and, of course, the heating system. Hopefully it'll all make more sense structurally and the overall layout will be more pleasing to the eye, with more exciting things to grow and harvest. You should be able to get some tropical fruit growing successfully all year round before long. If you wanted to, of course.' Isaac's aware he's stepping on toes.

Gilbert smiles. 'Tropical fruit. Whatever next.'

Isaac smiles in return and rubs dried mud from his forearm.

'Go and clean yourself up,' Gilbert says. 'You're caked in mud. And while they like to know we're busy out here with the soil they don't want to come upon us looking as if we've bathed in the stuff.'

Isaac laughs and turns his face up to the hot sun. 'Do you know? I think I might.'

He heads down towards the lake, appraising the tall dividing ash trees that hide the lake from view of the house. Come winter he has plans to fell them, open up the view, when the leaves are fallen and the hot unstable ground is a thing of memory. He's already planned to plant others elsewhere in recompense.

No one ever goes to the lake, other than Isaac when he's sure no one's around. Other than that odd moment last night that he now can't get out of his head. Although why is beyond him. Come to think of it, no one from the house ever really goes down to the cove either. The house has its own path to an inlet, a sheltered pale yellow sandy bay where the Atlantic swell and temperamental surf never reaches. He's not sure he has time to get down there and back by the time the bell rings for the servants' early supper, so the lake it is.

With the sun streaming down, warming his skin he cools off with a fast dip. Keeping a watchful eye on the tree line in case someone from the house should appear, he swims from one side of the bank to the other, disturbing the still water, watching it ripple and undulate around him. This isn't quite what Gilbert means by cleaning off, he's sure. But Isaac's done it now. And then he climbs out, picking his clothes up one by one, letting the warm dry fabric dampen slightly against his skin as he dresses behind a tree, out of sight. It's as he's doing this that he sees something almost white in the distance, nestled in the reeds by the side of the bank. He walks towards it and picks it up; it's one of her shoes. Ivory to match her dress, a low block heel, pointed. He casts around quickly, wondering if the other one might be nearby. It's not. He's been here longer than he should. But he makes a noise from the back of his throat – frustration at what he's about to do as he hastily undresses – then dives back into the water, covering as much of the lake as he can. It's on his fourth or fifth dive back under that he catches sight of the other satin slipper resting at the bottom of the shallows towards the jetty. He pictures her entering the water without care for her shoes, running and diving from the end of the jetty. He missed that spectacle.

Silently, he congratulates himself on having located something else of hers that was lost. There's a carelessness to her that seems completely at odds with how uptight she was when she chanced upon him in the garden today. It occurs to him she might not have chanced upon him at all. She might have come looking for him. And then he laughs at his own ridiculous vanity.

CHAPTER 6

CORDELIA

The next day she sends off for the chocolates for Clive as she knew she must if he is to maintain his silence and, knowing Mr Isaac Leigh is bringing her diamonds – she's asked his name now of Ada, her lady's maid – Cordelia will make the effort to find him today to get them back before they are missed more widely.

She knows all about him now. She knows he's twenty-four, that his father was some sort of university professor. She knows now that his brother accompanies him on these sorts of big commissions, is called David and is younger. A bit of a 'Jack the lad', always flirting with the kitchen maids when the outdoor staff joins the household staff for their meals.

Ada hasn't offered too much information about Isaac though and Cordelia has grown frustrated at the lack of detail, pushing gently to find out what he's like, what kind of man he is. Ada is too focused on David.

Cordelia wonders if Mr Leigh's inability to engage in a meaningful conversation is because he might not be particularly intelligent. This thought dances its way across her mind like an errant sprite. But as he's a professor's son, she doubts that very much. Which begs the question as to whether he is just a bit sullen and moody.

At the lake the other night when he'd come to help, he'd been completely different. Or had she imagined that? Maybe he'd been sullen at the lake too. Although she'd caught him stifling a laugh at something Clive had done. He probably thought she hadn't seen. But she had.

'Maybe he's just a bit shy around you,' Ada tells her when she probes. 'He's quite chatty in the kitchen when he pops in. All the kitchen maids have got the eye for him though.'

'Have they? Not for the brother, the Jack the lad?' Cordelia prompts, eager to hear more of the Mr Leigh from last night.

'For both of them really,' Ada says after a moment's thought. 'Nice to have fresh faces, although they've already been here a few months. But then we're not exactly spoilt for choice with handsome men down there,' she says indiscreetly. 'All the handsome ones are in the garden or the stables all day long,' Ada says longingly.

Cordelia laughs at that. 'We must make the effort to hire some more attractive footmen in that case.'

'Doubt you'll get the chance,' Ada says, curling Cordelia's long fair hair up and into place with a pin.

'What do you mean?' Cordelia asks.

'There's talk of a war coming. It's been spoken of in the servants' hall. Mr Richards tries to quash our chat about Serbia and the Archduke being shot but the butcher's boy who delivered today says it's coming. Won't all the men be sent there? If there's a war? That's what the butcher's boy says.'

'Oh that,' Cordelia says dismissively. 'The butcher's boy needs to keep his opinions to himself. Father says it won't happen, or if it does it won't affect us. We won't go to war for some duke in Serbia or Austria or wherever it was.'

Ada finishes curling Cordelia's hair into place and inserts the final pin. 'I'm not sure I know enough about it,' she says.

Cordelia opts for honesty as she appraises Ada's handiwork in the mirror. 'I'm not sure I do either.'

CHAPTER 7

ISAAC

He's in the kitchen garden again when she appears, examining a pile of bricks as the wall undergoes construction. The other gardeners are in there too and when he sees her coming he discreetly moves away. He knows why she's here.

'I brought them in my satchel,' he says when they are some distance apart from the others.

'Them?'

'I found your shoes too.'

She laughs. 'You found my shoes? But they were in the lake. Weren't they?'

'They were.' He offers no further information.

'How did you—'

'Mr Leigh?' The head gardener turns through the doorway of the walled garden and then catches sight of Cordelia. He doffs his cap to her.

'My apologies, Miss Cordelia,' Gilbert says.

'It's quite all right. How are you . . .?' she grasps for his name and Isaac saves her, whispering, 'Gilbert.'

'Gilbert,' Cordelia says.

The head gardener looks surprised that she knows his name. 'Very well thank you, Miss. And yourself?'

'Perfectly well. The weather is glorious again today and I was just discussing with Mr Leigh here how the flowers are looking beautiful and how wonderful a job you are all doing.' She sounds imperious. She turns back to Isaac. 'The flowers in the churchyard look especially fine at this time of year also. Wild,' she grasps for a word that might suit. 'Especially,' she says to Isaac quietly, 'at around seven o'clock.'

She gives him a pointed look and then, 'Well, I'll wish you both a good day.'

She exits the walled garden through the arch. Isaac watches her retreat, wondering if he's read the situation correctly – if she's just engineered a meeting in a churchyard with him, because that's what he assumes that was all about. And then he looks back to the head gardener who narrows his eyes and gives Isaac a look, the meaning of which he can't work out.

Isaac arrives at Pencallick Church at the appointed time – in between the supper he ate in the servants' hall at six and the upstairs dinner at eight. Her items are in his satchel. He's opened it once or twice during the day to look at them, telling himself he's just checking they are still within.

If meeting her here isn't what she means at all then at least there's no one around for him to feel a complete fool in front of. It's quiet, the song thrushes in the branches above are the only sound. The church is the last building before the village gives way to tenant farmland and estate grounds on one side and then on the far side of the village, the small harbour gives way to the bright blue sea. On Sundays the church is crowded and the vicar puts up a good show, spouting rhetoric that Isaac's own father would have argued vehemently against but Isaac only attends out of duty as it's expected of someone in his position to attend church on Sunday, be introduced to people. Perhaps he'll gain new commissions from neighbouring big houses if word gets around of who he is and why he's here. Today he spies wildflowers – sweet-smelling honeysuckle, purple-crowned knapweed and delicate scented chamomile – pulling them from near the hedge on his way and placing them on a grave. It's that of a child, no one he knows, someone from fifty or so years ago but he noticed it a few weeks ago and has remembered reading on the stone that today is the anniversary of their death so it feels like the right thing to do, fitting to place flowers on a child's grave.

He stands for a few moments and looks at the headstone; just standing in a moment of stillness, contemplation. He wonders what it would be like to have a child, to lose a child. It must be the worst thing in the world.

He breathes in, out, turns to look at the building. Architecturally, Isaac likes the church, if not what happens inside. He likes the building, likes the words on the war memorial plaque from the Boer War. When he learned to read and had run out of his own suitable books at home in Cambridgeshire, their nearest church was the one place he could come and always know there'd be something to read. He read all the graves in turn, all the plaques on the wall inside the church.

And when he'd run out of graves and tombs to read,

he'd found his way to Father's rather dry philosophy tomes and Mother's own gardening books and that's what had set him on his path. Perhaps if he'd have been gifted a few *Boy's Own Papers* he might not have become an architectural landscaper. He might have been an explorer instead. He laughs, thinking about this. No, probably not.

Isaac looks up at the clock on the church tower as a bell ringer diligently strikes the hour with a rhythmic peal of 'Oranges and Lemons'. The day isn't quite chilly but the sun is making its descent now in the evening hour, the staggering heat has long since diminished. And then it's ten minutes past and the bell ringers give him a cheery salutation as they make their way out of the church, through the side gate and down towards the village. Now Isaac knows he's misunderstood her meaning. He picks up his satchel and makes to leave and then he sees her as she walks through the main lych-gate, closing it behind her.

'Hello,' she says as she approaches him.

'Miss Carr-Lyon,' he says. And then he braves, 'Fancy meeting you here.'

She has the grace to laugh suddenly and it completely changes her face. 'Quite,' she says teasingly. And then genuinely, 'Thank you for coming. I wasn't sure you would understand my meaning.'

'I did.'

'I can see that. I thought it was safer if you gave my many things to me away from prying eyes.'

'So you chose a public place in the village?' he asks casting his eye around, although there's no one about. He didn't mean to sound impertinent. But somehow he can't stop.

'I'm not sure I thought it through too carefully,' Cordelia confesses. 'Perhaps we should walk round to the other side of the church. I hope you don't think I'm being silly,' she volunteers as they walk together towards the shaded part, out of sight.

'But really if you're seen giving me items of clothing back – the diamond hairpiece is bad enough but a pair of shoes as well . . . You can see how it would look. As if I'd left them with you at some point.'

He nods, looking down at her as he walks. She's a head height smaller than him and he's looking at her hair rather than her face. She moves away a bit and now he can see her properly. Meanwhile she's said all this without a hint of embarrassment at what she's just insinuated people might think they'd been up to. Quite thoughtless really, putting that sort of thing in his mind. Or purposeful. He ponders that for a moment.

'I can see what people might think,' he says as they reach the side of the building, hidden from sight.

'No one ever believes the innocent explanation,' she clarifies.

'I wouldn't know,' he says as she turns towards him. 'I tend not to get embroiled in gossip.'

'Saint Isaac?' she offers.

His eyebrows flick upwards and his lips part in shock.

'I'm sorry,' she says. 'That was rude of me.'

'I didn't think you knew my name,' he says, recovering.

'I asked,' she confesses. 'I know all about you now.'

His eyebrows refuse to lower. 'Do you?' he questions. 'What do you know?'

'Apparently you and your brother are the kitchen maids' dream.'

It's his turn to laugh loudly.

'I've surprised you.'

'Yes,' he says, still laughing. 'I wasn't expecting that. The kitchen maids' dream. Not all of them surely.'

'Some of them. Housemaids too, I shouldn't wonder. Or was it the housemaids that Ada told me about and not the kitchen maids? I can't remember now. Sorry.'

He chuckles.

'Now you're embroiled in gossip,' she tells him sagely. 'See how easy that was.'

'Hmm,' he says slowly and those blue eyes, smiling, laughing stun him again. He has to draw his gaze away and instead looks at her mouth, slightly parted, still smiling. That's not the right place to look either. 'Would you like your things back?' he offers. He needs to get out of here, keep his distance.

'Yes please. Or else I'll only have to conjure another way for us to meet so we may as well do it now.'

'Another way for us to meet?' he echoes her words in confusion. Her presence here is now making him dumb. He just feels stupid. As he should, he thinks.

He opens his satchel and hands her back her shoes. The ivory satin is water-marked but she says she can fix that easily enough or rather Ada can probably have a try.

'What will you tell her about why they got wet?' he questions.

'I'm sure I'll think of something.'

'I'm sure you will,' he says, not unkindly.

'What would you have done if Clive had drowned? Or I?'

'I'd have tried to save you.'

'How?' she asks.

'It was in a newspaper a few years ago. An advertisement for a contraption that covers your nose and mouth, pumps air into the lungs. A Pulmotor, although I'm not sure who would ever purchase such a thing.'

'Do you have one?'

He laughs. 'No.'

'Well then,' she says. 'It's rather the end, isn't it?'

'I was going to go on to say . . . I suppose you just do the same thing, cover the nose and breathe into the mouth.'

'Yes, I suppose you could,' she says thoughtfully. 'I wonder if that would actually work.'

'I hope never to have to find out.' He reaches for the diamond piece, which he's wrapped in a clean handkerchief and unwraps for her now.

'Thank you,' she says. 'Awful really, that I didn't even know it had gone. I'm sure when the items were due to go back to the bank in London that someone would have noticed.'

'Let's hope so,' Isaac says. 'Do you . . .'

'Do I . . .?'

'Have something of mine?' he hints.

She shakes her head. 'No.'

'No?' he dares.

'What would I have of yours?' She sounds genuine enough.

'My pullover?' She's probably thrown it to her maid, instructing her to use it for rags.

'Oh . . . that.' She thinks, then says slowly, 'I don't know where that is, I'm afraid.'

His eyebrows lift again.

'I'm so sorry,' she says.

He just nods. 'Right.'

'I think I might have put it in a pile for the laundry and then of course . . . it's not any of ours, is it? So the servants who do that won't know who it belongs to.'

The servants who do that. She doesn't have a clue who cleans her garments.

'I didn't think of that at the time,' she continues. 'Do you have more?'

He's slow to respond, and wants to reprimand but instead says, 'I do. One more.'

'Yes, I thought you must have. I saw one folded up next to you when you were digging.'

'That's my brother's. I borrowed it,' he says pointlessly.

'Oh. I . . . assumed you wouldn't miss the one you gave me.'

He offers no reply to this.

'Whose grave were you putting flowers on just now?'

'No one's,' he says. And then catches how rude that sounds. 'A child's. I didn't know them. Just seemed fitting to place some wildflowers on a grave when the date of death is fifty years ago today.' How had she seen that? Had she been watching him for a while before she entered the churchyard?

There's a slow silence between them and then she replies. 'My father speaks very highly of your work.'

He says, 'I should hope so too,' and then catches himself. He's never normally this rude to people. 'I'm pleased he's happy with the results so far.'

A horse and cart passes on the road nearby and they both turn to look until it disappears. Neither of them moves. Perhaps she's not so bothered if they're discovered here together after all.

'Do you know,' she continues, and he refocuses on her. 'I didn't know you had been the one to draw up the plans, to design everything. I just assumed you were some sort of gardener.'

'I am some sort of gardener.'

'No, you're quite a senior one,' she explains. 'With your own company.'

'Does that make a difference?' He knows exactly what she's trying to say, that he's worth talking to now, just that little bit more than if he'd been some sort of journeyman gardener, which he is really, just with an accent similar to hers.

But he's going to push her on this, this snobbery. Make her confess to it. It riles him that he finds her remarkably attractive, on the surface; dig a little deeper and he's not sure what he's discovering and whether he likes it. But he's intrigued. And that's enough.

'No. It doesn't make a difference,' she says and he's disappointed. He didn't exactly want a pointless argument but he was ready for one nonetheless. Perhaps he's being unfair.

'I'm just making conversation, telling you the facts I've discovered about you. I didn't have a clue who you were or what your name was.'

'Why would you? I don't suppose you've much call to think of many of the staff who live and work here permanently let alone some sort of gardener who's only been here a short while.' God, he's doing it again. What's wrong with him?

CHAPTER 8

CORDELIA

She should adopt a superior tone and say, 'Quite.' But she can't bring herself to do that, because it's not what she feels. It's not what she thinks. She feels silly now. He doesn't want to be here, doesn't want to be talking to her. She's held him here too long and she's saying silly things, which is quite unlike her usually. If it had been Clive or Edwin speaking to her like this she'd have launched into a loud defence but instead she breathes in deeply, exhales slowly. 'I'm saying all the wrong things,' she says suddenly. 'I'm not sure I know what the right thing is though. I just know I'm not saying it.'

She's done it. She's opted for honesty. He blinks. He's taken aback and she rejoices at this a bit with a slight smile that she doesn't know has crept onto her face until it's too late.

He smiles back, but it's curious rather than shared. Heaven knows why she wants him to warm to her a little bit more. He's gone out of his way to find her shoes, he's kept her jewellery safe when he could quite as easily have kept it, sold it, never told her as much. He's honest. A little too honest. Perhaps this is why she wants him just to come a little further. Just a bit further. Just for a few more moments.

They could never be friends, nor does she really want them to be if she stops to think about it. But it's a conversation and he interests her and she knows once it's finished, once they both leave the churchyard, everything will go back to how it was before. And she's not sure she wants that. She's not ready to resume her predictable evening just yet. Although she knows she must, soon.

Tennis, embroidery, reading, walking, parties, dances, the season in London. She's loved it. She's loved it all. But it's just a little bit too easy, which might be why she allowed herself to be kissed so often. The thrill. Something different. And then when she's married, which of course must happen soon, nothing will ever change again. Now is the time to kiss strangers behind potted palms at dances because all that will be over. And marriage . . . It's not going to be the grand adventure she's always been led to believe it would be. She knows that now. She sees that from her mother. Cordelia and her mother lead nigh enough the same life, only her mother wears a gold band and Cordelia does not.

Just a few minutes longer. Something different. Someone interesting.

'I must go,' he says, glancing at the clock and for unfathomable reasons she's disappointed that it's over.

'Yes,' she breathes and then lies. 'So should I.'

But he hesitates. 'I wonder if it would incite talk if we walked together. Perhaps you should go on ahead of me some way. A head start, if you like.'

'All right. Thank you again,' she says and hates this crestfallen feeling that's swept its way through the churchyard, blown its way over the headstones and settled itself on her.

He nods, expectant, waiting for her to leave. How he has commanded her in this way a second time is beyond her but she does what's expected of her: she turns and leaves.

CHAPTER 9

ISAAC
JULY 1914

In the servants' hall Isaac reads a copy of *The Times* that's worked its way downstairs after being read by Mr Richards, the butler. Isaac's already read *The Cornishman* that serves the household staff, picking it up by accident this morning after a quick breakfast, but he was quite interested in the view of the local newspaper as to what's going on in the wider world. A second opinion of world events never hurts. One should not only rely on a newspaper that echoes what one thinks.

He's always one of the last to read it. Not being one of the usual Pencallick House staff, he doesn't like to get in the way of things too much, overstep the mark. He spends his days not overstepping the mark with those upstairs and downstairs. It's only in the garden he has true autonomy and even then he's mindful of Gilbert's long-term place and tries not to offend him either. Today *The Times* is particularly crumpled and tea-stained. As if it's been passed around, paused over, many, many times.

He's been following the first few days of the reportage of what appears to be an impending war with only a vague interest. Britain can't go to war. It doesn't have an army – not a large and proper one. The very idea is ludicrous and he finds war, in all its guises, disgusting. He's never really thought himself political. He thinks of his father, his head in a cloud of books, a long-term disciple of Darwin and only actually able to explain the Boer War to Isaac after Isaac had begged him to help him understand how it was a war against Dutch farmers on horseback and had lasted over two years.

Another war, so soon after that, cannot happen. But as he reads what can only pass as predictions, he has to admit, it does look as if war might be a reality.

Declaration of War by Austria-Hungary on Serbia, he reads. *Britain is joined by close ties, though not by a formal alliance, to France and Russia, who count on her backing. Britain is bound to defend the neutrality of Belgium if her territory is invaded during a Franco-German war.*

Russia will defend the Serbians by force of arms.

Germany would then join the war.

France would have to take the side of Russia and Italy will take that of Austria and Germany.

There is also a possibility that the Balkan States – Romania, Greece and Bulgaria – with Turkey, may join the war.

There will be war. It will stretch across Europe. But as Isaac folds the paper over and leaves it on top of the piano for the next person to read, he ruefully hopes it will not stretch towards England.

* * *

'Britain has a duty to defend Belgium should war reach her,' Mr Trahair, the valet, declares at dinner later as he spoons mustard onto his plate, quoting what he's read in the newspaper earlier that day.

'But what does that mean for us?' Ada asks.

'Not a great deal, I imagine,' Mr Trahair tells Cordelia's lady's maid with a placating smile. 'It probably won't happen.'

'It will mean quite a lot,' David announces which earns him a warning look from the butler.

'David,' Isaac warns his brother, reaching across for the discarded pot of mustard. He gives him a look that says, *don't rattle the cage. We're guests here.*

'You were telling me this morning,' David says defensively, missing Isaac's warning. 'You were saying Britain has no real army to speak of, that we're an island nation and so our navy is impressive in order to defend our seas from attack or invasions but our army not so because we've hardly needed it. That any declaration of war would bring with it great upheaval on that front. You were saying it.' David finishes, looking to Isaac for confirmation.

The entire Pencallick staff look between David and Isaac. Isaac nods slowly, shifts in his chair.

'So if we go off to defend—' one of the housemaids starts.

'We don't know that's happening yet,' Mr Richards cuts in swiftly.

'Yes . . .' she repeats. 'But if we do . . . how will we do that with hardly any army?'

The table falls silent, only the ticking of the clock on the wall at the end of the servants' hall prevails. Isaac says nothing but he can feel the eyes of everyone on him. It's a good question – one he fears he knows the answer to.

CHAPTER 10

CORDELIA

She opens the parcel in her bedroom with a smile of joy. She found it waiting for her when she returned to change from riding with Edwin. It took longer than she'd expected for it to arrive and she had half a mind to travel up to London herself to fetch it. Only today it's here. She claps her hands together and then opens the box because she knows what's inside. Alongside the confectionery from Fortnum's is something else entirely.

'What's that?' Clive asks.

'How long have you been standing there?' She turns from her position sat on the bed to see her little brother standing in the doorway.

'Not long. Are those for me?'

'Yes,' she says, pushing the little box along the bed without ceremony. 'Take them and enjoy them. But not all at once for heaven's sake. And don't tell Nanny or she'll only take them from you.'

'And eat them herself,' Clive sneers.

'She wouldn't,' Cordelia says idly.

'She ate my mince pies last Christmas Eve.'

'The ones you were supposed to leave out for Father Christmas?'

'Yes, only Nanny ate them instead. I saw her. She thought I was asleep. I also saw her put the carrot for the reindeer in her apron pocket, which I thought was a tad selfish. Poor reindeer.'

Cordelia stifles a laugh. She wonders if Mother and Father know Clive is almost halfway to the truth.

'What's the other thing?' Clive asks, peering into the larger box.

She closes the lid. 'Nothing for you to worry about.'

Days later Edwin lifts his tennis racket high in the air and cheers. 'I win again.'

'Do you know how abominable it is to run back and forth in these long skirts?' Cordelia justifies her loss. 'It's almost impossible to win like this. I don't have the freedom of movement you do. But well done,' she concedes.

He cheers again.

'Yes, don't crow about it. Lemonade?'

'Yes,' Edwin agrees. 'After I've gloated a bit more though, I think.'

They sit at the wrought iron table on which a maid has placed a jug of Cook's fresh lemonade and a plate of oven-warm butter biscuits.

Cordelia fans herself and watches her brother pour for them. She sees one of the under gardeners pushing a wheelbarrow towards the rose garden and watches him thoughtfully. It's not him though. Not Mr Leigh.

But what he'd insinuated about her has seared itself into her mind.

'Do you know all the names of the servants?' she asks, still watching the gardener as he disappears into the rose garden.

Edwin looks thoughtful. 'I could probably work hard at recalling them if you put a gun to my head and forced me to but . . . other than that, they don't all immediately spring to mind. Why?'

'No reason,' she says. 'It just made me wonder. I found out the gardener's names this week from Ada and . . . anyway.'

'How many gardeners do we actually have?' he asks.

'Three,' she replies knowledgeably.

Edwin's interest wanes and then it picks up again. 'How many staff do we have in total?' he asks idly.

Cordelia smiles. This is such a silly conversation to be having. 'I don't know. You'll inherit,' she says. 'So you should probably make a point of understanding the running of the estate. Starting with the names of those who work for you.'

'Won't be for ages yet,' he says dismissively. 'Father is very much alive and kicking and besides, I'm not sure I want to inherit.'

'I'm not entirely sure you get any say in the matter,' Cordelia advises, leaning forward and picking up a biscuit.

'More's the pity,' he replies. 'Go on then, what are they?'

She's confused and it must show as he clarifies, 'The gardeners' names.'

'Oh. Gilbert. Then there's James and the one with the wheelbarrow who just went past is Talek. And then there's the landscaper and his brother. But they're only here for a while, I suppose,' she says casually, hoping Edwin will impart information, however useless.

'Yes, met the landscaper at the party and a couple of times around the grounds. And in London, when we were there for the season. Met him then too.'

'Did you?' she asks, shock lacing her voice. 'What was he doing there? Did he come to the London house?'

'Yes, twice.'

'Oh,' she says. 'I had no idea.'

'Why would you? Too busy editing your dance card or whatever it was you did all day.'

She throws a biscuit at him and he catches it, refusing to give it back. 'Father asked me to look at all the plans,' Edwin continues, 'when they were being drawn up, see if I could offer some input.'

'And could you?' she asks although she suspects she knows the answer.

'Course not. I might have muttered something about a tennis court but it's only because it was already on the drawing.'

'Ha!' Cordelia scoffs, leans forward and takes another biscuit as Edwin begins munching the one he caught.

'And what did you think of the plans?' She's hoping to hear that Mr Leigh is a genius. Or an idiot. She's not sure, quite yet, if she minds which.

'I had no thoughts at all,' Edwin confesses. 'I didn't see what was wrong with the grounds as they were if I'm honest but one can hardly say that, can one?'

Cordelia snorts. 'No, one can't.'

The glorious day casts its benevolence on them, the sun warming her face, her arms through the fabric of her cotton sleeves. Everything is perfect. Just as it should be.

Edwin echoes her thoughts. 'Three blissful months until Michaelmas term begins. My last year,' he says wistfully, leaning back, his eyes closed, face upturned towards the sun. And with that she knows the conversation has ended.

It's not quite dark when she escapes the house. Escape feels like such a terrible word when she thinks it in her head, as if she shouldn't be doing it – which she shouldn't really.

She arrives at his cottage and hopes it's not too late, not too undignified a time to visit. When else can she do it? She can hardly do this out in the open while he's working. What would people think? Besides, she owes him this.

But it's not Isaac who opens the door, it's his brother who stares at her blankly for a moment before collecting himself. 'Miss Carr-Lyon,' he says and blinks. 'Do you need . . . Are you all right? Is there anything you need?'

'No, I'm quite all right, David isn't it? Or Mr Leigh, I should say.'

'David will do just fine,' he replies. There's a resemblance between them; she can tell they are siblings. But David's eyes are blue rather than dark like his brother's.

'I wonder, is your brother in?' she asks.

'My brother?' he questions.

'Yes. Isaac, the other Mr Leigh. If it's not too inconvenient. I know the hour is late but I wanted to get something to him before he starts work tomorrow, in case he needs it.'

'He's . . . Come in, come in,' he says warmly. 'I'll fetch him.'

Cordelia is ushered into the small sitting room. The

fire is empty and the night is warm. It's sparsely furnished and even more sparsely decorated. She supposes two men who don't intend to stay for long have little use for photographs in meticulously polished gilt frames. Although now she looks harder she spies one on the mantle above the fireplace, but she can't work out who the people in it are. Parents, perhaps? And that's about it for signs of a personal touch in this small space that they will only inhabit for a few months more.

David climbs the stairs to fetch his brother while Cordelia stands, waiting for them both to return. She doesn't like to sit without an invitation.

It's Isaac who descends first and enters the room. He doesn't greet her, just watches her. He's in a state of undress and he hasn't bothered to put his waistcoat back on. His shirt is tucked in but it's open at the neck, a few buttons exposing just a sliver of skin. He's tanned there, on that triangle of skin and it makes her wonder how that could be possible when he spends all his days buttoned up to his neck. Perhaps he unbuttons when no one's looking. When David enters and stands behind him, he casts his brother a glance, visibly notices his unkempt state as Cordelia has and then looks towards her.

There's no hint of a smile on Isaac's face, which Cordelia didn't realise she'd been hoping for. Or at least expecting.

'I bought you something,' she says, realising she's miscalculated the response her presence here is bringing. 'Please excuse the late hour but this is the first moment I've had to get away.'

Isaac glances at his brother, ever so briefly, and then at the brown paper parcel wrapped in string in Cordelia's hands. She holds it out to him and he has no choice but to step forward, take it from her. Cordelia smiles, watches him as he takes it. It looks as if he takes great pains not to touch her today, when before he had no issue with holding her wrist, lifting her up and carrying her over the bracken. He pauses, his eyes on hers before he removes it from her hands.

'Thank you,' he says and holds it still.

Silence descends on the room.

'Would you like to sit?' David asks.

'No, I don't think she would,' Isaac dares, giving Cordelia a pointed look. 'The hour's late,' he says, his eyes still on Cordelia's. 'I think Miss Carr-Lyon would probably prefer not to feel obliged to sit or take tea at this hour. But please,' he says giving her a look that leaves her in no doubt she should leave, 'correct me if I'm wrong.'

Cordelia's chest constricts. He's dismissing her. Again.

'You're right.' She attempts to hide how seethed she feels. 'I won't put you to any trouble at this hour. I just wanted to make sure this was delivered to you.'

CHAPTER 11

ISAAC

'Aren't you going to open it?' David asks before Cordelia takes the opportunity to leave.

Should he open it now? Heavens knows what it is. He looks at Cordelia, silently seeking permission and she nods, a wide smile on her face. 'Please.' She gestures to the parcel. 'Open it.'

He wants to open it in private. He doesn't want his face to betray him in any way – not here, with her watching.

But he opens it, snipping the string, watching as the paper springs back unveiling the contents.

It's a new pullover. But it's not too grand. It's white, yes, which is a silly colour to purchase for someone who works with soil all day. The one she lost was a deep grey. But it's thick – not too heavy. He's never touched anything this soft before. Yes, he has. He's touched her. Gosh, where has that thought come from? He swallows. He's looking at it, turning over the soft wool in his hands, stalling for time so he doesn't have to speak.

'Is it not all right?' she asks gently, looking at him with concern. 'I can purchase another, better, lighter or . . . heavier?' She grasps at pinpointing the problem but there is no problem.

'It's fine,' he says and then puts it on the table and looks at it for too long, saying nothing, giving her time to make her exit, wishing she'd leave, wishing she'd stay. Why is she doing this? Why is she here? Half of him is elated she's thought to do this. The other half is horrified. No good can come of . . . whatever she's trying to force here.

'I must get back to the house,' she eventually says, giving Isaac space to breathe.

He nods, and automatically moves to the front door to open it for her wordlessly. She says goodbye and goodnight to David and then follows him to the cottage door.

Too late he remembers his manners. 'Thank you for the present,' he says stiffly.

Quietly she replies as she crosses the threshold and turns, 'There's no need to thank me. It was the least I could do. I'm only sorry I lost yours. Thank you for trying to help the other night and for the conversation in the churchyard.'

He narrows his eyes in curiosity at this. Odd to add conversation to a list of things to be thankful for.

Isaac stands at the open door, letting the cool summer night air into the cottage. He watches her retreating figure until she reaches the gate. He realises she'll have to turn back in order to fix it into the latch. She'll look up, she'll let those blue eyes fix onto his again and he'd happily let her. But if he does that, something will change and he's not sure what. He's just certain he needs to not let that happen. He closes the front door quickly, and hears the click of the latch. With his brother in the room he doesn't go to the window to watch her walk back silently towards the house, although he's desperate to watch as she walks out of sight. The lamps blazing up at the house will guide her safely.

He stands by the closed door, briefly, thinking. She's so far above him. The last thing he needs is her seeking him out again. But whether or not he wants it is something else entirely.

He turns back into the room. His brother is holding the pullover up to examine it and then he gives Isaac a curious look. 'What on earth was that all about?'

CHAPTER 12

CORDELIA

Over the next few days rain falls intermittently, confining Cordelia mostly to the house. She plays cards, eats, embroiders, reads the newspaper before it's discarded in the direction of the servants' hall and wonders how only a month ago she'd been in London, ending the season with parties, suppers and dances with young men who'd mostly bored her. And a few who hadn't. She'd never thought herself bored easily. But all of the men who'd asked her to dance never had anything interesting to say.

Thinking about it as she sits in the window seat of her room, waiting for Ada to dress her for dinner, she tries hard to recall some of their names, or their faces for that matter. They blur into one entity with nothing to recommend them other than the fact they were well bred and well mannered. For the most part, she thinks with a smile.

There had been no talk of the possibility of impending war in the ballrooms, or if there had been it had been far away from her ears. She'd had no real clue there was a sense of stirring interest in overseas events, or in fact what these events might be, until she'd returned home a few weeks ago. But then, as Father said, events appeared to be moving fast, almost too fast since the assassination of the archduke.

'How exactly does one become an officer?' Edwin asks over dinner. They've just finished discussing the upcoming charity bazaar her mother holds in the grounds every summer, and tonight is one of those rare nights when her father and mother aren't entertaining. It is just the four of them, with Clive already in bed after his supper in the nursery.

Mrs Emes has cooked five delicious courses, as usual, for dinner. The first few mouthfuls of dressed roast beef had been soft and delicious but with her brother's words about becoming an officer it is as if the food has hardened and now a piece of rock sits inside her mouth, waiting to be chewed. Cordelia forcefully swallows it down with wine, endeavouring not to choke on her claret in the process.

'What?' her mother splutters.

'How does one . . .' Edwin repeated.

'We heard you,' their father replies gruffly.

'Who does one have to know?' Edwin clarifies. 'What about our limping friend, Major Trevelyan? Millicent and Irene's father.'

'Retired,' Cordelia points out. 'Due to the limp.'

'Surely you won't need to.' Mother looks aghast. 'You won't be doing that.' She is forceful now. 'No son of mine is going to war.'

'Now, now,' Father says. 'We don't know that Britain will need to enter the fray.'

'There will be a fray then?' Cordelia asks.

She glances over her shoulder as behind her a footman clatters a salver on the sideboard.

'I think so, yes. But whether or not Britain is in it remains to be seen.'

'And if it is,' Edwin cuts back in, 'I should like to help in some way.'

'So should I,' Cordelia agrees.

'What do you think you'd be doing, young lady? Dancing your way through a war?' her father asks. 'It won't be like the Napoleonic campaign, women following the menfolk all the way to the action.'

'Darling,' her mother directs her attention to Cordelia. 'You already help. The charity bazaar for the Boer Veterans Fund . . .' she reminds her. 'Those poor soldiers who lost limbs, their livelihoods, the families they left behind, the proceeds will go to them and that's how you contribute.'

Cordelia fails to see how attending this once-yearly lawn event for soldiers wounded or killed in a prior war would at all help the efforts of a future one. She opens her mouth to speak.

'You'll be staying put,' her father cuts in before Cordelia can even speak.

'Will Edwin be staying put?' she asks icily.

From across the table, Edwin smirks.

CHAPTER 13

CORDELIA

The great and the good of North Cornwall are walking to and from the stalls and stands on the lawn of Pencallick House. It's one of those balmy summer days that's arrived to push the rain away. Cordelia adjusts her opulent ostrich-feathered hat that matches her cornflower-blue dress as she stands near the balustrade, looking down on the event. She'd only finished, late last night, the embroidery piece she is donating to the raffle. It is a series of daisies and other flowers that she'd slaved over for weeks and weeks while in London, pricking her fingers in the process many times. She hopes it brings someone joy if they win it. It had brought her many hours of despair, boredom and pain when she'd much rather have been doing anything else at all so some pleasure needs to come from it.

The sun has just passed the clock tower on the stables, managing to cast its rays gently onto proceedings after a brief hiatus. The white tea tent has a queue outside and she can see Mother's friend Lady Trevelyan being escorted in by her father while shortly behind them one of the kitchen maids and the hall boy are arm in arm.

Cordelia smiles at that and how easily, today, the villagers and downstairs staff mix with those above. Of course the two groups would not combine any further than that, other than perhaps for one of her mother's guests to ask Mrs Emes for a cup of tea in the tent. Cordelia hopes the cook and the rest of the staff have scheduled a good rotation so they get to at least experience the coconut shy, run by the verger.

She hadn't been looking for Mr Leigh when she sees him. But he is there, in the distance, laughing with one of the under gardeners – Talek. She's proudly remembered his name. They're lingering by a stand, tasting jams and preserves.

Cordelia doesn't want to move, doesn't want to go directly to Isaac and it is at that moment, while she is deliberating this that she realises she might just be in a little bit of trouble. She closes her eyes, resisting the draw Mr Leigh seems to have on her. It certainly isn't because he is doing anything to encourage her – quite the opposite, in fact. And she wonders if that might be the very thing that's interesting her. Because a passing infatuation with the landscaper doesn't really bear thinking about, does it? And yet she does think about it, does think about him, often. Too often. Curiosity has turned slowly into something else, although she's not sure what. The purchase of the pullover had been dutiful, something she had to do by way of apology for not returning his. But visiting his cottage to give it to him hadn't been any of those things. There'd been nothing untoward about it. She'd known his brother might be there. And she'd still risked it because it was better all round that they were chaperoned. Besides, it would be very improper to have entered his cottage if he'd been alone. But if he had been alone, would he have invited her in?

And more importantly, would she have accepted, entered the cottage at night, alone, and gone in with him?

Stop it, she tells herself. Just stop it.

But she'd wanted to see where he lived although it is only temporary until he moves on to his next commission. And she thought that might be it, might be all she needed. But it wasn't. She'd left unsatisfied but about what, she can't put her finger on.

It is while she is thinking about this, that she finds her feet propelling her, for an unknown reason, towards the jam and preserves stand. Clive darts past her as she makes her way there, shooting her a triumphant look, his face smothered in ice cream and an exhausted Nanny in hot pursuit.

Isaac is holding a jar and receiving his change when she arrives at the stand. He turns and sees her at the same time as Talek chooses to move off.

'Hello Mr Leigh,' she says formally when the under gardener is out of earshot.

'Miss Carr-Lyon.'

She expects him to continue speaking but he looks over her shoulder as Edwin appears.

'Mr Leigh,' Edwin hails him so easily, as if he is an old friend. He nods towards the jar. 'What have you bought?'

'Strawberry jam. Mrs Emes has been making and jarring them for weeks for this or so she tells me.'

'While we've been in London, no doubt,' Edwin says.

'Indeed, Mr Carr-Lyon. Do you intend to buy something?'

Cordelia stands impotently, unable to climb into the conversation, unable to converse as readily as her brother.

'Yes, I think I'll be in the tea tent snapping up all the cake,' Edwin replies. 'I'd like to say we get enough of it at home but a few extra scones each week wouldn't go amiss, eh? Cordelia . . . cake?'

'Yes, in a moment,' she replies. 'I think I'd like to buy something here first.'

'To do what with?' Edwin asks. 'You don't even eat jam.'

'To support Mrs Emes' efforts and the benevolent fund, of course. I'll gift it at Christmas,' she says.

'Righto. See you in the cake tent,' he replies.

'It's the tea tent. The cake is ancillary,' she corrects him and then wishes she hadn't. She sounds sour. But Edwin has waved merrily to them both and gone in search of scones.

'Hello,' she says to Mr Leigh when Edwin has gone.

He smiles and so does she. They've already done this. 'Hello,' he says again. 'What will you try?' Isaac asks, saving them both from an awkward silence. 'The marmalade's very good. There's only a few jars left. Not as many oranges in the hot house this year as there were strawberries for jam.'

'Perhaps I'll leave the marmalade for someone who really wants it then,' she says.

'Especially if you won't eat it,' Isaac points out.

'Yes, quite.' She's not sure if he is teasing her kindly or unkindly.

'Perhaps a jar of lemon curd?' she asks Jonathan the footman who is manning the stall. 'And I can pop a ribbon round it and make a gift of it.'

She hands over the money and with it a hollow

feeling arises. This is supposed to be how she is useful. If this is it, purchasing a jar of lemon curd is a muted sort of usefulness.

'Do we grow the lemons for this too?' she asks Isaac as she holds the jar up briefly. Should she know this?

'You do, yes,' he says.

She gestures that they should walk on as others want to look at the preserves table. Together they move naturally towards the next stall. The grocer has made his own toffee for the event and Cordelia says she wants to buy some to show some support.

'You might want to gift that on as well,' Mr Leigh says discreetly. 'Hard as nails, you'll break a tooth.'

'Oh.' She looks up at him and they exchange a conspiratorial look, a shared secret, a shared confidence. One of many now.

She purchases two large blocks of toffee and with her hands full, Isaac offers to carry something for her. They move aside to allow others to peruse. The sun is in her eyes so she moves her head a fraction so the brim of her hat shields her.

Gesturing to the curd, she says, 'How do you grow a lemon?'

He tells her, talking about evening sunlight, frosts and glasshouses, making it sound poetic, rather than functional.

'I think it's beautiful how you can create life from nothing in the garden. How do you know what to do?'

He looks at her as if he's not sure what she means. 'I learned,' he replies. 'From my mother, originally, before she passed away. And then I was . . . unofficially apprenticed, I suppose, when I was at university helping in the kitchen garden. And during all of that, I read a lot of books.'

'What sort of books? Just gardening?'

'All sorts,' he says as Cordelia spies her mother talking animatedly with Major Trevelyan by the second-hand book stand. 'Nature books might have been what started my love of the outdoors, now I think about it. But my mother's gardening books were what really did it.'

She smiles. 'I'm sorry your mother has passed away.'

'Thank you,' he says, his dark eyes penetrating hers. It feels like the first real conversation they've had. And then she ruins it. 'I've always liked gardens, especially ours.' Oh, why can't she think of anything better to say?

'Me too,' he says, probably to appease her. 'I like the peace and solitude of a garden and being useful in one, bringing something to life and making the most of what's already there. My brother likes fishing, always has done,' he says conversationally. 'I like gardening. We all have something.'

'Yes,' she says thoughtfully. 'I suppose we all do.'

'What's yours?' he asks as if he might be genuinely interested.

'I don't think I have anything much. I like reading. I embroider. I don't like it though. As a matter of fact I'm rather awful at it.'

'You should find something you're good at, and that you enjoy.'

'Yes I should. Will you teach me?' she finishes.

'Teach you?' His brow furrows in confusion.

'How to garden,' she replies. 'When to plant things – how to plant things. How to nurture them to life. It must be such a sense of achievement to watch something you've worked on grow and grow. I must admit

I had no idea what you meant by pinching tomato leaves or whatever it was you said to me before. I should like to understand.'

He pauses and his eyes narrow but there's a glimmer of a smile on his face, she can see it. And then he replies. 'I learned every spare chance I could. Always in trouble for putting aside my actual schoolwork in favour of picking up a spade. Always knew it was what I wanted to do.'

'That doesn't answer my question,' she says, although she pictures a younger version of Mr Leigh sneaking into the garden to dig when he should have been doing other things.

'I don't think I'm the right person. You should ask your head gardener if he'll take you on,' he suggests. And is it her imagination or does he back away a pace?

'Take me on?' she laughs.

'If he'll teach you, I mean. It's his place to do so. Not mine.'

She thinks about this.

'And it can't be taught in five minutes. You have to be patient with fruit and veg,' he continues.

'Veg?' She repeats his shortening of the word as if it's comical.

'Of course.' He misunderstands her. 'Where do you think all the food on your plate comes from?' He points towards the kitchen gardens around the far side of the house. 'And the meat and fish, from the tenant farmers and the fishermen.' He points vaguely behind them where North Cornwall's shores lie. 'And the cheese and butter from the dairy.'

'Well, of course I knew that,' she says. 'How long does it take?'

'How long does what take?' That smile is back on his face again.

'To grow vegetables.'

'It varies,' he says. 'It's not a hobby for the impatient,' he repeats.

'Do I look impatient?'

'You sound it, yes.'

She gasps a little and then laughs. Someone nudges her by accident and apologises but she barely notices. Isaac and Cordelia move further away from the crowd and she turns to him as they walk. 'You're trying to put me off.'

'Perhaps.'

'Why?'

'I don't know,' he says, looking into her eyes. 'Why not try then? Why not just come down for an hour? We'll find you something easy to do.'

'Easy?'

'Productive then. So you'll feel you've achieved something in a short space of time.'

'Now you're trying *not* to put me off,' she suggests.

That smile again.

'Or you're trying to patronise me?' It's her turn to narrow her eyes.

'I'm just trying to help.'

'With my impatient fancy?' she teases.

He smiles to someone in the distance, one of the villagers. How does he know them all and she doesn't? He raises his hand a fraction in jovial greeting. 'Is it just a fancy?' he asks, turning back to her.

He locks his brown eyes onto hers. 'I'm not sure yet,' she replies. Her breathing has slowed but her heart quickens. 'Perhaps we should find out together.'

The smile is gone from his face now, his expression unreadable. He says nothing for a while and she worries she's said something silly until, 'Perhaps we should.'

'What did you tell your brother about the pullover?' she questions. 'I realise now it was a silly thing to do, to come to your cottage. But . . .'

'But?' he asks.

'But I'm not sure I could help it. I wanted to come. I wanted to give it to you the very moment I could.'

'Thank you,' he says.

'So what did you tell your brother?' she repeats.

'The truth, or a form thereof. I said you were cold and so I'd offered you mine but you'd since lost it. I didn't say where and I didn't say when.'

Cordelia smiles ruefully. 'It was a silly thing to do,' she repeats.

'Which bit?' he teases. 'Not many young women would do what you did that night, I'm sure. Jumping in like that.'

'No?' she questions. 'What would they do?'

'Stand and scream idly, most probably,' he says. 'Wait for help to simply show up.' And then he follows it up with, 'I'm probably being unfair on your sex. I'm generalising unkindly. Ignore me. It was brave. That's what I mean.'

Cordelia walks towards the tea tent and Isaac naturally falls into step.

'And I imagine without context your brother now thinks I'm careless.'

'I wouldn't like to comment. I didn't ask. He didn't offer an opinion.'

'I find that hard to believe,' Cordelia says. 'I'd think I was a careless sort of person.'

'I disagree,' he says. 'You cared enough about your brother to try to save him. And to purchase me another pullover.'

In the tea tent she loses him but not before they fix a plan to talk to Gilbert individually and encourage him to take Cordelia on. 'If you're serious about it,' he clarifies as they enter the tent. Is she serious? It was a bit of a passing comment, really. Just a way to keep the conversation flowing, a byway to nowhere. And now she's nervous. What has she done? If she hates it she can get out of it easily enough without having bothered too many people. Besides, it will fill her days a bit. So she asks if it could be 'a sort of trial period'.

To which Isaac laughs and reminds her it's her garden after all. She can come and go as she pleases. She can command Gilbert to teach her if she so wishes.

'But I don't want to command anyone,' she implores. 'I should like him to want to impart some knowledge. I should want you to do the same without feeling as if you have to.'

'I don't feel as if I have to,' he says.

And then in the tea tent as two of her friends approach, he discreetly leaves her side so that when she starts to introduce him, he is already gone.

CHAPTER 14

CORDELIA

Cordelia sweeps the crumbs from the white tablecloth and then from her lap and places them onto the dainty china plate that holds the other half of her scone. Edwin has coerced her into eating a scone but, not liking jam, she is finding the experience a little unsatisfactory. She's sitting with her older brother and the two women who'd sought her out the moment she'd entered the tent with Isaac.

Millicent is Major Trevelyan's daughter, only a year older than Cordelia. Her flame-red hair struggles to keep within the confines of its hat and pins. She's buxom and beautiful compared to Cordelia's slight figure and pale hair. Cordelia has often thought she'd quite like to look like Millicent, as if she'd stepped out of a Rossetti painting. The families have known each other for years and Millicent and her people live at the eponymously named Trevelyan, a neighbouring estate. Cordelia has always liked Millicent, who doesn't have the foggiest clue how beautiful she is and is currently eating a piece of lemon cake voraciously, almost as if her very existence depends upon it. Edwin watches her in awe, which is when Millicent's older sister Irene chooses to turn her chair towards Cordelia, inviting confidences.

'Who was that I saw you talking with as you entered the tent a little while ago?' Irene asks.

Cordelia blinks in pretend confusion. 'I don't know, I'm afraid. What did they look like?'

'Handsome,' Irene says slyly. 'Not one of us though. One can tell.'

Cordelia restrains a sigh that threatens to escape her lips. 'Can one? I'm not sure he's a million miles away from being one of us,' she says.

'But then I imagine,' Irene continues salaciously, 'that him not being one of us is what makes him even more handsome.'

Cordelia looks over to where she knows Mr Leigh is standing, although he's hidden by James and Talek. The three of them are deep in discussion. 'He's Father's landscape architect,' Cordelia says idly, if only to stop Irene from continuing to probe. 'Brought in to change the grounds and parkland.' She's describing it badly, dismissing him on purpose.

'A gardener. Yes, he looks like one actually,' Irene says, her eyes roving the tea tent. James moves his head to talk to someone else, leaving Mr Leigh and Talek talking. She can see him now and so can Irene. 'He looks outdoorsy. Looks as if he sees the sun a lot more than some of our lot. Earthy.'

Earthy? Is that good . . . or bad? 'Yes, perhaps.' Cordelia is non-committal.

'I don't mind saying your gardeners are a little easier on the eye than ours. Ours are old. Very old. Still, at least they'll stay behind and the garden won't go to wrack and ruin when the war comes.'

Cordelia snaps her head back in Irene's direction. 'What do you mean?'

'There'll be a war, of course. Although for how long, no one knows. Father says it won't last long but Mother imagines the footmen all joining up the moment it looks likely. Especially given the way Father often shouts at them. They probably can't wait to leave. Any excuse.'

'He doesn't mean to be so angry,' Millicent pipes up, now her cake is finished. 'It's only his leg gives him so much pain and he has rather lost his patience over the last few years. I think patience is something one loses rather than gains, wouldn't you agree, Edwin?'

Edwin nods, still enthralled by Millicent.

Cordelia cannot work out what is happening here but her mind is drawn back. 'So you think there will be a war then? I mean, we've been discussing it at home but Father and Mother keep putting a stop to our conversations and I can't quite glean what it means for us all?'

'For us?' Irene offers. 'Nothing at all. Well, perhaps for Edwin if he so chooses.'

'I will choose. I do choose,' Edwin says, enthusiastically snapping to attention at talk of war.

Irene cuts back in. 'But they can hardly force people to hold a weapon, can they? They can hardly force a man to stand his ground and fight.'

'I'm not so sure,' Edwin says. 'I shall volunteer, happily.'

'So you've just said,' Cordelia reminds him.

'But as for you, and I, and Millicent, I imagine it means nothing at all. We shall continue on as we've always done, as we were always intended to,' Irene finishes knowledgeably.

Cordelia doesn't reply, instead reaches for her teacup and takes a sip of what is now lukewarm tea. The tent is getting hotter under the glare of the sun. She needs to be outside. She casts a glance at Millicent who also looks subdued by the prospect of carrying on as she's always done.

'I think I shall get us all some more scones,' Irene says, rising quickly.

'Oh, could I have another piece of lemon cake instead?' Millicent asks.

'And me,' Cordelia requests, pushing the detritus of her scone even further away. But Irene marches on, their requests unheard.

'I think I shall try to be a nurse,' Millicent keeps the conversation going.

'Really?' Cordelia asks, trying to be interested but watching Irene as she walks directly towards Mr Leigh. Cordelia strains to hear the conversation over the chatter surrounding them but she can't. Mr Leigh smiles warmly, which jolts Cordelia and not in a good way, and then Irene moves towards the long table of cakes and tea paraphernalia just behind him. He bends, picks something up, moves off after her and hands it to her. Now Cordelia can neither read what they're saying nor see their faces and the conversation appears to end.

Millicent and Edwin are staring at Cordelia, awaiting a response to a question she's not aware she's been asked.

'I'm sorry, pardon?'

'What will you do?' Millicent asks, obviously for the second time. 'Will you nurse as well? I imagine there'll be quite a calling for it.'

Edwin scoffs. 'Can't imagine Cordy mopping blood and stitching up wounded soldiers, can you?' Although it's not clear who he's directing the question to.

'All that gore . . . imagine,' he continues indelicately. 'Cordy can't even cope when she stubs a toe, or when it transpired Father had knocked over the goldfish bowl and the little mite was fitting around on the floor gasping for breath. You cried heaps.'

'I was Clive's age,' Cordelia replies acidly, reminded of the loss of her fish.

'No, Cordy won't be sweeping men's insides up from a hospital floor. Can't see that happening at all. But very best of luck to you, Millicent.' He raises his teacup in a strange form of cheers.

Irene arrives with a plate of scones and jam. Edwin, oblivious, reaches for one, while Millicent politely declines, now looking rather pale.

Somewhere outside, the local brass band strikes up. On the surface all is as it should be. Edwin tucks merrily into his scone and Mr Leigh stands by the tea table, talking animatedly to the outdoor staff. He glances over at her, gives a flicker of a smile that she returns before he looks away again. But her smile is not as wide as it should have been. Because somewhere deep inside, Cordelia cannot now shake the feeling that this bucolic summer is not going to end the same way in which it started.

CHAPTER 15

CORDELIA

'I admit the garden party was more fun than I thought it was going to be,' Irene Trevelyan confesses over dinner that evening, which makes Edwin and Cordelia exchange a glance.

Cordelia's mother, Mrs Carr-Lyon looks taken aback at Irene's forwardness as they finish their dinner of salmon under the ever present gaze of the Duke of Wellington.

Mrs Emes has made a dish of vanilla soufflé with strawberries to finish. Cordelia spears one and smiles as she realises they came from the garden – nurtured and grown.

Mr Leigh has no doubt, in recent weeks, helped where needed in the grounds. She wonders if he has helped pick them. Has he touched this one? And then, how does one go about growing a strawberry? She's going to find out on Monday. She's convinced Gilbert to let her have a dabble in the garden as long as she doesn't take up too much of the other gardeners' time. She knows Gilbert suspects she'll give up after half an hour. She knows this because he dared to suggest this to her – something that made Cordelia laugh in utter astonishment at his brazen accusation.

'What was more fun than you thought it would be?' Millicent and Irene's father booms.

'The garden party, Father,' Millicent offers in her soft voice. 'The coconut shy was marvellous. I won. Edwin helped a bit.'

Edwin smiles at Millicent. Cordelia doesn't miss Millicent smiling back.

'Edwin opened it for me and we drank the milk inside. It was absolute heaven.'

'Well done you,' Cordelia congratulates her. 'I never win those. So difficult. Better at hook-a-duck. I did win some embroidery material today.'

'Oh bad luck,' Edwin commiserates, 'I know how much you hate embroidery.'

'Oh I love it,' enthuses Millicent.

'Then it's yours,' Cordelia offers and Millicent smiles brightly. She really is a lovely girl, thinks Cordelia. Edwin seems smitten. He could do much worse. In particular, the older sister who is either rude, surly, catty or all three at the same time.

Millicent fans herself and Edwin jumps to attention. 'Would you like some fresh air?' he offers. 'A walk, perhaps? It's stifling, even with the door ajar.'

Millicent smiles gratefully.

'I'll escort you. Cordy, you'll chaperone, won't you?' Edwin says reluctantly, glancing at the parents but knowing it must be so. Cordelia knows he would rather it be her than their mother, or worse, Irene.

'Of course,' Cordelia says, rising and placing her napkin on the table. She pops a final strawberry in her mouth. 'Shall we?'

In the garden she gives Edwin and Millicent some distance, pausing, pretending to adjust her shoe and telling them to go on for a moment without her. She'll give them a bit of room to get to know each other better. Funny, she thinks. They've known each other for years but perhaps it is only now that they are beginning to really see each other. Edwin might not realise it, but he's in very great danger of falling in love.

Cordelia wonders if she will have that kind of love when it eventually finds her, slow and steady, gentle and unexpected. Or if it will crash into her with such force it knocks her from her feet. She cannot imagine either happening. She cannot imagine much happening to her at all. At next season's balls will she meet a new set of men or the same ones again? Or will most of them be married by then? Will she be married? Heavens, not to one of them surely. None had impressed her but there'd been a trickle of correspondence from some. She had yet to reply to those letters. She'd not known what to say and didn't like to encourage. She reaches, pulls a leaf from an ancient oak tree, its thick leaves and branches so low that the grass underneath – blocked from any hope of sunlight – has turned to dust. Edwin and Millicent passed by here a few moments ago. They were both just in sight in the darkness. Just. Edwin is taking the scenic route around the garden with only the moonlight to guide them on their path. She squints. Up ahead, are they holding hands? Oh, she does hope so.

And then she notices it. Cigarette smoke coming from the walled archway she's just passed, the one that leads to one of the newly constructed glasshouses and the route into the walled garden. She moves back, stands by the brick arch and places a hand against the wall, the new bricks telling a story under her hand of the day's intense sun.

In the walled garden, the moon casts a faded glow onto a man, smoking, leaning against the doorframe of the glasshouse, his head tipped up to the sky. The faint orange glow marks the cigarette out against his face and the smoke whirls from his parted lips. She knows who it is. That easy stance, as he leans, is unmistakable. Cordelia is entranced; she cannot move, cannot bear to move either away or towards him. She watches him through the darkness, with only the moon to guide her. But she won't go towards him. She won't. Edwin and Millicent are long since forgotten and she adjusts her feet on the gravel as she watches Mr Leigh, smoking in the moonlight. It is this sound that summons him from his reverie.

His sleeves are rolled up. She can see that now as he walks towards her. In this light he looks beautiful, there is no other word for it. Like a Roman statue, sculpted, carved. And then she blushes as she reminds herself those sculptures are hardly ever attired. She wonders if he's sculpted in quite the same way as a statue under his clothes. Would he be hard like stone to touch? She has no idea. As he walks towards her she has no idea of anything.

CHAPTER 16

ISAAC

He doesn't speak, just looks at her – takes in her appearance in her deep-blue velvet evening dress, her scooped lace and diamanté neckline, her fair hair pinned up. Is she alone? He glances behind her, expecting others.

'I'm not with anyone,' she volunteers, reading his mind.

It's as if her words jolt him into realisation that the two of them are alone, once again, when they probably shouldn't be, and he steps back from her a little. He can feel it, this gradual draw, this pull towards her and he has no control over it. The diamond hair ornament he found is back in her hair tonight.

'Is this the style you wore your hair the night you . . . went swimming?' He aims for lightness. He knows anything else is dangerous.

She smiles, replying softly, 'Yes. It's a wonder Ada found enough pins to hold the rest of my hair up. I thought I'd lost all of them in the lake.'

He doesn't reply. He can't think what to reply but she saves him from having to as she continues, 'I can't help feeling you're not supposed to be here at this time of night.'

'I can't help feeling the same about you,' he replies. At some point during this exchange Isaac has dropped his cigarette to the ground although at what point he couldn't have said.

'Where were you standing that night?' she asks. 'When you saw me running. When I had no idea you were there.'

He gestures to the other side of the wall. 'By the main glasshouse.'

'Why?'

'I like to come back, at night, after supper. I like to stand in the silence of the garden. The garden's different at night,' he says simply. He can't elaborate. His brother laughed at him when he said it and he wonders if she'll do the same.

'Yes,' she says, 'I can feel it is, in some way. A different kind of beauty. Private. Personal.'

He nods. An owl cuts through the silence of the garden, hooting from a tree, making them turn their heads in its direction although neither of them can see it.

She looks as if she wants to say something but instead she looks back at him and he waits for something conversational he can cling to, to fall from her lips. He steps forward, reaches out to her and then realising what he's doing, drops his arm immediately.

'Mr Leigh . . .' she starts almost desperately but she's cut off by the sound of Edwin summoning her.

'Cordy?' he calls. 'Cordelia? Where are you? We're heading back to the house. Have we lost you?'

Her eyes are desperate. Whatever she wants to say she needs to say it quickly. Her brother's voice is not far away on the other side of the wall. In a matter of moments he will walk past the open arch and see them both standing there. Isaac briefly considers pulling her towards him, the two of them running into the darkness of the glasshouse, out of view of the arch. Although why he'd do this is beyond him. And whether she'd run with him is another thing entirely. His thoughts are muddled so he doesn't know what he'd do if she did take his hand, run with him. Or if she didn't – what his next step would be either way. He just wants to talk to her, here, like this, under a moonlit sky, alone for a moment longer.

Regardless of the fact every conversation between them has been innocent, if he'd have stood there with her for much longer it might not have been. In some way, Edwin has been their saviour.

She still isn't saying whatever it is her lips are parted for. She looks anxious but their time has run out.

'Goodnight,' Isaac says softly and walks away.

CHAPTER 17

CORDELIA

Her back is still to the open arch, to Edwin when he walks past and spies her there. Isaac has gone. But Cordelia's heart is pounding against her ribcage. She was alone with Isaac Leigh and she hadn't wanted to be anywhere else. They had almost been discovered. Even if they had only been talking, they had almost been discovered. He had reached out for her – she had not missed that. But to do what? Was he going to touch her cheek, her hair, her lips? What had he been going to touch? She cannot bear this agony now of not knowing.

'Cordy?' Edwin says.

Cordelia spins around. 'Edwin. And Millicent,' Cordelia says with surprise, completely forgetting the reason Millicent was there, completely forgetting why she was in the garden in the first place.

'Are you quite all right?' Millicent looks genuinely concerned. 'You look flushed.'

'It's a wonder you can tell. It's so dark,' Cordelia says.

'Don't be snappish,' Edwin counters. 'What are you doing in here?' He looks around but of course Mr Leigh is long gone.

'Giving the two of you a little bit of breathing room,' Cordelia fibs.

Both he and Millicent have the good grace to look sheepish at their disappearance ahead of her but it is Edwin who replies quietly, 'Yes, well . . . thanks for that. Appreciated. Don't tell Mother you sloped off, will you? We'll none of us hear the end of it.' Edwin's gaze is directed towards the ground behind her.

'Of course not,' Cordelia says but she follows her brother's gaze to where the trailing amber end of Isaac's cigarette burns its last on the path.

CHAPTER 18

CORDELIA

Since her discussions with both Gilbert and Mr Leigh helped make up her mind that she would learn to garden and that they would teach her how, Cordelia's believed that's all she's wanted to do. But now she doesn't want to go into the garden. She spent all of Saturday evening and all of Sunday thinking about him, wondering what exactly he had intended to do when he'd stretched out his hand. She's been far too used to men's unwavering interest in her and this – Isaac's wavering between weariness at her presence and all-out interest – is confusing. She cannot fathom him out and she needs to. She needs to know.

Her reflection in the looking glass shows a young woman who has had no sleep, deep flourishes of grey underline each of her eyes and she pinches her cheeks together, almost painfully, to encourage a less sallow look on either side of her face. Before they left for home, Millicent confessed her older sister Irene uses a new form of rouge. Cordelia examines her face, deciding she will send off for some. She wonders if that's the sort of thing either Fortnum & Mason or Selfridges & Co might stock. Or perhaps a pharmacist might need to concoct it. She'll write to Millicent and ask her for proper details later.

She's told no one what she intends to do today. If she says it aloud, she'll feel incredibly silly. Pruning and snipping a few flowers for a display is perfectly reasonable but she knows Father and Mother will be apoplectic if she tells them she intends to truly muck in, as it were. Besides, she'll probably hate it, all that dirt and will vow never again. And then the family will tease her for this fancy if she harps on about it and then abandons it just as quickly. So perhaps just for today, she'll keep quiet. And then tomorrow, when her fad has passed, no one will have been any the wiser.

Mr Leigh is kneeling on the ground, his back to her when she arrives as he looks over the bricks, appearing to count them. It's a warm day and she can see his shirt clinging tightly to him where patches of perspiration hold it in place against his back. Fragments of delicious memory creep into her mind – him walking towards her in the garden, his hand outstretched to touch her.

He pauses, tenses. He knows she's there but he's refusing to turn and acknowledge her. Over the past few days he's been so warm and now he's so different. Before he wanted to be near her. Is this what has prompted the change in behaviour? He caught himself in time then. He won't do it again, this she knows from the simple fact he's still pretending not to notice she's there.

'Right,' Gilbert says as he strides into view. 'Are we starting with the easy things or the hard things?'

'I don't mind,' Cordelia says honestly.

He looks her up and down. She's chosen a deep maroon dress. She assumed a dark colour would be better than a summer pastel but Gilbert looks unimpressed and so she explains her rationale.

When she finishes, he simply says, 'I have spare things if you . . .'

A laugh comes from Mr Leigh, still kneeling on the ground, still not looking at her.

'What?' Gilbert asks. 'She's either doing it properly or she's not,' he snaps. But Mr Leigh remains quiet, his shoulders still shaking with the last of his now silent laughter. 'And besides, I meant an apron.'

'Perhaps let's start with the easy tasks,' Cordelia concedes to spare Gilbert's blushes, 'and I won't invite my parents' wrath by donning an apron or whatever it is. Just in case they should chance upon me.'

Gilbert shrugs. 'Suit yourself. Grab that trowel, we're digging up new potatoes.'

Cordelia stares at the row of small instruments laid out on the ground. No, she doesn't know which one is the trowel. Mr Leigh lifts the smallish spade, stands and turns towards her. Meeting his eyes for the first time since that moment in the walled garden on Saturday night, she thanks him, allowing her fingers to brush his on the trowel before taking it from his hands. She expects him to hastily remove his from hers but he doesn't, not immediately, and it startles her into letting go of a tight breath audibly. She turns away, following Gilbert, the trowel gripped firmly in her hand.

Gilbert teaches her what to do with the soil before standing up slowly, groaning as he does so, and allowing her to get on with it.

'You're very trusting,' she offers as she delicately digs out a handful of smooth-looking small potatoes.

'Don't dig up all of 'em,' he says. 'We only want enough each day for what Mrs Emes is going to use.'

'So she tells you what to dig up?' Cordelia asks. 'What she needs to cook with?'

'Not really. The garden sort of tells her what you're having for your supper each day. The weather is the master of all of us. What's ready gets harvested. What's not, stays in the ground or on the trees until it's ready.'

'I never thought of it that way.'

'You can go a bit harder than that with the soil. We're not excavating a site of historical interest, we're digging up potatoes. Just don't spear 'em with the trowel and they'll be fine.'

When the basket is full, she stands.

'They'll be in season for a while yet,' he says. 'So we'll come back every few days and see what sort of size we're at. Next, the herb garden. We'll go and take a look at the watercress for a sauce. Then we'll stop for tea and a rock cake.'

This all sounds very enjoyable and Cordelia picks up her trowel and potato basket, dusts the flecks of dry mud from her dress and full of joy, and dare she say it, excitement, almost skips after Gilbert towards the herb garden.

The other gardeners, James and Talek, filter into the potting room – the last of the long row of brick buildings at the edge of the kitchen garden. One of the kitchen maids has brought the groundsmen out an urn of tea and a tray of hard-wearing, plain white china cups and rock cakes and placed it all on a wooden table against which sit four sturdy wooden chairs. A slab of churned butter melts in a dish next to paper packets of seeds and assorted wooden posts waiting to be placed to identify things growing in the ground. The room is dusty and muddy, the white walls not quite white anymore. It's busy, well used and functional.

Cordelia follows Gilbert to the filling tap just outside and rinses her hands, drying them on her dress the way he does. Today has been enlightening; the gritty feel of the earth has found its way into the space between her fingers and under her nails but far from minding, she's managed to get used to the feel of it on her skin as she worked. She's never really understood the properties of different herbs (just always accepted which ones often went with which dish, according to Mrs Emes) until today's quick lessons in mint, parsley, thyme and its more superior cousin lemon thyme – far and away her favourite. If she could bottle it and wear it as a scent, she would. It was all she could do not to lay in among the herbs and eat them all as if she were a rabbit.

But now she eyes the rock cakes hungrily. She doesn't remember the last time she was actually hungry and she doesn't like to take one, to make herself at home in this masculine space.

Gilbert reads her mind. 'Hungry work if you're doing it properly. Don't stand on ceremony. You can either take a cake with your muddy fingers or I can offer you one with mine?'

She laughs, reaches forward, takes a cake, slathers the underside of it in butter the way Gilbert does (Mother would be horrified if she saw) and munches ravenously, forgetting herself for a few moments until she slowly becomes aware that she's invaded their precious free time – and they don't get much from what she gathers. There's no chatter between the men. Talek and James eat quickly, throw Cordelia a sideways glance then move in silent agreement into the sunshine to drink their tea. Normally they'd be laughing and sharing some sort of joke. Or rather James would be laughing and Talek – who is quieter – would simply be nodding along in agreement. She knows this because she's stumbled across them many a time and seen them together before they look away respectfully.

Almost as quickly as they came the two men are gone, cementing her feeling of awkward intrusion.

'Pay no mind to them,' Gilbert suggests. 'No manners. I'll have a word later.'

'No don't,' she says. 'Please don't. Where are the two Mr Leighs?' she asks, aiming for nonchalant.

'Rose garden,' Gilbert says with a mouthful of cake.

'Should I take them a cake and a cup of tea?'

'No,' Gilbert says simply. 'They know what time we stop. If they've chosen not to stop too then that's their lookout.'

'Oh. That seems a bit sad,' she says.

'We'll leave it out and they can always come and help themselves when no one's looking before one of the maids comes to collect the things, if that makes you any happier.'

She nods, satisfied but a little bit of her is uneasy because now she is certain Isaac Leigh is keeping away from her on purpose.

CHAPTER 19

CORDELIA

Later, in her room, bathing her face and hands in the water Ada has brought, Cordelia wonders how much of what Gilbert taught her has actually gone in, settled itself in her mind ready to be retrieved another day. How will she ever remember what's in season and what's not? When to harvest things, when to leave them? She should have brought some writing paper out with her so she could have recorded things.

But she sits at dinner, making polite conversation, eating her piece of delicate salmon, watercress sauce and new potatoes, with a warm, knowing feeling that earlier in the day most of her dinner had been in the ground and that it was she who had dug it up.

The next day, with her mother, Cordelia pays a call to the widow of the old rector. It was a call they often paid as the woman descended into her dotage and a visit, no matter how dull, would have previously been the highlight of Cordelia's day while she was in

Cornwall. But secretly she itches to be in the garden. She'd had her eyes opened to how vast the grounds are and how much opportunity they hold and yesterday she'd only worked in a fraction of it, just a few beds. She wasn't exactly a natural, but she had enjoyed it and it had made her hungry for more. On her return, she heads straight into the gardens, finds Gilbert and asks him to put her to use.

'When will you let me loose on some of the flowers?' she asks as she works among the redcurrant bushes, delicately picking their bounty without bursting them between her fingers.

'Is that what you want to do? The pretty things?'

'Not especially. But the garden is so beautiful and I should love to know how it gets that way.'

He nods and leans against his spade, which Cordelia notices he doesn't seem to use all that much. Is it for support, as the man grows older, rather than actual digging? She'll wonder more about that later.

'I did think about that,' he sighs. 'And let's see how we go, shall we?'

'You mean whether I'll stick at it?'

Gilbert merely grunts. 'Also . . .' he placates. 'If you stick at it, I wonder what use flowers will be to you over coming months, possibly years. Other than when we put the daffodils and the lavender on the train up to London to sell.'

'What do you mean, what use?' she says, turning around, the redcurrants forgotten.

'I won't be here forever.'

'Don't say that.'

'And I don't suppose James and Talek will be either, the way the world is going.'

'Don't say that either,' she says disconsolately. 'It's only talk, isn't it?' she appeases. She hasn't mentioned the word war but they both know that's what hangs in the air.

'It does make me wonder,' Gilbert thinks aloud. 'James and Talek have already said they can't wait to go and fight if there's a war. They understand what they read in the papers better than I do. In truth, I don't think I want to understand it. Some duke no one's ever heard of gets shot in a country I don't even know where it is and a rabble of gardeners in coastal Cornwall are talking about going and fighting. An adventure, they think it is. But of course, they can't know what war is until it hits them in the face, which it invariably will.'

She's silent. Taking it all in. The gardeners intend to leave. Edwin intends to leave too. Who else?

'I'd like to say there won't be a war,' Gilbert continues, 'but it's all any of that lot all talk about over the last few weeks. I'm going to have to ban them from taking their tea in the potting shed if they won't stop. I don't want to hear it.'

She looks at him sympathetically. 'I'm sorry.' But she's not sure what she's apologising for – who she's apologising for.

'So . . . as I said, I can teach you when to prune the roses or I can give you a book and you can go off and work it out for yourself. And we can get on with practical things, keeping this estate in fruit and vegetables. It's all well and good your father overseeing the running of the farm and the dairy but if you want to really do something useful, perhaps in addition to the practical elements of gardening, it would do you some good to know how to get a potato out of the ground without obliterating it, when to sow seeds, when to thin 'em out. It's up to you though,' he finishes.

Why would Gilbert think she'd be here, gardening if a war starts? She's only worked out here with him for one day. She won't be here, if there's a war on. Will she? She'll be off doing something. Millicent's going into nursing, or so she says. That's incredibly useful. But rather awful.

Is being here, planting and sowing, keeping as much food growing as possible, perhaps not just for the house and staff but for others if they need it – after all the estate has plenty and sells it widely – is that useful? Will no one else be here to do this? If not, Gilbert can't do it alone. More importantly, is this what she wants to do? Perhaps she should think about this further after a few weeks of gardening. She might hate it tomorrow. She doesn't know at the moment. But she does know this, that if a war comes, she'll have precious little else to do.

As she's kneeling, removing some courgettes to stop them turning into marrows, it's the shadow that falls over Cordelia that makes her realise there's someone standing behind her.

She holds her rather grubby hand up over her eyes to shield the sun so she can see who it is.

'Hello,' Mr Leigh says.

'Oh,' she breathes, betraying what's happening inside her. 'I didn't know you were there.'

'I haven't been standing here long,' he says, adjusting a stack of objects in his arms.

She doesn't know whether to stand up and engage him in conversation or let him say whatever it is he's come to say while she remains kneeling on the ground. She's at a loss.

And so is he as he looks at her handiwork and her pile of courgettes she's put in a basket on the ground next to her. 'You've been busy,' he says eventually.

She has no answer to this and an awkward silence that certainly wasn't there the other night descends over them.

He holds out the stack of objects he's been carrying. 'I was on my way to check the heating installation in the glasshouse and I was cornered. Gilbert wants you to have these, apparently.'

'Apparently?' she queries, reaching out to take them.

'Talek found me. He says Gilbert instructed him to give them to you but Talek would rather not. I don't think he's spoken to a woman since his mother passed away last year. Coming to talk to you would probably send him running scared.'

'Oh,' Cordelia says, shocked. 'Poor Talek.'

'Quite,' Mr Leigh smiles.

'So you're here.'

'So I'm here,' he says.

Cordelia looks at the objects one by one: a pair of thick gardening gloves, a cushion and a book about roses.

She smiles at the last one. So she'll be learning about flowers from books, as Gilbert suggested she should.

'That was kind of Gilbert,' she says.

'I'm surprised he waited until now to provide you with gloves and a kneeler but there we are.'

'Perhaps he was trying to make it as uncomfortable for me as possible so I'd give up faster.'

'That's quite astute of you,' And then, 'I'm sorry, that was rude of me.'

'It's quite all right.' In addition to the awkwardness, the sense of formality is back between them. But his dark eyes are trained on hers and she has to look away.

'I wonder if there's a book lurking somewhere about fruit and veg,' she continues, hoping her face isn't as flushed as she believes it to be.

'Veg?' he queries, smiling teasingly at her.

'That's right,' she teases in return. 'I too can shorten words down the way you do.'

He laughs loudly. 'Fair enough. I don't have one on me, no. But Gilbert might, up at the bothy. Or you will, no doubt, in your library.'

'That's a thought,' she says. 'Mother's drowning in gardening books, which is odd really because she never reads them and she's never outside putting anything into practice.'

'Well no,' Mr Leigh says with a smile. 'You've got staff for that.'

And then Cordelia remembers as she sees his muddy hands that he's part of that collective. Staff. Is he staff? Not really. She doesn't think of him as such.

He continues, 'See if you can find *Diaries of a Victorian Gardener*, that's the one I liked best. Quite famous. It's an easy read, seasonal. Practical. She might not have it but if there's something like it – month by month – see what you think. See if some of the information sticks. And if it doesn't, don't worry. You can come back to it later.'

'I will, thank you.'

'Why has Gilbert given you a book about roses in particular?' he asks, turning it over in his hand.

'It's a long story,' she says, not wishing to get into talk about a war quite so soon.

He glances at the courgettes in the basket and then steps forward to assess the remaining produce on the vines. 'I think that's probably enough for today,' he says kindly. 'The servants will be eating those for their supper for weeks if you cut any more.'

And then he pauses, seems to think. 'We're extending the rose garden,' he says. 'If you're interested in roses would you like to come and gain some practical experience with me for a moment?'

She brightens. 'Yes, I would.'

'Come on then,' he says. He points at the objects he's just given her. 'Bring the gloves, leave the rest.'

CHAPTER 20

CORDELIA

'And this is an old English rose,' Isaac says when they've completed a tour of the existing rose garden. 'They look best in tall vases, I think, so leave a lot of stem when you cut,' he instructs.

'Are we allowed to do this?' she asks, glancing around, feeling like a thief.

'Of course,' he says. 'It's your garden and your mother tells me she loves roses throughout the house at this time of year.'

'She does,' Cordelia replies.

'Which is one of the reasons she wants the rose gardens extended,' he counters.

Cordelia moves forward and her gloved hand touches his ungloved one as he moves it further down the stem. 'Like that,' he says as if he's not just touched her. 'But remember to take a few from all over or it will look a bit sparse round one side.'

She cuts ten and Isaac takes them from her one by one without comment, laying them down in the basket.

'James has already taken some up to the house, but you could present your mother with something from your endeavours today if you wanted to.'

She nods. 'Yes, I'd like that.' A reason for mother and daughter to bond, that might be very useful indeed if Cordelia is to find something beneficial to do if there is a war to come. A way to butter Mother up, especially as she hasn't *quite* let on to her family what she is doing out here each day. In truth, Cordelia hadn't been expecting to enjoy herself enough to keep doing this.

'And then we'll cut some tea roses,' Isaac continues. 'Do you remember which ones they are?'

She gives him a look. 'Of course. I'm not stupid,' she says.

'I never said you were.' He looks genuinely surprised by her remark.

'Mother likes tea roses so I suppose we'll have to cut them but quite honestly I prefer the climbing roses and the floribunda that you showed me earlier. That's what I'd have dotted around the house if it were me.'

'Why?' he asks, his eyes narrowed.

'Because they grow so wildly, clustering together, bursting to and from each other, completely unrestrained. Tea roses are too neat, too perfect.'

He folds his arms and looks at her.

'What?' she asks.

He shakes his head, still looking at her. 'You are a surprise, Miss Carr-Lyon.'

'Why? And you can call me Cordelia, you know.'

He looks at her. 'Can I?'

'Of course. And perhaps I may call you Isaac?'

He smiles. 'You may.'

'I don't much like my name,' she goes on as they

walk. 'And I don't like how it sounds when most people say it. I don't like how it sounds when I say it. But I think I should like it if you said it.'

'Why don't you like it?'

'Because I'm named after a very tragic heroine. Who dies.'

He suppresses a laugh.

'Of all of Shakespeare's heroines to choose, why one that dies?' she asks rhetorically.

'It's a pretty name,' he admits.

'It's not. Ophelia's much prettier.'

'She dies too.'

She looks at him. 'Does she? I forgot that. Have you read it?' she asks.

'Which one? *King Lear* or *Hamlet*?'

'Either.'

He nods. 'Yes. Forced upon me at school. If I read now it's most likely to be the newspaper or *Tomato Diseases and How to Prevent Them*.'

'Does that book actually exist?' she teases.

He smiles. 'No. Something like it does though.'

'I've never really been much of a reader,' she confesses. 'I've only just started reading the newspaper.'

'Not the greatest time to start reading it,' he says. 'But better late than not at all.'

'I don't like what I read in it so far,' she says.

'That's usually the way with newspapers.'

'Father says because the Russians will support Serbia who shot the Austrian archduke in the first place, the Germans will support the Austro-Hungarians.'

Mr Leigh nods. 'Your father is not wrong.'

'And there's talk that if that happens,' Cordelia continues, trying her best to remember the complicated alliances, 'that Serbia – through a variety of treaties – will be able to call for help from Russia, Belgium, France . . . and us because we are bound in treaty to the Belgians.'

Isaac nods. 'You make it sound quite simple.'

Cordelia sighs, tracing an invisible line in her mind across Europe, various armies racing to each other's aid. 'Actually, it sounds anything but. How could this happen? How could war stretch so far so fast? We'll go to war,' she finishes.

He nods again, watching her carefully. 'We probably will, yes. Not just us, but the might of the entire British Empire. En masse.'

'Edwin says he won't go back to university. That he'll try to join the army.'

'He might not need to join the army if he doesn't want to,' Isaac offers.

'Believe me, he wants to. Is there talk in the servants' hall of war?' she asks suddenly.

Isaac makes a thoughtful face. 'I'm only in there for mealtimes and Mr Richards is banning war-talk from now on but in a manner of speaking, yes. It's not so much putting names down to go, it's more general talk of what war will mean.'

'Do you think any of them will go?' she asks. 'The outdoor staff intend to, so Gilbert tells me. Will you?' This is what she's wanted to know most of all.

He shrugs, then focuses his attention back to the roses. 'Honestly, I don't know.'

'Edwin says it's a noble cause, to rush to the defence of our foreign friends, if need be.'

'I suppose it must be then.'

'You don't agree with my brother?' she pushes. 'He's going to try to be an officer, he says, if there's a war.'

'And if there's not a war?'

'He'll continue at university. He's thinking about medical school afterwards.'

Isaac smiles knowingly.

'What?' she asks.

'His options are to become a soldier and kill, or be a doctor and save lives?'

'I . . . I didn't think of that. You make it sound so simple.'

'War is simple,' Isaac says, his voice calm, monitored. 'It's about people like you and me . . . well, not you. It's people like your brother and me, being handed a weapon and told to kill someone we don't even know, who we'd probably get along with in everyday life. And all because someone, somewhere on a gilded throne or behind a big desk decides that's what we have to do.'

Cordelia doesn't speak. And then, 'Are you a Bolshevik?'

He laughs so hard it stuns her.

'No,' he says, eventually. 'I'm not.' But he offers no name to what he might be.

He's right though. She knows he's right. She hopes fervently now there won't be a war.

'I'm not sure how killing in war can ever really be truly justified,' he says finally. 'So whatever that makes me . . . I'm that.'

'Because we'll need to help,' she offers. 'Father says our foreign neighbours might need us and if that's the case, the country will have to send men to help.'

Isaac says nothing, neither agreeing nor disagreeing. Overhead the sun moves from its position behind a frothy white cloud, casting its generous glow on the gardens, its light shafting brightly towards the coast in the distance. Isaac follows her gaze towards the direction of the light to the sea. 'Let's hope our foreign friends don't need us then.'

She smiles but it's thin, contemplative. 'Do you think we're on borrowed time, here like this?'

He inhales deeply. 'Perhaps. Yes. Cordelia,' he continues and hearing him say her name, it's as if a rain cloud has been blown away, one she hadn't known was overhead. She cannot help it, her spirits lift.

'In the walled garden . . .' he rushes out.

'Yes?' she breathes.

'I . . .' he starts but he's struggling. 'I want to apologise.'

'You were going to touch me.' She speaks quickly.

A brief nod from Isaac – so brief she almost misses it. She didn't imagine it.

And then he says, 'Yes. Well, no. I don't know. I think it was simply an involuntary movement. Regardless . . . I apologise.'

'Why are you sorry?'

'Because it's not a good idea.'

She pauses, unsure they're talking about the same thing. 'What's not a good idea?'

'You must know.'

'I'm not entirely sure I do.'

He gives her a look so penetrating she has to look away. Her eyes fall to his lips and she wonders, not for the first time what it would be like to be kissed by Isaac Leigh.

But she's stopped from thinking this as she hears her mother's startled voice cry, 'What in God's name do you think you're doing?'

CHAPTER 21

CORDELIA

Later, Cordelia tries for the second time to explain herself – badly – to her mother. Halfway through Cordelia's careful speech, justifying why she is covered in dirt and spending so much time in the grounds, she knows she is failing as her mother puffs up even more than usual.

Edwin has walked into the music room to join them just as Cordelia is climbing to the pinnacle of her argument.

'It's because it's unladylike,' their mother retorts, struggling to keep her composure as Edwin pours tea, scouting around on the sideboard for his beloved scones that aren't there.

'What's unladylike?' he asks, biting into the edge of a fruit tart, obviously hoping for something more salacious than the word . . .

'Gardening,' Cordelia responds. (It is sweet relief to Cordelia that *this* is all she's being accused of and that fraternising so closely with Isaac went unnoticed.)

'It's not just gardening though, is it? You're outside all day, your skin is browning like a foreigner and by your own admission you're on hands and knees. It's unseemly,' her mother says.

'Don't be ridiculous, Mother,' Edwin starts, plucking a harp string absentmindedly as he moves towards the settee. 'You're out there cutting and doing whatnot,' he reminds her.

'Not on hands and *knees*. Not surrounded by men.'

'Times are changing, Mother,' Cordelia starts. She's seen articles in the newspaper about women in factories and although it hadn't appealed to her, women earning their own money did look rather . . . freeing. And on the other side of that argument is . . . 'Gertrude Jekyll does it. She's a woman and she's quite renowned for her horticultural flair, you know. And it's voluntary, Mother, in our own grounds, and educational. It's not in exchange for any actual money in anyone else's gardens.'

Her mother baulks, raising a hand to her heart. 'Could you imagine?' she asks, her eyes closed to guard against the vision.

Cordelia has only tried this counter argument on for size, just to see if her parents would be disgusted by the concept of manual labour. But she can see they really do think the idea of learning a trade and earning money from it is abhorrent. In this day and age, when Edwin intends to learn medicine . . . a trade of sorts. She had not known this about them before. She's never had call to discuss it. Now she does and she doesn't like it.

'And you want to do this?' her mother says. 'You actually want to be out there in all weathers, tending to the fruit and vegetables every day?'

'And the rest of the grounds.' Cordelia thinks it best

to get it all confessed now, while she is on the subject. No surprises later, reigniting a row. 'There are meadows that Isa . . . Mr Leigh apparently doesn't intend to change. I know because I've checked the plans. We could be putting them to better use, especially if a war comes. We could be producing so much more. We might need to. And not just for the estate and its surrounding environs. We already send daffodils and lavender up on the train to London. Why not do more?' She's repeated this last part about the flowers from Gilbert but the first part about the meadows she's thought of all by herself.

'What a good idea, Cordy,' Edwin says. 'Father will like the idea of more revenue for the estate. What do you suggest?'

'I have no idea at the moment but I've been reading some of the books in the library about gardening and I found one about crop rotation. It's actually quite fascinating and Gilbert and Mr Leigh are fonts of all knowledge—'

Her mother makes a despairing noise.

Edwin chips in. 'Cordy, do you intend to do this for a while? And by that, I mean . . . not just for a week.'

'Yes, Edwin,' she tuts. 'I'm enjoying it. I'm sure it will get harder in the winter months but I am genuinely enjoying the literal fruits of my labour. I know I didn't plant anything but all the vegetables you've been eating with each meal have been gathered by me. And that's just the start of it. There's so much I can do out there. The gardeners are very busy but incredibly talented. They grow food from tiny little seeds. It's almost akin to alchemy.'

'All right,' Edwin laughs and Cordelia can see his

mind working. His flighty sister is actually sticking at something. If he wasn't already thinking that, she's not going to voice it and put it in his head. 'I understand,' he says in jovial defeat. 'In that case, I fail to see the problem. In fact, it might be a solution to a problem we didn't know we had coming.'

Their mother's hand is against her temple, pushing slowly against it repeatedly.

'War's coming. Cordy knows it. We all do. Only you and Father won't see it. We can't help you get there faster, I'm afraid. I know you read the papers.'

'Sensationalist nonsense,' their mother says, but not convincingly.

Read beyond the headline, Cordelia wants to say but doesn't.

'Anyway,' Edwin continues. 'We'll probably lose a lot of staff.'

'Of course we won't!' their mother says. 'Who would voluntarily want to leave Pencallick House and their nice, safe employment to go and play soldiers? To play at war? Only the suicidal would do such a thing.'

'Call it suicidal but I have no doubt it will happen,' Edwin says, standing his ground. 'And when it does, when all the staff have gone to war and the gardeners have all joined up you can watch the estate decline or Cordy can roll up her sleeves, if she wants to, and grow food for the nation and light all the fires in the house at dawn and cook the dinner and carry the tubs of bathwater—'

'Yes, all right,' Mother says as Cordelia can't tell if Edwin is truly joking or not. 'Fine. Fine. Talk to your father about the grounds and if he agrees to you spending your days learning about . . . whatever it is you've been learning about . . . then who am I to stop you? I'm only your mother after all. I have no say, clearly, in the fates of my own children.'

Cordelia rushes over and kisses her mother on the cheek. And as Edwin mouths the words, 'You're welcome,' she rushes over and kisses his cheek too.

CHAPTER 22

CORDELIA

Isaac is keeping away again. She knows he is. And now she thinks she knows why. She cannot tell if there is something bursting between them or if it's all in her imagination. Perhaps him reaching out to touch her had been entirely innocent after all. Entirely unmotivated by desire. God, she hopes not. Although nothing can come of it, she knows that. It would be nice to know he felt . . . something, anything for her.

There have been days of glimpsing him around corners. And when she thinks she'll go and be friendly and simply say hello, she finds that when she arrives in the spot in which he's been standing he is either flanked by his brother, or by James and Talek as he issues general instructions to them about some garden job or other; or that he has long since gone entirely.

At first she thinks it is pure chance he keeps moving in the other direction and then she wonders if he might just be avoiding her on purpose.

A passing infatuation, that's what it is. And he must

feel the same. He was going to touch her after all. But what if she's attaching too much to that?

She could never be with someone such as Mr Leigh. Although he is educated and an architectural landscaper, where does he live? What does he do with his days? No. It's laughable. The more he keeps away from her, the starker that realisation grows in her mind. It is ridiculous, absurd, dangerous, embarrassing.

Cordelia's cheeks flush as she imagines a dalliance with Isaac Leigh. It would be something remarkable to look back on in later life. She imagines herself older, surrounded by a brood of children, giving a boring dinner for people whose faces she can't imagine and remembering back. *When I was a young woman I allowed the most handsome gardener to make love to me among the roses.*

But yes, it is ridiculous. Incredibly, undeniably ridiculous. She knows that. But where is the harm in being friends?

CHAPTER 23

CORDELIA

Cordelia has been dipping in and out of books about crops. After she had a conversation with Gilbert about making better use of the flower fields, now that war was likely and food might be scarce, they decided it might be useful to consider sowing vegetable seeds alongside the daffodil bulbs. Lettuces and parsley would be suitable bedfellows for the base of the tall daffodils and would not only provide food but would maximise space and also revenue.

But for something a bit lighter, this morning she ponders over the beauty of Gertrude Jekyll's recent publication *Gardens for Small Country Houses*, while her brother and father pore over the latest world news.

They speak of matters far outside any of their collective control: Germany having declared war on Russia but agreeing with Great Britain to maintain Belgian neutrality; France having mobilised troops to come to the aid of Belgium and Luxembourg; German soldiers being spotted in Poland and France without having made a formal declaration of war on the latter.

The newspaper is littered with detail upon detail upon detail including Foreign Secretary Sir Edward Grey's speech to parliament to recommend Britain enter the war.

She breathes in, breathes out as her family announce selected pieces of detail one after the other – something Edwin and Father had ever only done in morbid excitement once before, two years previously when news of the *Titanic* disaster had found its way to their quiet corner of England. Until they'd spotted friends' names on the list of the perished and the tone had changed decidedly.

'This is it, isn't it?' Edwin says bleakly when they finish reciting the news. 'We can hardly sit back and do nothing while all this is going on, can we?' And he sounds as if he's asking a genuine question.

Both he and Cordelia look at Father. Mother too. No one has the answer. 'I think we should wait and see what happens,' Father says eventually.

Edwin glances at the newspaper and then again at Cordelia. 'I don't think we'll have to wait very long.'

Cordelia forces her mind off Europe and back to the garden in order to distract herself. She's curious to know which of the new garden fashions Mr Leigh intends to incorporate. The plans – always on Father's desk – whetted her appetite for things to come. A wild garden? Would there be some sort of wilderness? Having now read all about them, she dearly hopes so. But with war coming will this sort of thing feel a little pointless, a little unnecessary and out of step with the wider world?

Mother and Father are taking an urgent trip to London today and will stay at the family's house in town. Father is visiting his banker to discuss matters now the London Stock Exchange is closing due to the situation in Europe, and Mother plans to do some urgent shopping on Father's recommendations. Mother finally understood that Cordelia is serious about her new pastime in the garden when she rejected the opportunity to accompany them shopping.

Edwin has taken the carriage over to visit Millicent, and Cordelia notices her brother hasn't extended the invite to her and so it transpires that Cordelia will have the house to herself, other than the servants downstairs and Clive who will be with Nanny for the most part. She can't remember the last time she was alone in the house. Has it ever happened? So she won't dress for dinner and has arranged with Cook to have a tray in the library where she can pore over the gardening books she's sent off for.

While she is on a ladder harvesting the few early pears, her mind is deep into the finer details of her plan to spread her books all across the floor for the rest of the evening and well into the night, scattering writing paper around, drawing diagrams and making notes.

And then Gilbert ambles past, instructing her to down tools, telling her he has no idea why she is still here as the other gardeners have already left for the evening. The other gardeners. She was sure that was a slip of the tongue. He doesn't see her as one of them, surely. She certainly doesn't. She hasn't earned that right. Has she finally found something she enjoys and is good at?

But he is too busy dismissing her to notice her mind wandering, saying she's earned the right to finish early in her own grounds if she so wishes, let alone finish late. She smiles, says something about how time has run away from her given that she's never had call to wear a wristwatch and says she will finish for the day after all.

The sun casts telltale long shadows as Cordelia cleans her tools and hangs them back in place on the rusty nails in the potting room. She looks down at her apron, which she's begun wearing over the top of her day dress. She isn't so much covered in mud but she is covered in a layer of grime. She can feel that dustiness on her face and in her hair. The day is far too hot to ask Ada to draw her a bath. The last thing she wants to do is wallow in hot water. But cool water might be just the thing.

Is she too old for a spot of sea bathing? She hasn't been down to the cove in such a long time. She puts her hands on her back as she walks to the house, stretching it out and tipping her chin up to the sun. The day is still warm and the tidal cove will have had the sun on the sand all day, warming the water as the tide returns. It is the most perfect time to take a dip.

There is a certain sense of delicious freedom about this afternoon. With no family at home, she can come and go as she pleases, reporting to no one but herself. She's already taken tea with Gilbert, James and Talek. Talek actually responded to her when she spoke instead of nodding or staring at the floor. She'd made a point of cornering him and speaking to him about his favourite subject – the new orchard.

If that is the only achievement of the day – that one discussion and getting Talek to converse with her – that will have made the day perfect alone. But the real excitement is for this evening: supper on a tray and books on the library rug and the hope that none of the servants walk in halfway through to see her snaffling her supper while sitting on the floor.

She climbs the ornately carved wooden stairs, crosses the landing to her room, puts on her bathers under a clean dress, takes her towel and with dreams of laying on her back, letting her hair fan out in the cool sea water, sets off towards the cove.

CHAPTER 24

ISAAC

'I think it's getting hotter,' Isaac says, standing on the soft sandy beach and staring up into the blue sky as streaks of orange and pink lower their way across the horseshoe-shaped cove. 'How can that be possible?'

David ignores him and yells, 'Last one to swim to the rock is a fool,' and he runs into the calm water.

Isaac cries out in frustration, still hopping out of his shoes. 'You've got an unfair head start.' He adjusts his bathers, follows at speed, running until he's knee deep and then swimming as fast as he can to beat his younger brother, although David is so far ahead he'll never reach him now. Their time off is precious. With every passing day, Isaac realises this. Never more so than now.

Both men carve through the calm water, sheltered as it is here in the cove. David reaches the rock first, as Isaac knew he would. The younger man climbs up the smooth rock. Soon the water will be above it, masking the rock entirely. It is when David wobbles unsteadily, rising and then standing up on both feet, that Isaac finally reaches him, conceding defeat.

Isaac climbs up, latching his knee into a groove before pushing himself up into a standing position next to David. He playfully jostles for space on the rock and his brother catches him before he falls. They turn away from the cove and stare far out to sea. Isaac wonders if he and David are thinking different things.

'Do you think it will always be like this?' David asks after a while and Isaac smiles because they are thinking the same.

'Are you getting sentimental?' Isaac suggests as above them seagulls swoop and soar, call out to each other.

'Maybe.' His brother sits down on the rock. 'All this talk of war . . .'

'It won't affect us if we don't let it,' Isaac says. But he knows he's clutching at a dying hope.

'But what if we want it to?'

Isaac laughs. 'Why would we want that?'

David shrugs. 'Adventure?'

'I don't think that's what it's going to be,' Isaac replies.

'We won't know unless we go.'

'I won't be going anywhere,' Isaac returns.

'You sound very sure. What if they make us?'

'They can't.' Although as he says it, Isaac isn't sure of that at all.

'You want to stay stuck here forever?'

'Don't do that,' Isaac replies. 'I know you've got delusions of grandeur . . .' David gives Isaac a shove that almost destabilises him. Isaac chuckles and continues. 'But I'm happy here. A roof over my head and enough food to eat, a healthy brother and a job I enjoy. And we're treated incredibly fairly. The families always seem to respect us, treat us well, speak to us.'

David makes a noise halfway between a grunt and a sigh. 'So far. That's not enough,' he says vehemently.

Isaac tuts. 'It should be. It's more than most men have and if you think war is going to bring you riches, then you're chasing a dream.'

'Of course not riches,' David concedes. 'But it's just something different isn't it,' he says. 'Maybe even if there isn't a war, all this talk of it, it's made me think.'

'Think what?' Isaac asks.

'Just think. No parents. Nothing to lose.'

'Everything to lose,' Isaac cuts in.

David continues on, 'And if I do decide to go off on an adventure, it means you won't have to see my handsome face, making you feel inadequate every morning.'

Isaac laughs. 'Other way round, you mean?'

At that David gives Isaac a proper shove and he slips off the rock and straight into the water.

When he resurfaces, he starts climbing up again but David stops him. 'Look,' he says, nodding his head in the direction of the shore.

'Good try,' Isaac replies, grabbing his brother's leg.

'No. Look.' Isaac spins around in the water and stares to where his brother indicates.

It's her. She's on the beach watching them, her hand clamped to her mouth, her shoulders shaking with laughter.

'Oh God,' Isaac declares under his breath. 'What's she doing here? We shouldn't be here,' he says.

'We've as much right to be here as her,' David replies. 'They don't own this cove. Gilbert told us as much the other day. He didn't think they even came down here anymore.'

'Well, one of them's here now. Come on,' Isaac mutters. 'We'll apologise and leave.'

'I'm not doing that. We've done nothing wrong.'

'It's respectful. Look how's she's dressed.'

'She's in her bathers like us. We come down here when the housemaids and the kitchen maids are bathing on their evenings off . . . It's just the same. What's got into you?'

'Nothing,' Isaac says, setting off. 'I just don't want to be here when she's here. It's . . . odd.'

'For you maybe.'

'Just come on,' Isaac calls back over his shoulder as he swims.

He doesn't know if he should swim in her direction, stand in front of her, apologise for encroaching on her space. Or if he should just acknowledge her from afar, keep his distance, swim to another part of the beach – the bit closer to the steps – and then leave.

But in the end she spares him the trouble of deciding as she walks towards him, holding her towel in front of her. 'Hello,' she says. She's still smiling.

'Miss Carr-Lyon,' he says and then at her disappointed look, corrects himself. 'Cordelia.'

'I can't tell from here – is that your brother?' She squints as she looks towards David, in the water, swimming painfully slowly on his back in the wrong direction as if to prove a point to Isaac.

'Yes. David.'

'I know his name,' she says, narrowing her eyes at his tone. 'He's on his back, I just couldn't see who it was.'

'No. Of course. Sorry.' He stalls. 'We're going to leave.'

She's fast to react. 'Because I've arrived?'

'We want to give you some space to swim without us . . . you know.'

'Being here? I don't mind you both being here. You were here first.'

'I know but it's . . .'

She's in her bathers and so is he. He's been avoiding her for so long and now they're dressed like this. He needs to leave. He can't even remember what he was saying.

'It's not our cove, you know,' she says. 'We don't own it. You've as much right to be here as anyone.'

He makes a noise that he doesn't mean to make.

'You've been avoiding me,' she says. It's not a question and he can't work out her tone.

Isaac glances around to where David still swims. This whole evening is becoming increasingly more painful. He looks back at Cordelia. 'You're very forthright,' he mutters.

'I might be forthright but I also hope I'm very astute. I'm right, aren't I? Have I offended you in some way?'

Her knee-length white bathers are tied in at the waist, her arms bare. He can't stop looking.

There is no chance for Isaac to speak as David strides out of the water, walking towards them. 'Hello,' the younger brother says.

'Hello,' Cordelia responds warmly. 'Apparently I've driven you both away, which is a shame because it's stiflingly hot today and you both appeared to be enjoying yourselves.'

David shakes his head, drying himself on his towel. 'Are we leaving?' he asks with a wicked glint in his eye as if Isaac hasn't told him this less than three minutes ago. 'I was going to try to catch some fish.' He gestures to where he's set up his bag and rod. 'Not often we're by the coast. And I thought before the tide comes all the way back in, I'd scour the rock pools for crabs.'

'Crabs?' Cordelia asks.

'Of course. If there's any, if you like, I'll show you how to catch some without getting nipped.'

'Yes please,' she says before turning and accompanying David in the direction of the rock pools.

Isaac can't help but stare as Cordelia and David saunter along to the edge of the cove talking about crustaceans like the best of friends.

'I used to watch the crabs scuttling along here when I was a child. Never thought to catch them,' Cordelia says conversationally as they both crouch down to look for the biggest ones. 'Will you put them back when you've caught them?'

David looks at her as if she's mad. 'No. I'll cook them. Then I'll have cold crab sandwiches tomorrow. Bread. Thick butter. Delicious.'

She looks impressed.

'I'll bring you one if you like?' David says.

Isaac can feel his teeth grinding together. He's trying his best to keep away and now David's forging a friendship. He just wants things to go back to how they were before that night by the lake, before that night in the garden when his hand lifted and he involuntarily made to touch her. He turns away, closing his eyes in horror at the memory.

'We only see some of the other servants down here from time to time, never your lot,' David prompts.

'It's not actively encouraged,' Cordelia confesses as she watches David pull a crab from the pool on a line with a piece of bacon fat on the end. He decants it and they watch it scuttling into the bottom of the pail he's brought with him.

'When we do come down there's a big song and dance about it,' she continues. 'Trestle tables full of food, sun umbrellas and windbreaks and, oh, everything. And then Father gets restless and Mother worries about the ferocity of the sun on her face and then we all traipse back up the cliff path again. There's a big song and dance about everything we do as a family but when it's just me . . .'

'Something a bit quieter,' David dares. 'Without all the show.'

'Yes. Do you know, you're not afraid to say what you think,' Cordelia points out. She throws Isaac a look. He's joined them quietly. He's behind David but he's watching, not participating. 'Unlike your brother. Sometimes I can't work out what he's thinking.'

'Isaac?' David asks Cordelia. He's utterly oblivious to the fact his brother is right behind him. 'That's a joke,' he says conspiratorially. 'He's the most outspoken person I know.'

'Is he now?'

Cordelia stands up and gives Isaac her full attention but it's David she's talking to, his attention firmly on the rock pool. 'What is it he's outspoken about?'

David stares into the puddle of water and reaches forward to pull out a crab. 'Oh everything. Life, politics, war, gardening, politics.'

'Really?' Cordelia asks David knowingly while still looking at Isaac. Isaac looks right back at her.

'Life, politics, war, gardening and more politics?' Cordelia teases. 'Which is his favourite subject?'

'All of them,' David suggests. 'He's boring about all subjects in equal measure.'

Isaac can't resist smiling at this and so does Cordelia. 'Is he now?' she asks. Isaac's smile is still on his face but he disconnects eye contact with her.

Politics and war are likely to prove the most salacious source of entertainment, so of course that's what she asks about.

'He thinks the government are idiots, obviously,' David confesses.

'Obviously,' Cordelia laughs. Isaac catches her eye. 'And that we're in danger of sleepwalking into war.' Isaac is going to stop David if his mouth runs away with him.

'What about you? What are your favourite subjects for conversation?' Cordelia switches to David. Isaac can't believe his own reaction: Disappointment that she's stopped addressing him.

David looks up at her. 'Fishing. One day I want to own a trout stream or a fishery. I'm not sure which yet. I love fishing. I can talk to you about it all day long.'

'Do you have a sweetheart?' Cordelia asks David suddenly.

'No.' He draws out the word. 'We're never around long enough on these commissions to form any sort of proper attachment. Might be for the best too the way things are going across the continent.'

David stands, collects his pail. 'Oh,' he says in surprise at seeing Isaac standing there. 'Got six of them.' He shakes to the crabs squirming in the bucket. 'Crab sandwiches tomorrow.'

CHAPTER 25

CORDELIA

David walks towards where he's left his fishing rod and begins setting up by the shoreline, leaving Isaac and Cordelia by the rock pool. She walks towards the water.

She can feel his eyes on her as she bathes and then suddenly she can't. As she swims on her back she glances at him – walking away, towards his brother. She sighs, letting the cool water engulf her, fanning her hair out behind her and it is every bit as delicious as she'd remembered.

'You've been doing this since you were children?' Cordelia asks when she emerges from the water, wrapping herself in her large bathing towel.

Isaac nods, doing up his shirt, finishing getting dressed. 'David has. I do it only for fun. I'm not a serious angler.'

'No, no,' Cordelia agrees. 'You've got far too much to be getting on with already what with all the politics, gardening, more politics and whatever the other things were.'

She watches him laugh and his face opens in such a genuinely warm way it quite stuns her. Warm. Cold. Warm. Cold. He's like the weather or the currents of the sea. He's unpredictable. She can't work out if she likes this interchangeability or not.

He moves away as the sun is lowering in the sky. Soon it will set over the house, the cliff casting long shadows onto the sand, onto them. She feels her skin dry under the towel, the sharpness of the sea salt crystallising on her limbs. She will need a warm bath after all. She should return to the house now she's achieved her aim of bathing a little.

But she doesn't. She wants to be here, just a little bit longer. David is adjusting the line on his rod and Isaac is sitting on the sand, some way away, lacing up his shoes. She joins him. Close but not too close.

Down here at the beach, like this she feels as if she's momentarily living a different life as a different person. Far away from her duties as the daughter of the house, far away from the words in the newspapers. But she'll return to the real world imminently, as she knows she must, before the household servants start to wonder where she's got to and send out a search party.

'What's David hoping to catch?' she asks, if only to continue the conversation.

'Not a great deal. Mackerel, sardines maybe. He might get a few or he might get a shoal. You can never tell with David. Luck of the devil.'

In the distance, where the cove falls away to the sea, the rock is almost covered as the tide sweeps its way across it.

'Do you often swim here?' she asks.

'Not very often,' he says. 'We've only been here since the end of spring. Only been warm enough for a few months. Sometimes I swim in the lake.'

'Do you?' she asks, shocked. 'I've never once seen you.'

'I'm very discreet,' he confesses.

'I suppose you must be. Do you know, I got stuck on that rock once,' Cordelia says, pointing out to sea.

It's his turn to sound shocked. 'Did you? How stuck?'

'Very stuck,' she admits. 'I'd just learned to swim breaststroke properly and I was very proud of it. Showing off. I swam too far. Climbed onto the rock and the water kept rising. I was with Edwin and Nanny but they'd neither noticed I was in difficulty. Or rather I don't think I wanted to admit I was. I screamed for help when it was too late, when the water rose. I didn't have the energy to swim back to shore. Edwin came to fetch me.'

'That rock is the cause of a lot of distress from what I hear.'

'What do you mean?'

'Many a boat has run itself aground or caught itself on that rock as it sought sanctuary in this sheltered space, or so Ada, your maid has divulged.'

She is unsure what she thinks of these shared conversations he has with other people, other women on the estate. Does he have many of them?

But, 'Really?' is all she replies.

'The entrance to the cove isn't as deep as others. If it's not the sandbanks, hidden when the tide's in, that runs a boat aground, then it's that blasted rock apparently.'

She knows. Of course she knows. She's lived here, off and on, almost her entire life. 'Have there been many shipwrecks?' she asks, knowing of course there have but none since she's been alive.

'Before your grandfather bought Pencallick House, the previous owners had been in this part of Cornwall since time immemorial. They had once been rich as Croesus. But,' he said, 'they lost it all in bad investments. Their money had come from wrecking. They had been villagers, back before Pencallick grew, back when there were only a few houses.'

Now she didn't know that at all. 'How do you know all this?' she asks.

He laughs. 'Your father told me when I was recommended to him. He told me some of the history of the house at our first meeting. And Ada filled in the blanks. Did you not know this?'

She shakes her head. Perhaps she had been told. Perhaps she'd not been listening. 'Go on.' She is enthralled as to where this story is heading.

'That rock,' he cuts to the thrust of the tale. 'Where was I? That rock, those sandbanks, wrecked ships. Right, I'm back on my train of thought.'

She laughs, hugs her knees to her chest on the sand and pulls her towel around her.

'A poverty-stricken villager decided to do something about his situation to improve his life and obviously end other people's.'

'End?'

Isaac turns to her. She can tell he is weighing up what to say next.

'I understand now. Go on,' she prompts.

In the distance, David whoops as the line on his rod tightens and he collects his bounty.

Isaac takes a deep breath. 'They took all the goods that were being transported, sold them on. Over time they had enough to build Pencallick House. And each time they wrecked ships, luring them in with lanterns onto the rock or the banks in the midst of a storm, they drowned the survivors that made it to shore so that no one would bear witness to the theft. That's what the rumours are. Of course, it was a hundred years ago or so . . . but descendants of the original team of wreckers still live and work here and in the village, which is *perhaps* why this rumour hasn't filtered its way to the ears of young ladies.'

'Staff? Which?' she asks, ignoring his latter comment, captivated by the gossip.

'That would be telling,' Isaac says.

'No,' she says. 'You can't tease me like that. You have to tell me. You must.'

'Must I?' he says. 'Well, in that case . . .'

He looks at her, the two of them on the sand but he smiles to himself and then stares back out to sea, remaining silent.

'I'm not sure I want to know. They drowned the survivors,' Cordelia repeats to herself and then exclaims, 'My word. Oh I wonder if it's Gilbert's ancestors. Or Jonathan? Is it Jonathan?'

Isaac laughs.

'It's Ada, isn't it?' she asks in mock-seriousness. 'Wink once for yes and twice for no.'

He splutters with laughter. She loves how easily she makes him laugh. She's barely had to try at all. Although she does wish he'd tell her which of the Pencallick staff have wrecking in their blood.

While David moves around in and out of the water collecting his catch, Isaac and Cordelia sit and watch him, telling each other the stories they'd been told as children of mermaids, other legends of Cornwall and the one that seemed to have enthralled both of them as children, King Arthur, with Cordelia freely admitting she'd only been interested in the story of Guinevere and Lancelot and that she actually didn't know what it was King Arthur was supposed to have done to make him so legendary, other than sit at a round table.

Isaac laughs at that but not unkindly and regales her with the story of Roman legions, the Lady in the Lake, Excalibur.

'How do you know all this?' she asked.

'Tales before bedtime. Books.'

'Oh, I wish you'd stop saying that,' she says. 'I feel very silly. I've not explored any of the library in the house in which I've lived most of my life. I blame that on being forever up and down to the London house where the library is minuscule. I shall correct my lack of intelligence and my general stupidity today,' she declares proudly. 'Although I'm starting with gardening books. I'm not sure I can face Arthurian legend tonight as well.'

'I loved those books as a child,' Isaac says wistfully. 'I'd happily read them again.'

'Would you?' she asks. 'I'll see what I can find in the library and fetch some for you if you like.'

He smiles. 'Yes, I would like that.'

The air has turned chilly and the sun finally hidden itself over land, the cliff's shadow engulfing them. The inappropriateness of how she and Isaac had been sitting – him now fully dressed and she still in her bathing suit – for the past hour or so suddenly strikes her as she draws her towel up around her shoulders. Neither of them seem ready to leave but in adjusting her towel like this she has brought about the end of their conversation.

'You should get back,' Isaac says softly, rising. 'Someone will no doubt be wondering where you are.'

'Yes,' Cordelia admits, standing, dusting sand off her legs. 'My parents are away tonight. Edwin too. So it's just me. Dinner alone.'

'But Ada will still have your dress ready for dinner? Your bath drawn?' he says. 'I'm envious of your warm bath,' he admits with a slight shiver.

Cordelia smiles but it's thin. Their differences are once again laid bare.

'By the way, you're not stupid,' he says, picking up on her earlier comment. 'Is that what you think of yourself?'

She shrugs. 'Not stupid then,' she agrees. 'But, uneducated, which is enforced stupidity by any other name. I'm willing to be educated but I'm going to have to do it myself. I feel I'm catching up after a lifetime of learning to ride, play piano, draw and not much else. I wasn't really encouraged to do anything else. Not encouraged to make genuine conversation about genuine subjects or to read. But I'm happy to admit I'm enjoying both now. I think perhaps I'm not *really* a reader of fiction. Perhaps I'd have done better with big factual books that charted intricacies of wars and battles,' she teases.

They walk towards David, but he's had similar ideas, moving on some way in advance of them, towards the cliff path, carrying his rod and the pail of crabs.

'You never know. You *might* prefer non-fiction,' Isaac replies.

'Perhaps not wars and battles though,' she reasons as she climbs into her day dress and notices Isaac politely looking away.

'Perhaps not for the time being anyway,' he agrees while looking determinedly up the cliff path. 'There's enough of that to contend with in the newspapers.'

'Yes,' she says. 'And I'm looking forward to an evening of gardening books and supper on the floor.'

'On the floor?' His eyes narrow and they begin to walk.

'Books spread out in front of me. The house to myself.'

'How many books?'

'All of them,' she cries joyously.

'And you'll read them all in one night?'

'It's not about the reading of them, it's about the looking at them. Just absorbing them.'

'But not reading them?' he asks, holding out his hand to help her climb the first few steps. She looks at it briefly and then takes it as they talk, allowing herself to be helped up steps she's never once needed help up before.

'Well, reading bits of them,' she says, noticing how rough his hand is but how she's enjoying the feel of it nonetheless.

'Which bits?' His brown eyes are curious. As if he's trying to look into her mind, to understand her better.

Looking into his eyes, her hand on his, it all quite catches her breath. But now she can't think. What were they even talking about? 'The interesting bits,' she says, eventually.

The path narrows and he takes his hand away, gestures to her that she should go ahead rather than trail behind him and their conversation is brought to a forced close.

As Cordelia walks she realises, madly, that this is the happiest she's been in quite a while and a wide smile finds its way to her lips. The entire day has been wonderful and still holds so much promise.

'It will be lovely, walking back through the garden at night,' she ponders. 'Although it's not dark yet, the garden feels completely different in the evening.'

'Yes,' he says, stopping on the path. 'Yes, it does. It's my favourite time.'

Cordelia smiles. 'The scents,' she says. 'I've noticed now that the jasmine really comes alive at night.'

'Yes,' he replies earnestly. 'And lilies too sometimes. And the scent of evening primrose as well. When it's dark you should venture out to find that one in particular. It only flowers after sunset.'

'I didn't know that,' she says in awe, still watching him and his infectious enthusiasm. 'Perhaps I should make a special trip to discover that tonight before bed.'

He looks back at her. 'Perhaps you should.'

CHAPTER 26

ISAAC

'I'm going back to the cottage to cook these crabs,' David announces when they reach the top of the cliff path. He says it so easily and without preamble. It's always stunned Isaac how easy David is with everyone, how little he cares what people think of what he says and how he says it. He lifts the pail of crabs into the air. 'I'll bring you a sandwich in the morning,' he says to Cordelia. 'If you like?'

'Yes, I would like, rather. If it's not too much trouble?'

'None whatsoever. I'll give it to Isaac in the morning and you can eat it in the garden, in the fresh air, where it's supposed to be eaten. It'll taste better like that.'

'Not on fine china in the dining room?' Cordelia teases back.

'Certainly not,' David says, waving. And without checking to see if Isaac's following, he leaves.

'Sometimes I'm not sure who is the older brother, him or me,' Isaac says in jest.

'He's very much his own person, isn't he?' Cordelia says in awe. 'Very sure, very at home being himself.'

'Yes, he is,' Isaac says, looking thoughtfully at David who swings the pail easily as he walks. 'Well, I should—'

'Would you like that book now?' Cordelia speaks at the same time and then laughs as their words cross each other in the cool evening air. 'Sorry, I didn't mean to interrupt. Would you like the book . . . the Arthurian one, I mean. You can take it tonight, if you'd like. A spot of bedtime reading. I'll find it in the library for you.'

'Thank you. Won't your father mind a book being taken from his library?'

'No, he always lets people borrow books. Prefers them being read to being stuck on a shelf.'

He considers this. 'All right then.'

'Come now, I'll give it to you.'

Isaac follows as Cordelia walks around the exterior of the house, climbs the stone steps and opens the French doors that lead into the room. The fire has been lit and he is immediately much warmer than he was a moment ago on the beach, not realising how cold he had actually been in the end.

He takes in the high ceiling, the arrangement of comfortable-looking settees set around a low mahogany table, beautiful leather-bound books, the fire crackling in the grate as the evening air changes temperature, the lamps around the room lit on dainty tables, ready for Cordelia's planned evening. He turns around to close the door, keeping out the chill and then looks through the glass and up to the sky. Over the sea, clouds gather forming a blanket of grey. It will rain soon. They escaped the beach just in time.

But inside, it's warm, cosy, a dominion of calm.

On the table sits a stack of gardening books. Presumably Cordelia has laid these out in readiness, and he walks over. 'May I?'

'Of course. I'm embarrassingly excited and have already pulled them from the shelves.'

He picks one up, turns it over, opens the leather-bound volume, noting the year of publication, the diagrams and instructions in *The Home Garden*, 1895.

'This might be quite dry,' he says. 'I wonder if hands-on experience might be the way.'

'No,' she whines. 'No, I've got my entire evening planned out. Don't ruin it now.'

'They're also quite old.'

'Has gardening practice and . . . I don't know . . . pest control changed so very much?' she asks.

He makes a face. 'Well, perhaps not.'

'Perhaps it's because you know everything there is to know already that you think these aren't quite the thing?' She walks over and removes the book from his hands, replacing it on the table.

He watches her as she pulls another book from the pile. He's completely forgotten why he's here.

'What do you think of this one?' she asks reading him the title: '*A Treatise on the Cultivation and History of The Rose*. Gilbert says if I'm to focus on the floral side of things I need to do that in my own time.' She waves the book at him to demonstrate Gilbert's meaning. He takes it from her as she holds it out to him.

'I've read this.' He flicks through and pauses at an etching. 'I should like to grow something like this one day,' he says, pointing. 'Something that's delicately scented, beautiful but doesn't know it. One day when I have my own proper garden again, perhaps.'

'Your own proper garden?'

He nods, still looking at the drawing.

'Where?' she asks. 'Where will you live?'

'I don't know,' he says. 'I haven't thought. I'm so used to this life, you see.'

'Nomadic?' Cordelia chimes in. 'What if you marry? You'll have to settle then surely?'

'Perhaps,' he says, not meeting her eye, his gaze still on the book. 'Perhaps, I'll go home,' he says and then snaps the book shut, holding it out to her.

'Home?'

'Yes. I do have one,' he teases.

'Do you? Where?'

'Fen Byron. Cambridgeshire. David and I inherited it. We've got tenants in there currently.'

'Tenants?'

'My parents both passed away when we were young. It's just David and me now. That's why we're together, mostly.'

'Oh,' she says. 'I'm so sorry. I didn't know both your parents had passed.'

'Why should you?'

'I can't imagine losing both my parents.'

'No. I couldn't either. And then it happened. Father's passing came as quite a shock, despite the fact he was a lot older than Mother. Seemed invincible though. But of course, he wasn't. And then Mother passed away only a year later.'

A quiet stills the room and he watches her as she thinks. She really has the most beautiful eyes and her skin is browning from being outdoors.

'Where did you live after your parents passed away?' she interrupts his thoughts.

'At school. We'd had a tutor at home but my uncle believed in the virtues of school so David and I were sent away to where he and my father had gone. My father had hated it, which is why he never sent us. Told us all the horror stories you could imagine, never once thinking we'd end up there. And then we did.'

'I'm so sorry. Was it awful?'

'Neither David nor I enjoyed it. Hence why I snuck out at every opportunity I could to roam around the grounds, helping the groundsmen. David's outlet was sport. We've been together ever since. It's never occurred to us not to be.'

Cordelia settles herself against the bookshelves, leaning back. 'So you're . . .'

'I'm . . .?'

'More a parent than a brother,' she attempts.

He looks awkward. He feels awkward. 'What? No. I don't think so.'

'I think you are,' she says. 'It sounds as if you are.'

He blinks, goes back to another time. It's always been just him and David. It always will be, he supposes. Until David marries. Or until he does. He looks up at Cordelia.

'Shall I ring the bell for tea?' She brings him back to the room.

'Tea?' he asks. He's not really supposed to be in here, alone, with her. The book. He's here for the book. He remembers now.

She looks at him as if he's mad. 'Yes. Tea. Brown. Comes in a teapot.'

He laughs. 'Right,' he says. He wants to say no. He wants to say yes. Instead he says nothing at all and she obviously takes it as read that he's staying and rings the bell pull. A footman will arrive in a minute. He'll see Isaac in here. He'll see Cordelia with her hair down from swimming. They're not dressed properly. Or rather, she's not, having just pulled her day dress over her bathers.

He acts swiftly. 'Actually, I think I should leave.'

'No, why?'

'You, dressed like that,' he says quickly.

'I've been swimming,' she defends. 'I'm dressed though.' Is she being ridiculous on purpose?

'But it doesn't look it,' he says, one eye on the door. 'And me . . . in here with you, while you're . . .' He can't think of a suitable word.

Cordelia looks down at her dress. 'It's *on*,' she placates. 'Although I look a bit haphazard. Are you really that worried what people might think?'

'Yes,' he says, unable to hide his exasperation.

'There's only one thing for it then,' she says. 'You're going to have to hide.'

'Hide?' he queries. 'Are you serious?'

They hear footsteps on the tread outside the door and without a moment's hesitation, Isaac launches himself behind the door just as it opens and a footman arrives.

'Good evening, Jonathan,' Cordelia says calmly. 'May I have a large pot of tea, a big pile of sandwiches, and as many cakes as Mrs Emes can fit onto the tray.'

The liveried footman stands there, obviously confused.

'I've been swimming all afternoon and I'm very hungry,' she explains. 'This can serve as my dinner.'

'Of course, Miss.'

With that he closes the door and Isaac, pressed up against the wall behind, is revealed. He can't think what to say. That was preposterous. Cordelia smiles and then she laughs. And then so does he and he moves away from the wall and walks towards her. What is he doing?

'That was a bit close,' she says. 'You'll have to hide again in a moment when he comes back.'

'I have to go . . . is what I actually have to do.'

'You can't go now. I've just ordered a mound of food and more cakes than I'll probably know what to do with. It would be such a waste.'

'Well, you did say you wanted supper on the floor. What's easier to eat on the rugs than sandwiches?' he says, deliberating. He should go. He should. But his feet aren't taking him towards the door. Not at all. *Dismiss me*, he thinks. *Send me away. Say it and I'll go*. But she doesn't.

'Let's find this book, shall we?' she offers and he nods his agreement. How easily he allows himself to be led by her.

'I'll take this side and you take the area nearest the door then you can hide easily again,' she says.

He sighs, exasperated with himself at how stupid he's being. But he agrees, 'All right.' He glances back and watches her climb the rungs of the wooden ladder positioned against the shelves. He shakes his head. He's an idiot. He's become a complete idiot all of a sudden. Or perhaps it isn't all of a sudden. Perhaps this idiocy has been growing for weeks. Since that night at the lake.

Isaac slides behind the door just in time before the footman opens it. He holds his breath as fear grips him. Is it worse to be found lingering brazenly, openly in the middle of the library or worse to be discovered hiding behind a door? Either one will get him fired, the rest of his commission over, his reputation in tatters. He won't work again. After the footman places the tea tray on the table he asks Cordelia if she'd like anything else.

'No thank you, Jonathan. This is plenty. And with it being only me here tonight, whenever you all wish to retire, please do so. I'll happily bring the empty tray down when I'm done. You can tell Mr Richards to lock up the other doors and I'll do this one now,' she says, pointing to the French door. 'Oh, and will you tell Ada that I don't need her tonight. I'm sure I can put myself to bed and I don't want to keep her up.'

'Very good, Miss.'

'Goodnight Jonathan.'

'Goodnight Miss.'

The young man leaves and closes the door behind him, once again revealing Isaac behind the door.

Isaac rubs his temples and gives Cordelia a look. This gets madder with every passing minute. She presses her lips together to stifle a laugh. Isaac shakes his head but whispers, 'God Almighty.'

'There's only one teacup I'm afraid,' Cordelia says. 'Do you mind sharing?'

'Of course not. Would you like me to pour?'

'Yes please.'

He does so and offers her the cup first. She takes it from him and sips. 'Delicious.' She hands it back to him and he drinks from it.

'The very thing I needed after an evening's swim,' he says.

'Would you like a sandwich?' she asks.

'Yes please.' And then he laughs.

'What?' she asks. 'What's funny?'

'Look at us,' he says. 'Look how we must look, see how we're dressed, me hiding behind doors, and us sharing a teacup because we can't ask for a second one and yet we've become so formal with each other again.'

'I feel,' Cordelia says, 'that we may have broken through the formality somewhere along the way.'

'I think so too,' he says against his better judgement. His eyes are on her attire, dressed but not dressed. 'But perhaps we shouldn't tell people about this.'

'I know,' she says. 'A shame really because we've nothing to hide, by being friends. But I see what you mean.'

'Is that what we are?' he asks. 'Friends?'

'Aren't we?'

He doesn't reply. He genuinely doesn't know the answer. Not friends, no. But they can't be anything else. Not really.

She steps over towards the tea tray, takes a sandwich in each hand and makes a point of not using a plate. 'See? Not so formal after all.'

'No,' he agrees, doing the same. And then teasingly, 'Just slovenly.'

'Well I say, you've become very opinionated all of a sudden.'

'Ha,' he laughs. 'Sorry.'

'Don't apologise. Sit down,' she says as she slides onto the settee. He sits next to her and they eat hungrily. Cordelia pulls the tea tray from the middle of the low table towards them.

Then when she's eaten her fill of sandwiches and poured them more tea she tucks her legs underneath her so naturally it's as if she does it all the time. She turns her body towards him and passes him the teacup.

'Do you think your brother's crab sandwiches are going to outshine Mrs Emes' cucumber ones?' she jokes, gesturing to the sandwich in her hand.

'No. I'm afraid not,' Isaac sighs, putting on a dramatically tragic face. 'He won't make it delicately. There'll be more butter than you know what to do with. And crusts.'

'Hateful crusts,' Cordelia plays along. 'I'm sure I can stomach crusts as long as the sandwiches are in neat little triangles.'

Isaac looks serious. 'Oh no. I'm afraid the entire sandwich will be as thick as your wrist, wrapped in brown paper and presented with no flourishes whatsoever.'

She laughs and then quashes it, putting her serious face back into place. 'Hmm,' she looks thoughtful. And then nods. 'All right. I'll brace myself. It will taste good though, won't it? If I'm to eat like a heathen then it ought to taste good.'

He glances around, pretending to survey the surroundings. 'You're already eating like a heathen.' He looks at the tray, piled with cakes and sandwiches, crumbs scattered all over their laps.

'So I am. So are you,' she says, accusingly.

'That's because I am a heathen.'

'No,' she says suddenly. And the game is over. 'No you're not. Don't say that. We're not so different, you and I,' she says. And it sounds as if she means it.

'Don't be ridiculous,' he says but not unkindly. 'On the surface maybe not. But dig deeper and of course we are.'

'No.' She's forceful. 'We're not. We live differently. I live in a house surrounded by parkland and you work on it. But we're not that different.'

'No?' he questions. 'How have you come to that conclusion?'

She thinks and he admires her valiant attempt to pretend there is no barrier between them. 'We love our families,' she starts. 'We care if there's a war. We don't want people to get hurt, lose loved ones. We love gardening, or rather you love it and I'm learning to. And we are all made of the same things. Blood runs through our veins. And our hearts . . .'

She trails off.

'Go on,' he says, captivated. 'I'm listening. Don't stop now.'

'Our hearts beat in the same way.'

'Do they?' he asks.

'Yes.'

He sees her eyes lower, watching the rise and fall of his chest and then she looks up. Her expression is unreadable. He has no idea what she's thinking, what's going on behind those blue eyes. And he wants to – he really wants to.

'How is it I'd not really noticed you before that night at the lake? That night Clive tricked us?' she asks.

'I . . . I really couldn't say. I noticed you when you returned from London though. Hard not to really.' The words are out before he can help himself. He leans forward, hoping she's not noticed his blunder, takes another sandwich triangle.

'Hard not to?' she teases.

He doesn't respond and then he opts for bravery, honesty. 'Yes.'

And then the room stills and he can hear nothing, not even the comfort of the log fire crackling in the grate. Everything has disappeared and there is only her.

'In the garden, when you wanted to touch me . . .' she whispers.

He nods, his eyes on hers. He can't speak. He's holding the sandwich but he can't eat it. It's as if his throat has closed.

'What were you going to do?'

He sighs, not sure this is a good idea. 'I was . . . I was going to touch your hair,' he admits in a voice that doesn't sound like his.

'My hair?' Hers has gone up an octave.

'A piece had fallen down.'

'You were going to pin it back for me?'

'Yes. No. I'm not sure actually,' he says and then mutters, 'Madness.'

'That *is* madness,' she breathes. 'Why did you want to do that?'

'I didn't want to. It was involuntary. It was a different version of me that wanted to do that. It's a different version of me when . . .'

'When . . .'

He smiles. Oh God, he might as well just say it. Although saying it is the wrong decision, he's too far in now to turn back. 'When you're near,' he says. And now he's done it. All the hard work he's put in to keeping that feeling in abeyance has gone. It's all gone. He can't put those words back into his mouth. They're out.

'A different version of you?' she asks so quietly she's almost whispering.

'The Isaac that wasn't thinking wanted to see how soft your hair was.'

She gasps. 'Really?' Is it his imagination or has she moved closer on the settee than she was a moment ago? Or is it him? Has he moved towards her? He can feel the warmth of her breath. She's too close. She must know that. He knows that. She should move away. Or he should. Only they're both different versions of themselves near each other. They must be or else they wouldn't have let this get so far.

'And where is the Isaac that isn't thinking now?' she asks. She's far too close.

His gaze falls to her mouth and he can't help himself.

'He's here,' he admits. And his lips brush hers, softly, so gently. 'He's here. And he knows he shouldn't be.' And then he kisses her, his mouth on hers, her soft lips kissing him in return. He's lost. He's entirely lost with her and she with him. He kisses her neck, his fingers weaving into her hair, feeling the sea salt that coats her hair, her skin. And then his mouth finds hers again and she kisses him back softly and then harder, her fingers touching his chest where his top shirt button has come undone.

'Cordelia,' he says, whispering her name, touching her fingers, pulling back and looking up at her as she has somehow ended up on his lap. He brushes her unkempt sea-salted hair from her face. She looks messy, beautiful. He has no idea how he looks. He only knows how he feels; that this is beyond stupid, beyond dangerous. Because he is not of her class. Because there is a war coming. Because this will not end well. But he cannot help it, all the same.

She interlaces her fingers in his and says his name. And then she kisses him. And he is a lost man all over again.

CHAPTER 27

CORDELIA

Somewhere over the blue Cornish sea the sun has risen, heralding the fresh beginning of a new day. They sit on the settee, kissing, drinking cold tea until the pot is empty, eating sandwiches left out so long they start to curl; lust has made them so hungry they neither of them mind the now-stale bread.

It had been unexpected, he leaning forward to kiss her. She had wanted it, oh how she had wanted it, but she'd never expected him to be the one to kiss her. She'd assumed she might have to summon up a level of courage she didn't think she had. And now they had kissed. And it was everything she'd ever wanted and hoped it would be. It had felt like no kiss she'd experienced before. Soft, gentle, delicate, fierce, hard, passionate. A heady mix of all of it as the night moved on. But throughout he'd remained a gentleman, which is what she'd known he would be. Just kissing. But what kissing. What utterly delicious kissing. And then they'd held each other, talked into the night, their fingers entwined within each other's.

'You have very rough hands,' she says, almost admiringly.

'A lesson in wearing gloves. Yours are so wonderfully soft. Wear your gloves each day or yours will soon look like mine,' he says kissing her fingertips.

They talk of nothing, of everything and the clock strikes the hour two or three times, the fire in the grate falling to embers. And then when they are in danger of discovery, dawn breaking, and the threat of a housemaid coming to light the fires, they part; Isaac keeping to the borders, outmanoeuvring the approaching rays of sunlight that threatens to betray his presence here as he runs back to his cottage, while she creeps upstairs silently towards bed.

There had been no plan, no checking what to do, how to behave with each other. It was unsaid. They had to try to find a way to be together as they had been for those few hours, even if it was simply snatched moments in the garden. They would not find another night such as the one they had just experienced, the house empty in such a way. Cordelia realises this as she lies in bed, still covered in crisp salt from the sea, realises that what they have will be hampered by so many factors.

When she awakes, the day is warm, the sky already a deep shade of blue. She has woken late, a cold cup of tea on her bedside table, the milk already filmed over. The fire is burning brightly. Strangely she feels as if she's had enough sleep and, looking over at the ornate gilt figurine clock over her mantle, she sees that she's slept away most of the morning.

And then she remembers the reason she has overslept – she and Isaac in the library – and she folds herself back inside her bed again, reliving the events of last night: his touch, his warmth, the feel of his mouth on hers and she lets the blankets hold her in a warm embrace.

CHAPTER 28

CORDELIA

The day has brought warmth after last night's rain. The summer showers have refreshed the grounds, water droplets still adorning petals and blades of grass and all around is the crisp, fresh scent of a garden recently rained upon. Cordelia inhales pure contentment: the perfection of the sun, the sound of the birds, the Cornish parkland, the garden, Isaac, all of it.

She sees the morning newspapers on the breakfast table but she will not look. She will not read them.

And then the crab sandwich is brought to her wrapped up in paper and ribbon after Ada bafflingly confirms with Cordelia that she is in fact expecting such a strange offering. She supposes David has provided neither the ribbon nor the paper and that the kitchen maid has been ordered to make it look more presentable. But as Cordelia makes her way through the grounds to where she is expected in the walled garden, she holds the sandwich in her grasp, remembering all of yesterday: the beach, the library, the kiss.

When Isaac crept out this morning it was with fast, heady kisses and the unspoken promises of more of everything, more of him, more of each other. Let the others fear the war. She cannot bring herself to do that today. Nor does she need to worry, not really, other than Edwin's insistence that he's joining. And she cannot stop that even if she wanted to. It would take a force greater than Cordelia, Mother and Father combined to stop that. A force stronger than Mother might not exist.

The gardeners are dotted all around the walled garden when she arrives. Isaac catches her eye and smiles knowingly. It's all she can do not to laugh joyously at their new, shared, secret excitement but she keeps a straight face, continues to put on her gardening gloves and start on her list of jobs, remembering his touch of her fingers and his comments as to how soft her hands are.

After a few minutes, Isaac lifts a small bundle of books from where he's working and walks over to her. Ever aware they are under the watchful gaze of three other men, he turns his back to them all.

'I brought these for you to look at,' he says a little louder than necessary. And then quietly, so quietly, 'In a minute, follow me.'

'Where?' she whispers, pretending to look at the books he's pretending to show her. Just his presence, after last night, is enough to unsteady her.

'The lake,' he whispers.

'How can I get away?' she whispers in return and then more loudly for the benefit of others, pointing to the book. 'Oh, I've not read this one. But I think Mother has one similar.'

'It's your garden, your house. Make up an excuse. I have to see you. I have to be near you, Cordelia.'

She's sure she's flushing, her breathing quickening, her pulse betraying her excitement. 'All right,' she says. 'Ten minutes?'

'Yes, all right. I'll leave them with you then,' he says loudly, confusing her until she understands and takes the books from him. She stifles a laugh. How strange that he doesn't need to tell anyone where he's going; that he can simply come and go as he pleases but she has to make something up to Gilbert so she can exit.

She does, telling the head gardener she needs to dash back to the house for a moment. 'A glass of water and a hat with a wider brim to shield the sun, perhaps. A headache has been coming on since last night.'

'Must be the change in air pressure,' Gilbert says knowingly. 'The rain.'

'Yes, perhaps.' And then she's gone, keeping out of sight of everyone, she hopes, until she disappears into the tree line at the lake.

There is no stopping her when she sees him and she runs into his arms, letting herself be kissed and kissing him in return. His lips are warm from the sun, his skin too as she touches his face, running her fingers along his cheekbone, his chin, his neck where his tanned skin disappears into his shirt collar.

They stand on the jetty, entwined in each other as he holds her waist, pulls her against him. It does delicious things to her, sending jolts of something far in excess of excitement to within her core. The sound of seagulls crying overhead as they make their way over the water stuns them both.

And then he pulls away. 'I'm sorry,' he says throatily.

'Don't be. I wanted that. More than you could know.'
He laughs. 'Me too.'
'I could tell.' She's enjoying this far too much.
His hands still round her waist, gently resting, he looks at her. 'This is madness.'
'I know,' she agrees. Then a thought strikes her. 'I don't want to be one of those girls, those women, who imagine something where it isn't, who imagines a feeling, pines, wondering, only to find out it's one sided.'
'That's not what's happening,' Isaac says. 'I promise you.'
She closes her eyes with relief, then opens them. 'Keeping this a secret . . . I understand why. I do. And I agree in these . . . early stages it's for the best. But could you . . . do you . . .'
'I like you, Cordelia. Is that what you're trying to ask me? I like you far too much to hurt you. We live in uncertain times. This war. It's coming. It's weeks away, days away. The upheaval here will be astronomical. I think it's for the best we keep this, fledgling, beautiful thing just between us for now. Until *we* understand what we're doing, I don't think we should let others in on it. Let's let your father deal with the upheaval the war will bring. Let things calm down, let things settle here. And then if we still feel the same way . . .'
'You can be the hero of the hour,' she says and she's not teasing now. 'You can be the capable pair of hands my father needs,' Cordelia suggests. 'The only man of fighting age staying behind, by the sounds of it.'
His forehead creases into lines.
'That's not what I mean,' she says quickly, realising her blunder. 'I don't mean that. I mean that you will

be the immovable rock that keeps things moving outdoors. Or else there will be no one young and capable.' She's not recovering the blunder well.

'I know what you mean,' he says softly. 'Don't worry.'

'You do mean it, don't you?' she replies. 'That you won't enlist, should it come to it. You're principled. I admire that about you, that strength.' Her eyes search his.

'I won't enlist,' he says forcefully. 'I don't agree with any part of this coming war. I won't enlist.'

She pulls his hands away from her waist and holds them within her own.

'Thank God. I can't find you to have you go to war. That's just not fair. It's not the way it's supposed to be.'

'I feel the same, Cordelia,' he says before dipping his head and kissing her again. 'I should go,' he says. 'We've been gone long enough.'

'And I have a terrible headache,' she points out.

'Do you?' Concern finds its way onto his face. 'I'm so sorry.'

'No. It was my fib to leave the garden,' she says far too proudly.

'So you'll be in the house for the rest of the day?' he asks with a knowing look.

'Of course not,' she replies. 'I'll rally suddenly in about ten minutes with a wider-brim hat upon my head and will see you back in the walled garden where you left me.'

He chuckles, kisses her, and then he's gone.

CHAPTER 29

CORDELIA

Cordelia spent another night in the house without her family that evening. By the time she'd had word from Mother and Father that they were remaining in London for another night (too much business to put right, too much shopping for provisions for the impending war) and from Edwin that he would in fact be returning from the Trevelyan estate the following day, it had been too late to slip from the house with any ease. The servants were everywhere and the evening so bright she'd never have been able to run to Isaac's unseen (although what a salacious thought that was) to spend a second, unexpected and precious night curled up with him, kissing. Just kissing.

She cannot stop thoughts of him flitting into her mind. Those kisses in the library, the passion by the lake. She touches her lips, remembering. She's sure she can still feel him there.

When Ada arrives the following morning, it is to dress Cordelia for another day in the garden. Ada's learned to stop grumbling about the kind of clothes Cordelia pre-selects for her tasks: looser, darker, more freeing.

'Good morning, Ada. I cannot *believe* how late it is,' Cordelia exclaims as she stretches happily. For once she has slept soundly. 'Would you mind drawing me a bath? I'm of a mind to be lazy this morning.'

'Miss Cordelia?' Ada starts.

'I don't suppose my parents are back until later but is Edwin?' Cordelia slices in, before realising she's interrupted Ada. 'Sorry . . . you wanted to say . . .'

'No Miss. Your brother isn't back yet either. Miss Cordelia?' Ada attempts again as she removes the cold cup of tea and replaces it with a fresh one.

'Yes?'

Ada does not respond and Cordelia turns to look at her maid. 'What is it?'

'It's happening. It's been in the newspapers this morning. It's all we can talk about downstairs.'

'What is?' But she knows. Of course she knows and a chill rolls itself gently over the room, bringing with it sadness and fear.

'War, Miss. It's here. England has declared war against Germany.'

CHAPTER 30

CORDELIA

'I can't bring myself to destroy that willow tree,' Isaac says when he turns and sees Cordelia approaching. He's standing by the jetty looking thoughtful. It's taken her an hour but eventually she has tracked him down to the lake, tipped off by James that he was headed there.

'I should think not,' she says. How different it all is today, here in this same spot, compared to yesterday.

She stands next to him and he transfers the plans he's holding into his other hand and then holds hers. Together they both look towards the water, still on such a hot day. Every now and again a bubble rises to the surface as an unseen fish makes its presence felt.

The feel of his hand in hers brings comfort, but only a small level. She'd known war was coming. So had he. And now it's here. Neither one of them wants to say it. Perhaps if they don't say it, it won't be true. And it can be just them, here by this lake forever, a landscape in a frame of time.

Next to her, Isaac sighs. 'You've heard?' The moment is over – the frame shattered.

She nods. 'Ada told me. I've just woken up.'

'Have you?' he asks. 'I didn't sleep well last night.'

'Why not?'

'I couldn't. Impossible to sleep, memories of you on my lap, and then kissing you here yesterday kept me wide awake.'

She smiles at the heavenly memory. 'You don't regret any of it?'

'I regret it for you,' he replies, turning to look at her.

Cordelia doesn't know how to respond to that.

'I'm hardly the kind of man your parents will approve of. Sleeves rolled up. Arms covered in mud. Hands worn with work. Forever moving from house to house, garden to garden, commission to commission. As if that wasn't enough uncertainty for you . . . now this,' he says, referring to the war.

'I don't care,' she says and Isaac laughs.

'No, I know you don't,' he says. 'But I do.' He lets go of her hand and brushes his fingers against her cheek. Her eyes close involuntarily and she feels his lips against hers kissing her softly. It is as wonderful as it was the last two times, even more so. Today it feels more real, or less real. She cannot work out which.

He looks at her. His dark eyes connecting with her blue ones. 'I wanted to pull you out of the arch and into the glasshouse.'

'Pardon?' she asks.

'You asked me what I was doing when I reached out to touch you in the walled garden. I lied, about wanting to touch your hair. That's not what I wanted to do at all. I wanted to pull you towards me. I wanted to take you into the glasshouse and I wanted to kiss you. I wanted to talk to you. I wanted to know how you felt in my arms. I wanted to know how soft your skin was, your hair was. I wanted to know what it would be like to be out of the way of everyone and be near you.'

She smiles at the confession. 'You've found out now,' she teases.

He laughs. 'Yes I have.'

'I would have come with you,' she says. 'To the glasshouse. If you'd have taken my hand and led me there, I'd have come with you.'

'God, would you?' he says. 'Well, now I know that, I feel like I've wasted precious time.'

It's her turn to laugh. 'You have. *We* have.'

'But now I'm sorry it's happened.'

'What?'

'Cordelia, if this *is* a passing infatuation on your part then today seems as good a time as any to end it. Everything has changed.'

'Nothing has changed.'

'Of course it has. Or rather it will,' he states.

'Then we must try not to let it because this is not a passing infatuation. I thought it was, at first. I hoped it was. But I'm afraid it's not. Is it for you?'

'No,' he says immediately. 'I'm almost sorry to say it's not for me either.'

Cordelia smiles and so does Isaac.

'What are we doing?' he asks.

'This,' she says and steps forward to kiss him. Then they hold each other tightly as behind them a fish rises to the surface and then disappears into the depths of the lake just as swiftly as it rose.

* * *

'I've proposed,' Edwin says. 'And she's accepted.'

Cordelia is caught at the French doors in the library, the quickest way into the house from the garden. She has left Isaac reluctantly as he is meeting the fountain craftsmen in Bodmin. Edwin is sat exactly where Cordelia was when she kissed Isaac, a copy of the newspaper spread across his lap, a tea tray in front of him. But he's nursing a whisky.

He sees her frown at the whisky and then he points to the headline. She understands now. 'I thought you were excited about war,' she says, moving back into the room. She helps herself to a sherry from the decanter in order to be sociable.

'Excited isn't the right word,' he says.

She follows it up with, 'Congratulations.' She raises her glass to his and then sinks into the settee opposite. 'I wondered if that's what you were doing. To Millicent I assume. Not to Irene?'

He laughs. 'Of course to Millicent. Don't know why it took me so long to realise what was right in front of me all this time. Friends for so long, you know? But now . . .'

'Thoughts of war pushing you into fast decisions?' she says taking a sip.

'Something like that,' Edwin admits. 'Her father thinks we're both a bit young, though. Asked us to wait, which we've reluctantly agreed to. I've a year left at university anyway although heaven knows when I'll get back there again. So we've made a commitment to each other. And should I die—'

'Should you die!' she exclaims.

'Out there . . .' He points towards the sea, which categorically does not face Europe but she knows what he means.

'I see,' she says. 'So you are going then?'

He nods and downs his whisky. 'Spoke to Major Trevelyan about it all. Along with asking for his daughter's hand in marriage we talked about him getting me an "in" with his lot. Army. I should be able to leave at the end of the week. Officer training.'

'Good God,' Cordelia exclaims. This is all happening too fast. Her eyes are suddenly damp. 'That soon?'

'That soon. Already got a lot of officer training under my belt at university. Helps things along a bit. Was just a bit of fun though. Didn't think I'd ever actually need it.' Edwin looks at his sister and smiles ruefully.

'I'll miss you,' she says.

'No you won't,' he rallies. 'I'll only be gone a short while. If what most people are saying is true, I'll probably spend more time in training than I will in battle. Apparently it'll all be over by Christmas.'

Cordelia spends the rest of the evening working on the vines on the newly assembled brick walls. She finds she cannot simply sit around indoors waiting for news of war to filter in. She blushes every now and again when she remembers Isaac's words that he wanted to take her into the glasshouse, kiss her, hold her. She remembers the taste of him and his kisses. The memory does things to her that memories of kissing other men has never done before. This is different. Everything about this feels different.

Isaac is not at his cottage that night and after a fruitless search for him long after the last train from Bodmin should have arrived, she has to contend that his business has taken him away overnight. This, she reminds herself, is what makes Isaac Leigh different from those other working men. He isn't so much from a different class to her. As long as what he promised to do for her father gets done, he can come and go as he pleases, whereas of course none of the other outdoor staff could ever do such a thing. She knows she's hanging a lot on this fact, one that she might need to use in an argument one day with her parents.

After a quiet dinner shared only with Edwin, discussing war and his nuptials with Millicent, Cordelia says goodnight, and heads towards the library to replace her gardening book and fetch a new one.

While she is in there she hears voices from the drawing room. Mother and Father have returned home, and they and Edwin are discussing Edwin's recent choices and the war – no longer impending but here. They all appear to be talking at once and Cordelia reasons that she has no place in that particular bear pit. She silently wishes her older brother luck and climbs the stairs to bed.

The next morning she feels as if the world, already on fire, is burning rapidly to the ground. The household and outdoor staff have all been summoned to the terrace, the only location where they can all feasibly fit. The senior staff, Mr Richards the butler and Mrs Venning the housekeeper stand a slight distance away from the staff, discussing with Cordelia's mother and father. Cordelia can hear snippets. She's been called over from the garden along with Gilbert, James and Talek where they had been propping up the heavily laden fruit tree branches.

She looks for Isaac but cannot see him.

And now she stands near her mother, father and

Edwin. Clive and Nanny are the only two not here. Presumably this announcement does not affect them.

'By now we are all aware that Britain is at war with Germany,' her father begins, his words casting a chilling spell across those gathered. 'And Britain expects us to do our duty, so do our duty we will. For those men wishing to give the Boche a taste of good Cornish medicine – and I know there are many of you – those men ready to take up arms and fight, men from Pencallick House and Pencallick village will be forming a battalion together alongside those men mobilising from the Trevelyan estate. Major Trevelyan has suggested something called a pals battalion so you will not be dispatched to battalions far and wide without friend or acquaintance. Instead you join as a battalion of rifle volunteers as a division of the Duke of Cornwall's Light Infantry, alongside friends, family, men you've worked with and grown up with, brothers, cousins, schoolfellows, men of the estate, men of the village and surrounding hamlets. You will be joining together, training together, leaving together, fighting together. Giving the Hun a good Cornish beating – together.'

The rallying cheer that emanates casts a shadow over her and she closes her eyes, briefly. She wishes she could close her ears to it, to ward off the men's happy cries. It is a sound she thinks she will never forget. One of the kitchen maids is sniffling and Ada nudges her and mouths kindly, 'Stop it.'

Cordelia knows the majority of the men on the estate will be even more encouraged to join up by this. And for those who hadn't considered joining, this speech, these cheers, this hearty mass enthusiasm will hardly put them off. She looks around as excited chatter begins as her father finishes talking. James and Talek nod to each other, having already decided to join. Cordelia cannot see the reaction on Gilbert's face because he's looking at the ground. She spots a rabbit and its baby on the lawn. They stop, intrigued by the gathering of people then as quickly as they came, continue on their way.

The footmen, of which there are six, all from large families, are standing together nodding their agreement, smiling. How many men, boys, in each family will join together? How many of them will return safely? How many of them won't?

Is Millicent's father standing, ten or so miles away on the grounds of his estate, making this sort of announcement to their workers? How many men up and down Britain are making this decision right at this very moment as she stands here and casts her eyes around for Isaac?

She draws in a sudden sharp breath. He is here. Isaac. He's lost in the crowd, behind Kenneth the hall boy and one of the housemaids. She sees him but he doesn't see her. It's as if he is looking through her, through them all. Here but not here.

This doesn't affect him. He doesn't live here to be able to join the pals battalion. He's passing through, temporary. He will leave in the winter when the majority of the landscaping has been achieved. That will be a blow. Will he ask her to marry him before he leaves? Will she leave with him? Either way, he won't go soon, he won't go to war. They have a bit longer together. Until the winter, she thinks. She holds on to all of this, grasping at these collective facts while all around her people talk. And then Isaac sees her, holds her gaze, smiles sadly at the occasion, the words being spoken. This doesn't affect him. He, at least, will be safe when others won't be.

She wants nothing more than to go to him but she can't. Not here, like this. She must stay where she is, disconnect her gaze before someone sees how intently she's watching him. She looks at the ground, at her father, at Edwin, at anyone but not at Isaac. David, just behind Isaac, is smiling at the turn of events and slaps his brother on the back but Cordelia cannot fathom why anyone would want to go to war. It is war, it is unknown, it is looking death in the face and inviting it to do its worst. It is all of these things and more.

After the servants disperse, Cordelia stands with her family and listens to words she cannot understand form sentences she cannot grasp as they discuss commanding officers and ranks. Those men who wish to enlist as part of the pals battalion will accompany Edwin on the hour to Bodmin where a recruitment office has been set up. 'You want to get there in good time. They are expecting a long queue of men,' Father says.

She half listens and half waits until Edwin and her parents have finished bombarding her with logistical information and then manages to speak. 'I thought you'd be devastated,' she says to Mother.

'It is not the time for women to weep,' her mother replies. 'It is our time to support our men who are bravely leaving to fight. Your brother has made a choice to fight for his country and we must support him.'

'But he's not fighting for our country,' Cordelia protests. 'We're fighting for someone else's.' Although at this point she's not sure which country Britain is springing to the defence of. All of them, it sounds like.

'That is unpatriotic,' her mother hisses.

'Be that as it may,' Cordelia says, 'everything we feared is coming true. Edwin is going. Most of the staff are going. You can see it on their faces.'

'They will go, yes,' her father says. 'They will and it is our lot to bear it and wave them goodbye. For now. They'll be back soon enough,' he says dismissively as he crosses the now empty terrace and enters the library, as if it is already decided. They will leave. But they will return. Father says so. And so Cordelia takes heart at that.

In the garden she finally finds Isaac. He's inside the newly dug pit where the fountain is to be built. He's kneeling on the mud, plans laid out in front of him, but he's staring into the distance. He hears her approach and stands up to face her.

'I was hoping you'd come and find me,' he confesses.

'Where have you been?' She does not dare approach him. They are in the centre of the formal garden in full view of anyone who chooses to look out of a window of Pencallick House and see them.

'Bodmin,' he says. 'To meet the fountain engineers.'

'I knew that. I didn't know you were staying overnight though.'

'Our meeting overran and we missed the last train home. Easier to stay overnight in an inn and get the first one back this morning. I'm sorry.'

'You don't need to be sorry,' she says. 'Although I did wonder if I'd driven you away. I think I was more worried about that rather than your actual location.'

'Drive me away. Never.' He walks towards her, holds out his hand.

'What are you doing?' she hisses. 'They might see.'

'Helping you into the pit. Come and stand in here with me. Just for a moment.'

He helps her in, holding her by her waist, his hands comforting around her. Her feet land with a quiet thud in the gravel and mud. She moves away a respectable distance, should anyone see.

'I'm besotted with you,' Isaac says. 'You have to know that. I want you to know that.'

She wants to rush the few feet towards him but knows she can't. 'I feel the same.' Although she thinks 'besotted' might be a light word. She thinks so much more of him than that. But it's so early to know this . . . isn't it?

'Cordelia,' he says. 'Just let me look at you for a moment. Let me sear this moment into my memory.'

She glances around at the muddy pit surrounding them. '*This* moment?' she queries.

'You then,' he replies. 'Let me sear you into my memory.'

She stands uncertainly, smiling as he examines her, as he looks at every inch of her face. She sees something in his eyes. Sadness? Then her smile fades as she realises what has happened.

'Oh no,' she whispers, tears collecting behind her eyes. And then she dares to ask the question she already fears she knows the answer to, 'You're enlisting, aren't you?'

He takes a deep breath, exhales slowly. And then he nods.

'Why?' she asks. 'Why? You hate war. You said you won't go.'

'David,' is his only reply.

'David?'

He nods again, looks away from her. 'We have no one else. We only have each other. We can go together, be together. I can look after him, protect him.'

'On a battlefield?'

'We don't know what it's going to be like,' he says.

She has time. They aren't leaving to enlist until the clock strikes the hour. She can talk him out of it. 'It's a war,' she replies snippily. 'It's going to be like a war.'

'I know that,' he says. 'I'm expecting it to be like wandering into hell.'

'So why would you do that? It's not your responsibility to go with David into hell.'

'It is,' he says. 'Of course it is. I have to be with him. I just didn't realise it until . . .'

'Until now?'

'Yes,' he says softly.

He's leaving me . . . so soon, she thinks, *when he said he wouldn't. He said he wouldn't.* She still has time. She calms herself, counts to three, begins again.

'David will be all right without you. He's a wanderer – he'll be all right wherever he goes.'

'Probably,' Isaac acquiesces. 'But it's my job, my responsibility as his brother to be with him for this. You heard your father. Men are joining as a pals unit, with their families for this particular reason. They don't want to be separated and neither do we.'

'Isaac,' she cries. 'Please don't do this.'

And then she realises. 'Oh God. You've already done it, haven't you? In Bodmin. You've already done it.'

He nods. 'Cordelia, please understand I felt I had no choice.'

'There's always a choice.'

'David said he was enlisting this morning when we woke up at the inn and . . . and I couldn't let him go on his own. He walked into the recruitment office on the way to the railway station and I went in with him. I couldn't talk him out of it. Believe me, I tried. Patriotism be damned, I tried to stop my brother going to war. I didn't want to do it. Please believe me. If David hadn't have done it, I would never have enlisted. Cowardice, if you like. I'm not too proud to call it what it is. But I couldn't stand there and watch my little brother enlist and make the choice to let him do it alone. I just couldn't do that.'

'I understand,' she says but she's not sure she means it. She looks down at the mud of the fountain pit. 'But it doesn't make it any easier to accept.' She chokes her words out.

'I've just spoken with your father to tell him what I've done. I'm leaving his commission halfway through. He understands and supports me wholeheartedly. He shook my hand, says he knows a retired Major who might be able to step in as we've only just enlisted and help David and I get moved into the same pals battalion as the others.'

'Is that what you want?' she asks quietly. Her world, so new and perfect is being ripped apart so suddenly, so horrifically.

He cries in exasperation, 'I don't want any of this.' He inhales. Exhales. And then more calmly, 'But it's kind of him to try for us. We may as well go where we know people. We may as well go with your brother, with Talek and James and the others.' He kicks a bit of dirt disconsolately.

She nods. They are all going then. 'When will you leave?'

'I would imagine immediately,' he says softly, reluctantly. 'There will be officer training for David and me as we both did that at university.'

She looks up at him. 'Did you? I thought you hated war.'

'I do. But it just seemed to be the done thing at university. I didn't think I'd ever use it.'

'That's what Edwin said.' A rueful laugh escapes her lips.

'Then after we've completed that, I believe we join the rest of the battalion soldiers after their training and we'll go together.'

'Go?'

'To war,' he says quietly.

Cordelia wipes a tear from her face. 'Oh God,' she whispers again.

'Don't cry,' he says. 'I'm sorry to tell you like this. I should have taken you somewhere private but getting you alone is . . . Someone will no doubt be along in a minute to put an end to this. I had to do it now, before someone else told you in passing that I was going, not imagining you'd care. I didn't want you to betray yourself in front of them.'

'Thank you,' she says. 'I appreciate that.' She is formal again.

She looks at him, her eyes feel raw. She will cry many times before this week is over.

'I truly am sorry,' he says, soberly. 'I didn't want it to be this way. I didn't want to start falling for someone and then it all end.'

Her heart leaps and then crashes. 'Has it ended?'

'How can it possibly continue with me leaving? It would be unfair to both of us.'

'I don't care,' Cordelia replies. 'Do you?'

He smiles, 'I care for you.' He steps towards her, stops himself at the last moment, remembering the danger of being seen.

'I should like to see you as much as possible,' he says, scanning her eyes. 'Before I go. And then when I go, perhaps that should be an end to it.'

'No,' she says. 'It won't be an end to it. Ending it so suddenly would be crueller than knowing you're mine, than knowing I'm yours even though you're not here.'

'I don't know how we do this then. I don't have long.' His voice is urgent now as he glances over her shoulder and out of the muddy fountain trench. She turns briefly and sees Gilbert on his way towards them. Her heart races, her mind a whir.

She says the only thing she can think of. 'I'll come to you. Tonight. To your cottage.'

He looks shocked and nods, before Gilbert greets them both, telling Cordelia she's wanted at the house.

CHAPTER 31

CORDELIA

She waits as somewhere deep inside the house the faint chime of the grandfather clock strikes once; signalling she can release a breath she feels she's been holding all night. The house is quiet. All are asleep or at least in their beds. There has been no movement on the landing or the stairs for quite some time and so now she moves silently, deftly, risks being seen sneaking out. But it is a risk she knows she wants to take – must take.

She's in her nightdress, her coat wrapped around her, shoes in her hand until she reaches the French doors, unlocking them gently, slipping her shoes onto her feet and through the soft chill of a summer's night with the breeze rustling the trees, she runs to him.

Through the darkness she sees the lights of his cottage, muted oil lamps flicker in the window highlighting him as he waits, watching for her. She sees him walk from his position in the window, appearing a second later to open the door wide for her as she runs across the lawn towards him and into his arms.

She closes the door behind her. The reason she is there remains unspoken.

'I wasn't sure if you'd come,' he says, touching her face, his hands slipping into her hair. 'I thought you might change your mind. I wouldn't blame you if you did.'

'I haven't changed my mind,' she admits, breathless from running, as his fingers wind themselves gently into her hair. 'Where's David?'

'He's gone for a final spot of night fishing for a few hours,' he says quietly. 'I asked him to make himself scarce.'

'Does he know why?'

'I think he's guessed, yes. Only he's been gone quite a while and we might not have too long before he returns.'

Cordelia smiles and breathes deeply, her chest rising and falling from her run, from her excitement, from her panic. She's never done this before. She's guessed what happens but isn't quite sure what to expect, what she's supposed to do to make it happen. Kissing is one thing but this is something else entirely.

Isaac watches her carefully, the movement of his hands on her scalp, entrancing her. 'We don't have to,' he says, removing his fingers from her hair.

She removes her coat, slips off her shoes, stands in her white cotton nightdress and fixes him with a determined look.

'Yes we do,' she whispers.

In the end it's she who takes him upstairs, taking his hand in hers and holding it as they climb the stairs, as they kiss in the hallway, as they close his bedroom door behind them, as she slips the nightdress down a little – just a little – exposing her shoulders and then steps back so she can look at him as he undresses. But he doesn't move a muscle, just looks at her, his lips parted and then, as if from a dream, he reaches forward and gently slips her nightdress down all the way, letting it fall to the floor, pooling at her feet.

She should feel vulnerable, exposed but for some reason she doesn't. His awestruck face gives her a newfound level of confidence, trust and she can't resist smiling as she watches his expression.

He lifts his gaze and his eyes lock onto hers as she – bravely – undresses him, while he helps her unbutton his shirt, unbuckle his trousers. He reaches out to touch her, gently tracing his fingers – roughened from work – along her jawline, her neck, her chest and down, down towards her navel and around her waist, making her shiver in anticipation, bringing her towards him, bringing her with him to the bed.

And then everything that had been slow becomes fast, desperate and she holds on to him tighter and tighter as they move together, his mouth on hers until he pulls back to watch her. And then just when she didn't believe anything could be this wonderful, she closes her eyes, lifts her body into his, holds him tighter than she's ever held anything before, and feels her breath quicken, her hands tighten even harder around his waist and everything around them falls away as her body's involuntary reaction matches his.

And then they allow themselves to collapse together laying entwined in his sheets for so long after, his eyes remaining on hers as both the world and time begin conspiring against them.

* * *

After, she lies so happily in his arms, her body fitting so snugly against his. She marvels at discovering the places where the sun has tanned his body. And where it hasn't, tracing lines with her fingertips over all of him. She learns the various curves and grooves of his torso, trying desperately to remember, commit it all to memory, until the next time they do this again. It may be months before they meet again, before they lie like this again. They interrupt their kisses and caresses with their own battle plan.

'I don't know where I'm being sent for training yet. But I know now we're to go the day after tomorrow. The Expeditionary Force is preparing to go to France.'

'The army is going already?' she asks, from the safe space she's found herself, her lips brushing his neck.

'Volunteers won't be far behind them. I'll write to you,' he promises, holding her hand and tracing an invisible path around her palm.

'My parents might find that a bit interesting,' she tips her head back to look at him.

'Should I not write?'

'No. Do. I'll need it. I'll need to hear from you, to know you are well. Pretend it's about the garden. Give me plans or instructions as to what to do. Things you think Gilbert will need help with now that James and Talek are going too.'

'It's about maintenance at this point,' he says. 'Fruit and veg. Knowing when to plant to keep the estate and the village in food. Flowers if you can still manage it but it's going to be a big job. You might need help.'

'Sssh,' she says, planting a kiss on his lips as he turns in to her. 'Tell me in a letter.'

'All right.' Then he adopts a serious tone and looks at her. 'Cordelia, can you do something for me?'

'Anything,' she says.

He pauses, weighing up his words before saying them. 'Please don't come to the railway station to wave us off.'

'Why not? I'll be expected to. To say goodbye to my brother. To say goodbye to them all.'

'Oh, of course. I'm sorry. I shouldn't have asked it of you. I understand, of course I do.'

'Why don't you want me to come?'

He sighs, kisses her lips gently, so gently. 'Because I'm not sure I'll be able to stand there, patiently waiting to board, watching you, seeing you. And not run towards you, kiss you, hold you, say goodbye to you. They will all see. They will all know.'

'I don't care if they do.'

'You will. You will,' he soothes.

'You'll be an officer,' she says.

'I'm still a journeyman gardener. Don't pretend my actual occupation no longer exists because I've been handed a uniform and will board a train. Your parents won't want you to marry someone like me, someone who travels for employment. And I can go months at a time without a single commission. You do know that don't you? It's happened to me before. That is not stability.'

'I don't care.'

'Stop saying that,' he teases.

'They will come to think as highly of you as I do,' Cordelia says. 'My father shook your hand, you said.'

'I doubt he'd do that again if he could see us like this.'

'No, perhaps not,' she agrees, trying not to laugh. She strokes the light hairs on his bare arm. His forearm is tanned where his sleeves have been rolled to the elbow. It feels like hours ago David returned home, discreetly closed the door to his room and went to bed. He'll have seen her coat, her shoes, left downstairs, she thinks. But she doesn't care.

'I must get back but I don't want to go,' she says quietly as outside the birds begin their dawn chorus, ruining everything.

'You must.'

'I know,' she sighs, rising reluctantly, picking up her nightdress from the floor and slipping it over her head.

'I want to hold you a moment longer, remember you, in my arms, remember this feeling. With you,' he says, standing, pulling on his trousers and moving towards her. 'Nothing will compare to this.'

'Isaac, if you really don't want me to come to the station, I won't,' she says reluctantly.

He lifts his head. 'I feel it will be better for both of us if you don't but you must do what you feel is right for your brother, for the estate workers. I'm going to have to work very hard at ignoring you on the platform. It will kill me. I won't be able to keep myself together if I see you.'

'Neither will I,' she confesses. 'I will crumble.'

'Then let's say goodbye now,' he says, examining her face to remember her.

'It might not be for long,' she insists. But these words don't ring true.

'Yes,' he agrees. But it's equally as half hearted. 'It might not be.'

They descend the narrow staircase and he helps her fasten her nightdress, pulls her coat around her, a sad smile on his face as he looks at her. The sun slices a thin orange line over the sea, forcing her exit.

‘So this is it then,’ he says. ‘This is goodbye.’

‘It’s only goodbye for now,’ she says. ‘And then you’ll come back to me.’

‘Yes,’ he says, holding her hands.

‘Isaac,’ she dares. ‘I love you.’

‘I love you,’ he says as a wide smile forms. ‘And I will come back to you.’

‘Yes you will,’ she says, touching his face one final time. ‘You have to.’

CHAPTER 32

CORDELIA

When the time comes, Cordelia says goodbye to Edwin at home, finding him in his room as he's strapping up his kit bag. He'll be flanked soon enough on the steps of the house by staff not travelling to the station; those wanting to wish him and the others well.

She is going to do as Isaac asks. She is going to stay behind, telling her parents she feels too unwell to wave them all off.

'I'll miss you so much,' Cordelia says into Edwin's shoulder as she hugs him. 'Please, for God's sake, *do not die*.'

He laughs. 'I'll do my utmost to stay alive.'

'Oh Edwin.' She holds him tighter and feels the harshness of salty tears sting her eyes.

'And if I do die,' he says, 'you've still got Clive. Heir and the spare and all that.'

She steps back and looks at him with a half-hearted smile. 'Yes,' she says with mock-seriousness. 'That's true.'

On the steps of Pencallick House, she watches as the

horse and carts are loaded with kit bags and household staff while Edwin, Mother and Father are squeezed into the back of the Austin motorcar awaiting departure. She looks for Isaac, but he isn't here. He's already gone on ahead with the outdoor staff.

This is it. Her brother, the men, are all going to war. How quickly it has happened, when it should never have happened at all.

'Wait,' she says, without thinking. She doesn't have her hat but she's not going back now. 'Wait.' She runs forward, opens the door herself, steps on the tread board and hurls herself into the spare seat next to the chauffeur.

'Changed your mind?' Edwin leans forward and says. 'Not going to cry on me again, are you?'

'I might,' she says over her shoulder as the motorcar departs. She feels his hand on her shoulder comfortingly and places hers on top of it for a moment. 'I just might.'

At the station the train is ready and waiting, steam billowing around them and fogging Cordelia's vision. It's pandemonium with tearful wives and sisters bidding their men farewell. Men who yesterday were footmen and stable hands are now soldiers and are not quite willing to get onto the train until the very last second, jostling each other for space on the platform. No one wants to miss precious time with loved ones. Who knows when they'll return to embrace them again?

The rush starts as the stationmaster announces the train's departure and she cannot see him – Isaac. She cannot see him anywhere. She holds Edwin tightly, kisses him on his cheek as her parents begin a long farewell and then Cordelia is gone, rushing along the platform looking for him. She said she wouldn't come but now she is here she has to see him. Even if she cannot go to him, she has to see him. She has to look at him one last time. He has to know she was there, that she loved him too much to stay behind.

Through the steam the men lug kit bags onto shoulders and make their way with bright enthusiasm onto the train. Cordelia is lost in a sea of khaki as she pushes her way through, crying 'Excuse me, excuse me.' But she cannot see him.

She reaches the front of the platform and knows now she must begin looking through the carriage windows while still scanning the platform for any sign of him.

Cordelia turns, pushing her way towards the end of the platform, and still she cannot see him. The rush is over and the slam of train doors closing is replaced by the noise of men calling from windows, opening them hastily to hang out, wave their hands through – faces close to windows. Women cry and cheer and still she cannot see him.

And then he's there. At the window, looking out directly at her. She sees him and it's everything she knew it would be. The pain cuts into her. They can do nothing. They can't reach each other. He smiles and she watches him take a deep breath, in and out, but neither of them moves. She tells him silently that she loves him. He nods at her, as if he knows, as if he can hear.

And then a whistle blows, the men cry goodbye one final time and those straggling board the train, crowding those already inside. Isaac disappears from the window, moved along by someone else wishing to wave farewell to those left behind.

She's lost him. She can't see where he is, which window he is now in, if at all. She moves along, looking in the nearby windows, waving to the men she knows, footmen who have served and the boys who she's spent the last few weeks with in the garden. She sees Edwin in a window, waving madly at her and she waves madly back. She bumps into Millicent on the platform who has come to say goodbye to Edwin and the men from her father's estate who have boarded the train too.

And still she cannot see him.

The steam blows in even greater plumes as the train sets off, surrounding them all on the platform and still she cannot see him.

And then there are only those left behind on the platform, some waving, some already turning to go, some talking to friends and neighbours who will remain behind. And Cordelia stands wide-eyed. Because at the end, she could not see him.

PART TWO

CHAPTER 33

AUTUMN, 1914

Letter from Isaac to Cordelia

My darling Cordelia,
I couldn't picture what it would look like, the front.

But now I have been here a short while I am suddenly reminded, only in part, of the freshly dug fountain pit you and I stood in on what I now think of as the last normal day I had. Oh that day.

I used to think I knew what mud was, having toiled in it almost every day I've been alive. This is a different sort of toil, a different sort of life, a different sort of mud.

You wanted me to be honest with you about what it's like. I will but if I am too honest then you must tell me and I will stop. The norm is that we sit in trenches, quietly by day, quietly by night but at least at night we can move around under cover of darkness. The chance of getting shot is still the same, as it turns out.

You asked how we end up in trenches. When one is fired at, one finds the nearest ditch or makes a dug-out and stays safe. That ditch or dug-out now extends as far as the eye can see and we live in a never ending network of tunnels and trenches and, I won't say, hell but it doesn't quite have the same gravitas of Pencallick House.

The rain doesn't help as we attempt not to be waterlogged. Warmer clothes would be a boon. Thank you for the package you sent, preparing me for shortages. I was particularly buoyed by the cigarettes and the fruitcake, which I have shared around. I hope you don't mind.

While I think of it, here is your latest gardening instruction so you may pass this letter off to your parents as being entirely innocent and not laced with regret at having left you. By now leaves will have begun falling and autumn will be reaching its way towards Pencallick. Rake up fallen leaves to make leafmould. Gilbert will no doubt have a pile forming somewhere. You can get ahead in the vegetable patch by sowing broad beans. It's a bit early but you can start now; sow sweet peas in the hot house.

When I am not undergoing gun training and all the other things I must contend with, my thoughts are of making love to you. I can't stop thinking about you. I fully understand if you wish to burn this letter in the fire for the sake of modesty.

Tell me how you are and how the garden is. All I see is khaki and mud. But at night I picture the greenery of the parkland, the blue of the sea, and you.

All my love,

Isaac.

Letter from Cordelia to Isaac

Isaac, I cannot tell you how I blushed over breakfast as I read and re-read your words. Thoughts of making love to me. Is it terribly unladylike to tell you I think about that night quite often?

I cannot say any more without blushing again. Thank you for my gardening instruction, but do you know, Father doesn't so much as look at me at breakfast anymore, let alone quiz me about what I'm reading as we eat. There is a black hole where Edwin sits. He stares at the black hole often. And because the casualty lists are printed in *The Times*, he scours that eagerly every morning too.

I could be wearing a plant pot as a hat and he wouldn't so much as notice. But I find that I am not in the least concerned by this, mostly because I do not have to justify your letters to me. But perhaps an instruction every now and again from you might not go amiss. Just in case the inquisition begins at random and I find myself unprepared on the spot.

I am sorry about the mud. I have nothing to compare it to, other than the fountain pit. I wonder if you have heard – although how would be an interesting discussion – that the fountain is not to be completed after all. Not now anyway. It is a task for when all of this is over. The fountain men are too skilled to remain in Cornwall and have gone off to the Royal Engineers, or so I am told. And so, like you, I will look at mud fairly often as well. Although not, perhaps, as much as you.

As you hinted at the unkind weather I have

asked Father's permission and sent off to both Thomas Burberry and Aquascutum for gabardine waterproof coats for the officers and Pencallick staff. Please distribute them among the men. I hope there are enough.

I wish there was more we could do from here. I believe knitted pullovers will be making their way to you also from the voluntary association of which Mother has become patron, but as I can purchase coats quicker than they can knit pullovers, I win in the race to make sure the pals are warm.

Please tell me how you are all getting on. Does Talek talk yet?

I am due in the garden with Gilbert where I shall obviously carry out your instructions to the letter. I am doing the job of two gardeners and I'm working at speed, which is incredibly tiring and I find by bedtime I'm utterly exhausted. Poor Ada has never had to draw me so many baths, I'm that filthy.

We are producing more and more of everything and have roped in the hall boy and the dairymaid to fetch and carry in addition to their duties. Would you believe we have already lost a laundry maid to a factory? The pay is better, apparently.

Gilbert tells me the hall boy would be gone too, only he messed up his birthday when in the recruitment office and now they know he's only fifteen. Apparently he's been reciting his pretend birthday every now and again and intends to return to sign up in a week or two when he's quite been forgotten. And we will be down yet another helping hand.

You have been gone for weeks and weeks and moved out to war so quickly that I find myself wondering how often you will get leave? I assume they won't send you all at the same time so who will come back first and, where will you go? I never asked if you have extended family – will you go to them? Can I brazenly ask if I can meet you there if you do need to pay visits to family on your precious time home from wherever it is you are?

Or will you come here? Or somewhere close by where we can meet? I don't want to put off an awkward discussion so let me tell you here that I am happy to pretend to be Mrs Isaac Leigh and meet you at a hotel. I can pretend to Mother and Father that I am visiting my good friend Tabitha. I'd best write her a letter to butter her up in preparation. We met at a boring house party when I stumbled across her and one of the housemaids in a laundry cupboard. Yes, you read that correctly. The party stopped being boring at that point. I have told no one. Other than you. She is scandalous enough that she will vouch for me if questioned. But no one will question. I am getting ahead of myself. You have not said if you will get leave at all yet. But I hope beyond hope that you do. And soon. Please look after yourself.

Yours, Cordelia

Letter from Isaac to Cordelia

Darling Cordelia,

A housemaid? Well, I say. This has brightened my day considerably. What did she say when you discussed that event afterwards? I find I must know this detail. I find I must know every detail relating to this story.

I write this sheltered near a stove in what can only be described as a muddy, reinforced cave as the rain beats down torrentially. The rain here has been utterly relentless. We are all working to prevent flooding while waiting for orders. Until then we simply hold the line with our presence.

I have been on sentry duty now enough times to know we may be attacked at dawn. It is unnerving but also, is it mad to say reassuring? To know we are here for a reason. Drowning in mud, drowning in boredom. Although I find I must remind myself of the reasons why we are here daily, hourly. I am here for David. He is here for adventure. There are enough here who are all present for King and Country.

No Man's Land at night is a thing of bleakness as I look out. It is a thing of bleakness during the day too – perhaps even more so during the day when I look across at what must have once been a delightful landscape. Although there is no hint left of what it once was. I cannot imagine what it must have looked like before our arrival. Artillery shells have seen off all the trees and where there have been fields there is now a wasteland. I am on duty again in a moment, standing silently, awaiting movement, hoping there is none.

Yes, Talek talks. It is just you he is scared of. You and the Germans. I hope you smile at this. I cannot picture you doing otherwise. He brightened visibly when the waterproofs arrived, your parcels coming down the line to us. We all did. We are warmer, drier. The idea of pullovers warms us too.

I am soaked to the skin and cold to the bone despite the little camping stove providing a modicum of warmth (that and your housemaid story). A cup of tea in a tin mug is imminent, as is one of your cigarettes you sent me. As for leave, I do not know when this will be. There are rumours we may have something big to contend with here and for fear of giving you too much detail and having my letter redacted by the censor I will leave it there for now. I will let you know the very moment returning to England looks likely. I do not think it will be for some time. But a hotel, Cordelia. A hotel.

I love you,

Isaac.

Letter from Cordelia to Tabitha Bowes

Darling Tabitha, how long it has been. World events have quite overtaken me. Overtaken us all, I shouldn't wonder. Are you still at Bowes Grange or have you, like so many others, gone nursing? I send this letter to you there in the hope that if you are away, it will still reach you. (Do you remember Millicent? She is away, training to be a nurse with the Red Cross.) I am still at home, gardening. But the parkland is soon being dug up on the recommendation of the Board of Agriculture and turned into fields and I seem to find myself in charge of such things as crop rotation with our head gardener. We're having to think about pastureland for cattle now too. I am off to canvass opinion of our tenant farmers about that.

But I wanted to say hello and find out if you are well. How is your brother? Wasn't he already in the army before the war started? Did he avoid training he'd already done and was one of the first at the front? Edwin has gone. They've all gone from Pencallick House, mostly. How are your parents?

With love, Cordelia Carr-Lyon.

Letter from Tabitha Bowes to Cordelia

How wonderful to hear from you. Apologies for the delay in this letter. Bowes Grange thrives, I am sure. Only I am not there. Your letter was sent on to me by a housemaid who still resides there, who whipped it off the postman before my parents could get wind of it – as she does with most of my letters.

I think you might remember her.

I am too unruly for my parents to contend with, or so they say, so I now live in the Lake District, quite alone on a smallholding. I am used to it (but I can quite wonder at your face on hearing this for the first time).

My parents believe sending me away at the age of twenty-three was punishment. It is in fact, bliss. They give me an allowance so I can keep up the appearance of grandeur and not bring further shame on the Bowes name. I am squirrelling the money away for when it is truly needed.

I will have a visitor at Christmas but after that . . . you must come if you can get away. Why not come for New Year and stay as long as you like? I can't promise a party atmosphere but I remember you being one of the fun ones. Not too stuffy. You haven't become a traditionalist, have you?

From your letter I glean that you and I are kindred spirits in what I hear being bandied about as 'war work'. I too am outdoors most of the day here. I am farming, although animals not crops. You call what you do gardening, but darling, are you sure you haven't accidentally become a farmer?

Oh, dear Millicent, yes I remember her. Wouldn't say boo to a goose, would she? Does she intend to nurse in France? She's braver than I am. I simply couldn't. My brother Rupert was at the front, yes. He was one of the first casualties at Mons. I believe my parents are devastated. I am devastated.

I'll sign off now for fear I start crying. New Year? A trip to the Lakes?

Your friend, Tabitha

Letter from Cordelia to Tabitha

Darling Tabitha, Rupert was such a fine man. I am so incredibly sorry. I cannot imagine the pain you must be feeling. Please accept my heartfelt condolences to you and your parents, although I have told Mother and she intends to send a note to Mr and Mrs Bowes.

A trip to the Lakes to see you sounds divine. I would be overjoyed to come. Perhaps I should get away quickly before any of the other staff leave us. Gilbert – our overworked head gardener – and I are soon going to be quite alone if this war keeps up and we keep losing stable hands and housemaids who have been willing to help us out here and there.

But travelling, to you, for fun seems such a foreign, decadent idea. The last time I was away was because I was in London for the season. That seems so long ago now but it was only the summer and how the world has changed since then. I have no words to convey quite how I feel about you running a smallholding. I am in awe. You will have to teach me everything you know. It sounds idyllic. I assume it is not.

With love, Cordelia

CHAPTER 34

CORDELIA

'Not another servant gone?' Cordelia asks despairingly as she finishes shovelling the horse manure into a barrow. The last stable hand left last week. Gilbert says he has a plan for the manure in the garden.

''Fraid so,' Gilbert says, leaning against his pitchfork. 'Dairy maid this time.'

'What is it about factory work that seems more appealing than this life? Other than the money, obviously?' Cordelia asks. She's filthy. Wet mud has dried on her face somehow – at least she hopes it's mud – and her hair has long since come loose from its pins. What few remain have been pocketed. She's tucked her blonde hair into the collar of her dress. It will have to do.

'I can't think,' Gilbert says with a knowing smile as he steps round the manure, produces a piece of garden string and gestures to her hair.

'Oh, thank you,' she says attempting a crude sort of style with it. 'We didn't have them doing the kind of jobs we wouldn't have done ourselves,' Cordelia protests.

'I know. But you can't stop this war effect, I'm afraid. One goes with stars in their eyes and the whole lot want it. It's excitement. The only excitement they'll probably get.'

'But a factory?'

'They're making bullets or . . . I don't know. But it makes them feel they're doing something of actual use,' he reasons.

'I suppose,' Cordelia says reluctantly. Inside the stable a horse whines. 'Father's thinking of offering the horses to the war effort,' she says thoughtfully.

'To what end?'

'I'm not sure even he knows. To a cavalry unit I suppose. But he says there will be powers put into place over us soon as part of the new Defence of the Realm Act. He says if he shows willing, offers up things of use that he thinks they'll probably take anyway, we might get to keep other things.'

'Such as?'

'The motorcar.'

'There's no chauffeur to drive it now he's gone to sea.'

'Yes, quite,' she replies with a sigh. 'I don't know. It's just talk. He might not.' Cordelia glances towards the stables. She's had no time to ride the horses, to keep them exercised. Clive's been doing as much as he can and so has Father. The vet suggested selling them while they'd still fetch a good price. Not that money is an issue.

'Look on the bright side,' Gilbert offers. 'If the horses do go, you won't have to shovel their manure each day.'

'Oh yes.' Cordelia brightens then rubs the twinge that's formed in her lower back. 'I hadn't thought of that.'

CHAPTER 35

Letter from Millicent Trevelyan to Cordelia

Cordelia, I have a little free time before I ship out to a field hospital in Belgium so I wanted to let you know where I will be. I have written the forwarding address above and I should so like a letter from you every now and again. I know you are busy. Irene will write, I am sure, but it's not the same as having a true friend and hearing how things go at home.

I write to Edwin and he writes to me. (He apologises through me for having not written to you yet. He intends to. He is muddy. And cold. I think they all are.)

The main purpose of my letter was to thank you. That night, in the garden, when you hung back purposefully as I suspect you did, it brought Edwin and I closer together. It bought us time to be together. If I'd known what little time we'd actually have before he left, I should not have suggested we turn back to check you hadn't stumbled into some sort of hole or other. Forgive me for that thought. Proposing to me on the eve of war seems so romantic, all the nurses here coo at that story. But the reality is my fiancé is fighting at the front when before that night he would have just been a man I loved from a distance. I'm not sure what is worse. Forgive me, I am writing in a ramble.

Will you write if you have time? Don't worry if you don't. I understand how busy you must be.

Soon to be your sister-in-law,

Millicent Trevelyan

Letter from Cordelia to Millicent

I hope this letter finds you well. I assume by now it will find you in Belgium via the pure magic of the forwarding address you provided. Are you up to your eyes in handsome soldiers? I wonder now why I didn't hop on a train with you to become a VAD.

Strange to think of you and Edwin over there somewhere, together but apart. You in some sort of hospital, him on the front. I wonder how close to each other you are. I don't suppose you can know that, can you?

The nurses should coo at that story. It is terribly romantic. Millicent, can I trust you with some romantic history of my own? I have told absolutely no one and ask the same of you. I believe I've reached the stage when I shall burst if I don't tell someone. I too am in love. If I tell you it's with a gardener I might be playing it down somewhat. Although it does feel more sensational to call him that. It is Isaac Leigh, Father's landscape architect. I am so in love it hurts just thinking about it. There, I have said it. I am smiling as I write.

We have made no plans, unlike you and Edwin. Isaac and I started incredibly slowly and then it all happened in such a rush. I would not like to tell you what happened just before he went away but I would like to say war does things to people. I think you will understand – it happened to you and Edwin too! That slow burn and then the sudden flicker of flames that can't be fought.

There is so much more I could say about Isaac but I won't for fear of embarrassing myself. He shipped out with the Pencallick staff and your Trevelyan lot. There's so many of them. About two hundred and fifty men in total gone from the surrounding villages as well. How lovely that they'll all know mostly everyone they are fighting with. At least they are all in it together. I do worry for them all though. I don't worry that Edwin doesn't send me letters, but I do miss him. The house is so quiet without him, without them all. Most of the servants have gone. It is most strange. And now Clive is being sent to school. He is livid. Wants to lie about his age and join up. He's six. Feels very left behind. I've come to rely on him helping in the stables.

Edwin's not one for letters so I am jolly pleased he's using up all his letter-writing energy on you. Millicent, would it be incredibly odd of me if I told you that you are one of the nicest people I've ever met. If not the nicest. And I will be incredibly happy when you become my sister-in-law.

Write to me with your exciting VAD stories. I will not bore you with crop rotation and potato tales.

Cordelia

Letter from Edwin to Cordelia

I'm sorry! It's taken me so long to put pen to paper to you. I am terrible at writing letters but then you know that. My trunk home each holiday at university was always full of letters you'd written to me and that I guiltily realised, far too late, that I'd never replied to. Forgive me.

We do well here and by well I mean it is boring, wet and cold. I live in constant fear of getting sniped. Do you remember the landscaper, Isaac Leigh? He's quite a useful sort, always busy, strengthening the trenches from total collapse (the rain, Cordelia, the rain!) or building up the sides to make them higher so we don't get shot in the head every time we forget to crouch. He's been at it for weeks.

I snuck out last night with him into No Man's Land with a little rabble of equally brave soldiers. Two officers shouldn't have gone really but have I mentioned the boredom? (I do hope the censor skips past this bit.) But Leigh went too. He volunteers for most raiding parties. He's very good at that. Look at that, I've written three whole paragraphs. One for every month I've been away. Your loving brother, Edwin.

Letter from Cordelia to Edwin

The shortest of letters from me. What is a raiding party? Why do you carry it out at night?

Letter from Cordelia to Isaac

What is a raiding party? Why do you carry it out at night?

I have asked Edwin this same question but he will not reply for weeks, or at all.

Why do you volunteer for these things? He says you volunteer for most raiding parties. In the same way you wanted details about the housemaid story I want details about this. I suspect for very different reasons. Quickly please. Full letter to follow. Cordelia.

Letter from Isaac to Cordelia

My darling Cordelia,

It was your turn to write anyway but I wasn't expecting such a short missive. *Quickly please* gave me a rare moment of laughter. A raiding party is a trip across into German territory. Sometimes not very successfully. If we can capture a German we bring him back with us where we hand him over to some greater power who no doubt questions him about tactical plans. God knows what they expect to get out of some foot soldier. We know nothing here until the final moments. We survive on a diet of bully beef and rumours.

Yes, we have to cross No Man's Land to do it. But we are silent and we are careful and it is not all the time. Does that allay any fears? I am being careful. I promise you. I think of you and me and what might happen after the war. I think of this far too often to be anything other than careful.

I love you,

Isaac

Letter from Millicent to Cordelia

Cordelia,

Please do tell me your gardening tales. It won't be boring, I'm sure. It is something useful, isn't it, food production? We are all doing something useful, in ways that suit us. I am surrounded by handsome soldiers. But they are injured. At first it was just a trickle of them but more and more wounded enter the tents. You should see it after an order to go over the top has taken place.

I am far behind the lines, organising boat passages, writing letters home for those in the long queue to be transported home and other menial tasks for those who are injured but it is becoming apparent we are needed further up the line, where I think real nursing – that which I've been trained for might be the order of things. I am being moved to a casualty clearing station imminently. I was told indiscreetly by a soldier on his way home that it is probably going to be the worst thing I've ever seen. I am to brace myself. But I think I will be fine. It's the men who are not.

Yes, I believe I am fairly close to Edwin although

he can never actually say in his letters exactly where he is. Given where I am going, I hope I do not see him. If he stays safe and alive, I would be happy not to see him until this all ends. I am lucky to receive mail from him fairly quickly though. It all comes via here anyway before it reaches England. Speeds things along.

As for your garden landscaper, Mr Leigh, I'm sorry I didn't meet him. I'm sorry he wasn't introduced to us. Was he at a party in summer? If so, perhaps I remember him after all. Perhaps not. I'm sorry. He's with Edwin's lot, you say, but if you wish me to keep it a secret I will not mention it to Edwin in a letter.

I do rather hate it when love has to be kept secret although I think when this war is over, none of that will matter anymore. Mother and Irene are sticklers for respecting the class divisions, and by that I mean that Mother and Irene are rather snobby. Isn't that awful of me? I hope I am not and I hope to shake hands with your Mr Leigh when the war is over. Imagine us all sitting at the dining table at Pencallick House. Imagine us all on the lawn, picnicking. It feels hard to imagine any of that at the moment. I am growing morose.

Since writing the above, Sister has popped her head into the tent to tell me to pack. We move up the line first thing in the morning. I send this letter to you now, wish you well and tell you how I glowed red with happy embarrassment when you said you were looking forward to being my sister-in-law. I, too, wait eagerly for that happy day.

With love, Millicent.

Letter from Isaac to Cordelia

You have not replied. Are you upset? Or has a letter gone missing in the post? It's a long way from Cornwall to CENSORED. I wish my letters could grow wings and reach you swifter than the mail train. I have a little more time to spend on this reply than I did with the last one. The last one, I felt, had to reach you in good time so you knew that I wasn't lost or forsaken, while also justifying my volunteering for raiding parties. I promise not to volunteer too often but one doesn't like to let the side down by sending others all the time.

I've been on ration parties also quite a bit, which involves heading back down the line, out of the labyrinthine trench network, out where the snipers cannot reach us, out where the tents hold the other battalions, waiting to swap with us when our tenure here is over. It's all very civilised up there compared to how we live in the trenches.

How I long to sleep in a tent again. How I long to be with you. How I long to go to the CENSORED hotel in CENSORED. Ordinarily I would have loved to have been there with you. Instead I got your brother.

Edwin and I went in, on a rare twenty-four-hour pass, dined, drank good red wine and then because we were on a pass, hired a twin room and slept like babies.

Your brother snores, or so he tells me. I could not hear him for the guns firing in the distance that madly lulled me to sleep. The guns are always a bad sign. When the artillery shells end, it usually means over the top. Lucky we weren't there. Although that is why we are, generally, here. Over the top will come at some point and we discussed this in some length, alongside home and what it meant to us. How much I concealed about what home means to me now, because it has to be you, Cordelia. Home will be returning to you and not on a bit of leave. But at the end of all of this.

I note that your brother can drink. So can I as it turns out. Although I think it is a new habit for both of us, to drown out this new world of mud, guns and rain in which we now reside. He told me all about Millicent. I very nearly told him all about you. He invites confidences. I told him I was in love. I was vague about who she was but not the sentiment behind her . . . I mean you. See, how well I can lie when forced. I surprise myself. I told him when all of this is over I intend to propose. I have seen things, Cordelia, that make me realise life is far shorter than I ever thought it might be. God I miss you. I'm not sure who the devil was who kept bandying about the phrase it will be over by Christmas. It will be anything but. But when it is over, I will come home. To you.

Letter from Cordelia to Isaac

Isaac, I do love you. Since I received your letter I am tense with nerves. But please do not think I need you to dim down any feeling behind your notes. If you are scared you must say. The things you have seen. I dread to think. I do not want you to hide it from me. I want to know and I don't want to know. I wish that you weren't there. I wish that you weren't seeing these things. Whatever they may be. I suspect from what Edwin's Millicent tells me she sees that they are horrific and otherworldly. She is brave and I am not. You are brave. You and David and Edwin and the vicar's son Reginald and James and Talek and Jonathan the footman and . . . all the others, you are all so brave.

In answer to your question, yes I think a letter has gone missing. I replied to your last practically screaming at you for going on raids so in a way it's good you were spared that one but I am pleased you've been switched to ration parties for the time being. Long may that continue. And a hotel, with wine and beds. Your version of heaven for now. It will do until you and I can share wine and hotels and a bed.

For now my latest news is the glorious parkland has become both arable and pastureland and the tenant farmers are chipping in their help here. Cows roam wildly and I often find them up by the house. I've had to have fencing installed around the fountain hole so they don't fall in.

Sadly the green pastureland is far out of sight of the house so when I look out of my window I see nothing but muddy vegetable beds all the way to the lake. I believe now we are going to have to enlist some voluntary help given the sheer scale of it all. Gilbert and I have put our heads together to see what can be done.

Oh, before I forget I must tell you that your

last letter was censored! So it's true, people are reading our words to each other. Still, I don't care. I'm going to talk to you about bed all I like. I hope it gives someone some titillation somewhere. They black it out with heavy ink. I have tried holding up the letter to the light to see through it but it's no good. So I have no idea which hotel, which town you were in. I should so like to hold up a map of Belgium and put a little pin in it to mark where you and Edwin are, where Millicent is. You are all so far away from me. At least one of you has to get leave soon, surely. Although Millicent has been moved further up the line so no hope for her for a while, I think.

I hope it's you first. With love, Cordelia

CHAPTER 36

CORDELIA
NOVEMBER 1914

Cordelia wakes to find a bounty of birthday cards and letters, presents and flowers adorning the breakfast table. Her parents are too busy scanning the casualty list in *The Times* to notice her arrival.

'Good morning, darling,' Mrs Carr-Lyon says when Cordelia moves into the room properly and heads towards the breakfast dishes laid out on the sideboard. Mother's bright smile tells Cordelia that Edwin is still safe – that his name is not on the list.

Cordelia greets her parents with a slightly embarrassed smile when they both cry in unison, 'Happy Birthday.'

'Thank you,' she blushes. 'Anyone we know in the lists this morning?' she dares. Best to ask now. Best to know now. Get it over with. Usually she'd have a look herself. A quick scan. Just to be sure. She'll look in a moment regardless of what her parents tell her. Just to see that Isaac's name remains blessedly absent.

'Yes, I'm afraid so,' Father says. 'Remember that chap who was here in summer.'

Cordelia stills. Her legs waver and she grips the edge of the sideboard, threatening to upset the kedgeree. Oh God. 'Which chap?' she says with an air of calm she doesn't feel.

'That fellow Edwin was at school with,' her father states. 'Mungo William-Lloyd. Here for that final party we had. Not that we knew it'd be the final one. Do you remember?'

Oh thank God, she thinks as relief sweeps over her in waves of heat and then realises that any death is horrific. Mungo. Poor Mungo. But not Isaac. And not Edwin either.

'Cordelia?' Mother prompts.

'Yes,' she says but her breath is a whisper. More clearly, 'Yes, I remember Mungo. Poor boy.' Because he is a boy really. Not quite a man. 'They both went up from school to Oxford together,' Cordelia thinks aloud, attempting to cover the silence she'd created a few moments ago.

'Well, the young man won't be going back now,' Father says abruptly. 'And if this war lasts much longer, I don't know how Edwin will be able to go back either? One can't be in their mid-twenties trying to get back to university, surely?'

'So many unknowns,' Cordelia's mother says absently. 'I'll write a letter of condolence to his people.'

'Shouldn't you wait,' Cordelia suggests. 'Just in case they don't know yet? Do you think they get an official letter before the list is printed? Or after?' Cordelia asks. 'Do you think they find out the way we've just done, by looking in the newspaper? It can't be that way round surely? How cruel.'

'I don't know and I hope never to have to find out,'

Father says, folding the newspaper over and discarding it on the table. And then more softly, 'Sit and eat something and let's change the subject. This is not good birthday conversation.'

'Mrs Emes has made your favourite,' Mother says. 'As it's your birthday. Porridge with fresh cream and berries from the hot house. You should be so proud of those berries.'

'Yes,' Cordelia admits 'Yes, I am. Thank you. And Gilbert, of course. And all the rest of the gardeners.' Who aren't here now, she thinks.

No one's here now.

Letter from Edwin to Cordelia

Happy Birthday old girl. See, I remembered. I've made this card and drawn the picture myself even though art was never my strong suit. What do you think of the picture? Are you laughing? I thought it rather clever but when I showed David Leigh, he said he hadn't a clue what it was. You can tell what it is, can't you?

We are not on the front line! I can hear your cheer from here. We've been relieved by the CENSORED battalion so we spend a blissful few days down the line in a series of white tents. Not so white as when we were last here however. Bit grubby now. But there are beds, and hot food cooked in a canteen and not cooked by us on a camping stove. It's the same food, mind. I am forming an aversion to tins of bully beef and biscuits. Not the biscuits you are thinking of. These are like dominoes. Only harder. And I think a domino might actually taste better. Autumn has gone and it feels as if winter proper has arrived. December looms. I should imagine the garden is chilly. It's freezing here. Hard to believe we are in CENSORED. I feel as if someone upped and moved us all to the North Pole overnight. A polar bear will meander past my tent any moment, I'm sure.

How do you intend to spend your birthday or how have you spent your day depending on how long it takes the bally post to reach you? One assumes tea and cake and some presents. Did Mrs Emes and Mrs Venning make a fuss of you? I hope so. I hope Mother and Father rallied a bit or are they still staring at the space at the dining table as if I was dead and not alive and kicking in a field in CENSORED.

The censor will probably get at this, no doubt but one has to try. I hope this card finds you well. Thank you for your kind presents of chocolate and cigarettes. And those coats you sent. Marvellous work, Cordy.

There are rumours of leave! Although it might equally be rumours of going over the top so I must not get anyone's hopes up. Especially not my own.

Do you know where Millicent is? I have not heard from her in a while and I am starting to grow twitchy. Last I heard she was working at a casualty clearing station and no harm can befall her there, surely. So far back from the line, so far back from the guns, I thought. I'm sure she's just busy but if you've heard in the last week or two will you just pen a quick note to say? How I wish we had married before I went away. Learning about widow's pensions was an eye opener and I would so like her to have something of her own if I die. As a fiancée she is entitled to nothing. We planned this badly. Never mind.

A final Happy Birthday from me so you know I've really not forgotten.

Love, Edwin

Letter from Cordelia to Edwin

You wrote to me! And you remembered my birthday. It was spent with Mother and Father and tea and cake and they sent off for some books by Gertrude Jekyll. And a lovely watercolour set so I can paint the garden. Although it's not in bloom at the moment. My days this week have been spent fixing the heater in the greenhouse that decided to give up the ghost. I had to send off to the original manufacturer, describe the problem and ask him for step-by-step instructions as to how it should be fixed. It took forever. And weeding. I'm picking up quite a speed now.

No. I have no idea what you'd drawn. Mineral or animal? I couldn't tell. A man, perhaps? No clue. Sorry. But the thought and the effort you put in was enough for me. I hugged your birthday card and it has pride of place on my dressing table.

Sorry, no, I haven't heard from Millicent since she said she was moving up the line. I expect she's busy if she is, as you say, safe. I will send a little note to her just to see all is well.

I'm pleased you are away from the front line for now. And in tents. What luxury. I'm thrilled about your potential leave. Will it be before Christmas? I see Christmas approaching and passing us by without proper celebration. But if you return home, it would be the best gift of all. Enclosed are more cigarettes and some toffee I saw for sale when I went to the greengrocer, the kind I bought at the fair in the summer that breaks your teeth. Gosh that day feels so long ago. Another time. Perhaps you can put it in some hot tea and see if it softens. The postmaster and the tobacconist are both doing very well out of me since you all went away. The tobacconist in Bodmin is purchasing additional cigarettes just to appease me so there will no doubt be more coming your way soon.

With love, Cordelia

Letter from Isaac to Cordelia

Belated birthday wishes, my darling Cordelia.

Your brother mentioned in passing. All I could do not to rush off and write a letter to you there and then, for fear of giving the game away. Had to walk off discreetly and pen you this very quickly so you had a little something from me as soon as possible.

He must have told you we are away from the front line for now. Although we are never quite away for long enough. I am being sent on machine gun training so that alleviates some of the boredom of parade and sitting around. Although catching up on missed sleep is never a waste of time.

Edwin is correct in that there are rumours of officer leave. Obviously not at the same time so it's pot luck which of us gets to return. I'm not sure who starts these rumours. Probably the same person who mentioned the war would be over by Christmas, which is only weeks away. What will you do? Ours will be dire. I will either be on leave or I will be back in a trench as it will be our turn again, I'm sure.

I miss you. I long for you. I cannot wait for the day I hold you in my arms. That day cannot come soon enough.

Isaac

Letter from Millicent to Cordelia

Happy Christmas! I'm writing this in advance so I hope by the time you get this it will not have passed yet and that this letter reaches you before the day. I envy you, your Christmas. It will be lovely and normal. It is my favourite time of year and I will spend it in a tent, in the cold, with a rushed dinner of some kind and then back to the wounded. I do not mind though. There will be other Christmases to look forward to.

And happy birthday. I missed it. Edwin told me in a letter. Saying that, I realise it is mine in a month or so. No doubt the date will rush past me. Yes, I am alive. I have been so tired I collapse into bed every night. Each day is so similar to the last and they all merge into one long day treating soldiers and bandaging them up and preparing them for emergency surgery and . . .

oh everything. And so I didn't realise the days passing. I kept saying to myself, tomorrow I will write to Edwin, Mother, Irene and Cordelia. And it has been weeks, I am sure. Although you and Edwin were the only two to write to confirm my alive-or-dead status.

Does Edwin write to you much more or is he still as awful? I hope your Mr Leigh is a bit more useful in the letter-writing department.

Write soon! Millicent

Letter from Tabitha Bowes to Cordelia

Cordelia,

Enclosed are your instructions to reach me. Trains, where to change, that sort of thing. I'll meet you myself when you arrive at Windermere station. I have a little motorcar, can you believe? (I have been squirrelling my funds and then spending them wildly.) It's not far from there to Rose Cottage. Will you just send me a note as to what day you wish to arrive? Then I will know at what time and day to meet your train. You could stay for absolutely ages if you like. Doesn't have to be a short visit. So bring enough things for a lengthy stay. You can always change your mind halfway through if I bore you. You can help me in the garden and with the animals if you like? Or do you just need a good rest? Either is fine. I'm excited to share in your company. It's been so long.

Love, Tabitha

Letter from Cordelia to Tabitha

I intend to arrive on the 30th of this month but, Tabitha, I may have to telegram you at the very last minute and postpone because Edwin may be due some leave. I don't wish to simply not turn up. But I would like to come so if I have to postpone my visit, would you mind? It may only be for a week or so. We doubt he'll get longer than that. Or any at all the way things sound.

I'm so incredibly excited!

Cordelia.

Letter from Cordelia to Tabitha

A letter to you quickly flying on the heels of my first. Can we postpone my visit? First week of January all right for you? Edwin has leave. A note has come through today to Mother and Father to tell us so. Do you mind? I am so excited to see you. You mentioned a long stay so I hope you are still available first week of January for me to arrive? I cannot believe we are soon entering 1915 and this fray continues. I digress. Write back when you can to confirm. Yours eagerly, Cordelia

Letter from Isaac to Cordelia

Cordelia, I waited in a hopeful kind of non-expectation for rumours of my leave to be real and to be able to return to you before Christmas but alas it was not to be. (Although more on that in a minute.) I was overjoyed for your brother that he had news of some and we were told one other officer might be able to return to England a few days after he left us but that's all over now.

Leave is cancelled all round this side of Christmas.

Which is never good I'm sure as it can only ever mean one thing. So I think I need to tell you things. Lovely things. Things I want you to know before I go over the top, because presumably that is what is about to happen.

I love you. I think you know that, I've told you often enough but here it is for you in block capitals so you know I mean it. I LOVE YOU. There, am I making a fool of myself? I do hope so. A man longs to be a fool in love. I've never known it before you. Why did I spend so long fighting those feelings, when I should have just given in from the outset? You knew better than I did. I should have trusted your judgement and not mine. I do rather worry we wasted those weeks when we could have been doing other things, falling in love, learning more about each other. A few days doesn't feel like enough time to admit how one feels about someone and then be shipped off to the front. But I suppose war speeds things along. It sped us along. Perhaps we should thank it for bringing us together rather than cursing it for separating us. War is temporary, but you and I will be forever. It is wrong to make plans in this state and so I won't but I want you to know there is a promise of plans. In my mind there are plans – in yours too, no doubt. Let us keep them there, ours and unsaid. Let's not tempt fate by declaring them loudly. But know we have them.

And now I'm going to leave you just here on a high note. I've been told I may have leave at the very end of December. Nice to actually be told something, however vague. No date yet. Will believe it when I hear a fixed date. We will see.

Prepare yourself because I'm going to shout my love to you in capitals again.

I LOVE YOU.

Isaac.

Letter from Isaac to Cordelia

I've had confirmation that my leave is to begin on Boxing Day! I am sorry to miss Christmas with you but I hope my arrival will be a good, belated Christmas present. Rest assured I will be eagerly awaiting the midnight hour on Christmas Day so I can make my way directly to you on some sort of truck convoy towards the boat train (there's always something coming or going bringing food and the such). Then I will be on my way home to you. I have a week. Now for our very own battle plan. Where and when shall I meet you? Let's fix it now so we are sorted in good time. Can you get away and pretend you are going somewhere else – to a friend?

I can telegram a hotel in London and book us a suite. We can live like kings in each other's company. I have a week with you. Food, wine, bed, you, theatre? Is the theatre still on? I've rather lost touch with what's happening away from here.

Or perhaps leave will all be cancelled again. No, I won't talk like that. I must believe this is happening. Cordelia, I need to be away from here. I need to come back and be with you for a bit. I just need it.

I feel bad because I seem to have overtaken your brother when it comes to leave. Edwin was scheduled for 22nd December but has been shunted back into January. How I've overtaken him I do not know.

He will follow on after me so you get two of us, one after the other. David and Reginald, the vicar's son and the other officer in our merry band do not have their leave yet and we'd dearly like to send some of the other younger boys back home to see their parents. We all needed it weeks ago and now we really need it. I, selfishly, am exultant I am coming home to you, albeit briefly. This is going to spur me on for the next few weeks until I see you.

Yours, lovingly and forever, Isaac

Letter from Cordelia to Isaac

Isaac, I cried when I read your letter. Both in sadness for you and in happiness that you are coming home. To me. I cannot believe it.

However, I cannot get away from here to travel on Christmas Day itself. Mother and Father will be furious if I skip off on the big day so I shall wake at the crack of dawn on Boxing Day and I will say this is the day I am due to visit my friend Tabitha Bowes. (She of the housemaid story.)

I am due to visit her in January regardless so I shall simply pretend to Mother and Father that I am on an extended stay with her then no one is any the wiser. Then on Boxing Day I will make my way to whichever hotel you book in London. Perhaps you could leave a telegram at the hotel for me to pick up so I know you are boarding the boat/already on the boat and how long it will take to reach me. Unsure how that works but sure you will think of something.

I will arrive in London late that evening, the trains being far removed from what they are in normal times, I may even arrive the next morning! But I will arrive. And so will you. I cannot believe it. I am going to hold you so tightly, Isaac Leigh. I will try not to squeeze the very life out of you.

All my happy, happy love, Cordelia

Letter from Isaac to Cordelia

Will you be quite safe with she-of-the-house-maid-story?

One, rather excitedly, imagines all sorts of things. I have booked a room for us at Brown's Hotel in Albemarle Street under the name Lieutenant and Mrs Leigh. Keep on your gloves on arrival if you cannot ferret a piece of jewellery that resembles a wedding band.

I shall endeavour to find something for you at a jeweller's as I pass through London on my way to you in order to save your modesty and reputation.

Cordelia, if I intended to propose to you – what would you say? I don't mind telling you, from my side, that you and I . . . this, us, is not a passing fancy. This is not something to cherish now and then forget later. Will I sound trite if I say one of my dearest wishes is for this to be forever? Actually, it is my only wish. (That and all of us in our little band of brothers surviving this war but I feel that's a given.)

And, if I am to propose to you, and if you are to say yes, we would need to tell your parents. I am getting ahead of myself. I have not asked you yet (nor am I going to in this letter). And you have not given me an answer to a question I am not asking you here. Can you see me smiling as I write this?

I was always of a mind that there are no certainties in this life but of one thing I am certain. I am in love with you and I want you to be my wife. Would you like that? God, let this war end soon. In case the mail is slow or our letters pass each other, I will be at Brown's Hotel on the evening of Boxing Day. If I am late, blame the trains.

All my love. Isaac.

Letter from Cordelia to Isaac

Isaac,

I am scribbling this quick note as I prepare to rush into the garden. We have had a terrible storm last night and I must hurry to help Gilbert who is attempting to lift fallen branches, at his age. Father has run out to stop him as we can see him from the dining room windows trying to load a wheelbarrow. (But I must quickly dash this letter off to you to catch the post.) We have so many trees felled on the estate and the hall boy (he was rejected by the recruiting officer again who remembered him!) and I are going to have to chop them up for firewood. Even Father has volunteered. Mother and I are mourning the loss of so many of the plants in the formal garden, especially as it was the only garden completed during your short time with us. I hope you do not wince unhappily at this news. By the time you are next here, all will be well again. I will have put it all right. Which brings me on to my next point.

You have not asked me to marry you (but what a hint to it!) and I am glad you have not officially asked me in a letter. But if you did, Isaac. If you did ask me when I next see you . . . I think you must know what my answer would be. You must know. My stomach tightens with excitement at the thought of it. So please, visit a jeweller as you pass through London if you have time. And I will see you at your room in Brown's Hotel in the evening of 26th December.

Yours,
Cordelia

PART THREE

CHAPTER 37

ISAAC

25TH DECEMBER 1914

Isaac stands in the dark of the trench and looks through the periscope over No Man's Land as Christmas Eve becomes Christmas Day. One more day until he comes home to Cordelia. He's smothered his feet in whale oil to ward off trench foot. The water levels have been rising consistently since . . . he can't remember when and his boots are always full of rainwater or ground water or both. He's used to the weight and feel of it all now. There are no guns, no sound of any kind, no movement from the German trench, which looks eerily close through the viewfinder. The stillness around him is neither worry nor comfort. It simply is. There are no working parties, no ration parties, no raiding parties. Not today.

'The only thing we have to look forward to today is lamb and veg stew,' David whispers as he joins Isaac.

'And the fact it's Christmas Day.'

'And that,' David acquiesces. 'No different to any other day though. Not here.'

'Maybe not,' Isaac says as he looks through the periscope over No Man's Land.

'You go home tomorrow,' David says. 'To her,' he says vaguely, glancing around for fear of Edwin or others hearing.

Isaac nods.

'I'm happy for you,' David says. 'That day on the beach, she was nice.' In the end, Isaac had to tell someone. He had to tell David. Odd to be here, sharing the prospect of death and not confess to his brother how ridiculously in love he is and how he plans to marry Cordelia.

'I'll try not to think of you lording it up in some hotel while I sit here and eat tins of bully beef,' David sighs. He lights a cigarette, shares it with Isaac. The amber glow, deep in the safety of the trench, the only light out here. That and the moon. The night is cloudless.

'It'll be your turn next,' Isaac says, pulling his gaze away from where the Germans sit in their own trench only two hundred yards away and inhaling on his tobacco. It's heaven. It's the only thing out here that is. He hands it back.

'End of January now, apparently.'

'That long?' Isaac says.

'On rotation. Waiting my turn. I assume.'

Isaac nods, looks back through the spyhole. 'Made any plans yet?'

'I'm going to take myself off to see Cyril Dunholme from school. Remember him?'

'I do, yes. Didn't he join up?'

David shakes his head. 'Medically unfit. Rheumatic fever as a child did something to his lungs. That's why he never played much sport at school. Lives near a trout stream these days so we'll have just under a week's fishing together.'

Isaac looks away from the spyhole and inhales deeply on the cigarette. Exhales. He looks back through and tenses. He can see lights coming from the German trench, slowly, hands are rising with lanterns and candles.

'What?' David asks. 'What can you see?'

'I'm not sure. I think I'm going mad.'

'God we're not being raided, are we? On Christmas bloody day.'

'No,' Isaac says as across the distance of No Man's Land a makeshift choir of enemy soldiers begins singing 'Silent Night' in German. 'No, I don't think we are.'

'Hey, Tommy. Come out,' shouts one.

'We want to talk to you. Hey Tommy?'

'*Frohe Wienachten*. Merry Christmas.'

'There is no shooting. It is Christmas Day. Come and shake hands with us.'

'Bloody hell,' Edwin says sleepily as he arrives. 'Am I hearing this correctly. Do we think this is a trick?'

'No sir,' Isaac says, his eyes on the viewfinder. 'They're standing up. They're not carrying guns. Have a look.'

'God alive,' David says. 'Are they mad? Do they want to die?'

Edwin looks through the viewfinder. 'My word.' He stands back, obviously thinking as men gather from their sleep. Reginald, the vicar's son arrives. 'Are we going over to say hello?' he says excitedly.

Isaac can't help it. He laughs. These are men they've all been shooting at ever since they arrived, men they've been crawling through barbed wire to get to in order to raid. Any day now they're going to be told to go over the top and kill as many as possible in a dawn attack.

Isaac looks at Edwin. It's his decision. Quite frankly, he can't think of anything more ridiculous than going over the top in order to say hello. But then on Christmas Day, he can't think of anything better. The officers look at Edwin, the men look at Edwin and Edwin looks through the viewfinder again and sighs.

He nods, reluctantly and then says, 'I apologise in advance if we come to regret this.'

'And this,' a German officer tells Isaac as he holds up a lantern in the halfway space between Allied and enemy camps and shines a dim glow onto a small photograph. 'This is my daughter, Vicki. She is named after your Princess Vicki – the mother of our Kaiser.'

'She's very sweet,' Isaac says truthfully. 'How old is she?'

'She is only five. I hope to see them again soon.'

'I'm sure you will,' Isaac says. Around them other men have paired off or stand in groups sharing stories and cigarettes. Someone has started a game of football, just a kick about from what Isaac can determine but there is laughter when there hasn't been any in such a long time.

Isaac sees David open a jar of something and offer it to the German foot soldier he's conversing with. 'Plum and apple jam,' he explains. 'The only sweet thing we often get. Afraid I haven't got any bread to put it on. All ours is stale.'

'I have,' says the soldier. 'It is pumpernickel bread. If I fetch some, will you try?'

'Oh yes,' David says. 'Bring a spoon or a knife or something back too? I forgot mine, sorry.'

The soldier agrees and scurries off. David and Isaac look across the small patch of No Man's Land they're standing on and exchange a disbelieving glance. And then they laugh. This is mad.

The soldier returns with a spoon and some blackish bread and David and he eat merrily. 'The jam is good,' the German says.

'So is the bread. Never seen it this colour before though.'

Isaac looks back to the soldier and then glances behind him. There are bodies lain about from both sides, a stark reminder of their purpose here: kill or be killed.

'I wonder,' Isaac says and the German follows his gaze. 'I wonder if our time might be best served by burying these men?'

The German nods as he too assesses the bodies. 'Did you lose people from your battalion?'

'Not out here.' Isaac gestures around them. 'Not yet, anyway. These are a different battalion.' He thinks those fallen might be from 1st Battalion, Queen's Own Cameron Highlanders, although there have been many that have come and gone since. He can't see tartan on the bodies. He can't see anything. Just mud.

'We did lose the village baker's son a few nights ago when he stood up too quickly and forgot to crouch. He got shot in the head. By the time he made it up the line he'd already died.'

'I am sorry.'

Isaac doesn't reply. He tells the men over and over again not to stand up to their full heights. Every now and again someone forgets and he has to write a letter home to their mothers, explain how they wouldn't have felt a thing. In all honesty, he has no idea if this is true.

'I think the more this continues the more reluctant we find ourselves to be here,' the German says. 'There are some who sit in the trench even now and will not come out and enjoy this . . .' He grasps for the word.

'Temporary truce?'

'Yes.' The German lifts his shoulders. 'They believe too strongly in the cause.' And then he smiles. 'My name is Gunther. What is yours?'

'Isaac.' The two men shake hands. The morning has moved on at quite a pace, the sun high in the sky. 'I believe our chaplain speaks English and German,' Isaac says. 'If we bury the bodies perhaps he can conduct a service for all our lost men.'

Gunther nods, soberly. 'I will fetch some spades.'

'We commend unto thy hands of mercy, most merciful Father, the soul of these our brothers departed, and we commit their bodies to the ground, earth to earth, ashes to ashes . . .' The chaplain finishes and speaks it again in German.

Isaac and Gunther have dug all afternoon and are steadily joined by other members of the German unit and the pals battalion – a shared effort to bury their fallen. The task of picking up men long since dead and placing them into graves adjacent to where they lay is something Isaac never wants to relive. In a way, it is a relief to think this truce will probably only last the day. He cannot see it happening again. For one thing German and British command would never officially endorse this one, let alone another. This is just for today, he thinks. And then tomorrow he will see Cordelia and put all of this out of his mind. One blissful week. Just one. But it might be enough to save him, to stop him from going entirely mad.

He knows when he returns here, he'll have to relive memories of Cordelia to sustain him. He feels bile rise in his throat as he considers returning here.

But he swallows down the dread, says, 'Amen,' at the end of the prayer and decides although he's not much of a sportsman, he will join the game of football if it restarts again, cook stew on the camping stove for supper and perhaps they will share their meals, this strange assembly of two warring factions, brought together for just one day. And then the December sun will set and the day will end. And while they all shake hands with men they are soon expected to recommence shooting at, and then return to their positions in their respective trenches . . . and while his men sleep, Isaac will take his bag – already packed in earnest – and he will walk through the network of trenches until he reaches the camp, join any trucks heading towards the English Channel, and board a boat home to England.

And to Cordelia.

CHAPTER 38

CORDELIA
CORNWALL
CHRISTMAS DAY 1914

Cordelia's trunk is packed and she is ready to go to him. This time tomorrow she will be in his arms. But even after a wonderful day of Christmas dinner with her parents, the church service and catching up on soldiers' news home from the pals battalion with the various families she sees at church that morning, sleep still evades her, as it so often does.

She must endure these last few hours of sleeplessness before she is up and ready to go to London to meet Isaac (where she has resigned herself that she'll look awful and sleep deprived), for their blissful week ensconced in a suite in Brown's Hotel, and then on to the Lake District to stay with Tabitha.

Of course, her parents believe she is spending the entirety of her time away in the Lakes. A part of her should feel awful that she's lying so brazenly. But nothing feels awful about this. Everything feels exactly as it should be. Everything *is* exactly as it should be. Tabitha should have received a letter from Cordelia by now, boldly begging her to lie should any sort of telegram or emergency summons arrive at her home for Cordelia while she is with Isaac.

Tabitha is under strict instructions not to write back for fear of it being opened in her absence. Instead, she is to send word to Brown's Hotel. Cordelia sent the begging letter far too late, fully expecting to receive word from Isaac that his leave was cancelled. But the stars have shone down on them and now it is past midnight and Isaac will already be on his way to her.

The December weather is biting and the fire has all but gone out and still Cordelia cannot sleep. She hates trying to fall asleep after the fire has died; the chill makes it twice as hard. She opens the curtains to let in the moonlight as she pads around the room, almost blindly opening drawers in order to find something warm to wrap around herself, a shawl perhaps. She puts her hands past the soft linen and the thin silk shawl, her hands groping at the back of the large drawer until she clasps something that feels thick and soft enough to suitably engulf her in warmth. The moonlight shines through the window and Cordelia walks towards the pane of glass, holding the item of clothing up to see it better. It's a pullover, only it isn't hers, of that she's sure.

It takes her a moment or two to place this item and then she does. She remembers what it is or more importantly she remembers *whose* it is. It's Isaac's. She smiles in surprise as she recollects that night all those months ago. Back when she didn't know him. Back when she didn't care to know him.

She remembers how she came to be wearing it, how she snuck through the door and up the staircase while wearing it, shivering after having jumped into the lake to find Clive. She remembers how she entered her room, hair damp around her shoulders and her clothes wet under Isaac's pullover. She remembers how, when she heard footsteps on the tread outside her room, and knowing Ada would enter at any moment, how Cordelia had quickly dragged the pullover over her head for fear of questions, how she had stuffed it into the drawer containing her shawls. But now it is folded, Ada having found it at some point soon after and replaced it in the drawer neatly and without question. Good old Ada.

That was so long ago. Cordelia has spent more time away from Isaac than she has with him. But their love has only grown, not diminished, while he has been at the front.

Cordelia had told Isaac she'd lost it. And so she thought she had. Until now. It is a piece of him brought to her. How she'd longed for something of him and there had been something here all along. She puts it on, smelling it, and deciding that although she wants it to smell of him, it simply doesn't. Not now, not after all this time. But she will cherish it all the same.

She sits in the window seat. It is a crisp night, dew shining on the blades of grass, forming a glistening crown to the garden. In the distance, a man walks towards the house. Cordelia frowns, pushing her face up to the freezing pane of window glass in order to better see who it is. Who would be here at this time of night? But it's no use. She cannot tell at all who it is. And then she thinks she can and she stands up, an involuntary action that she's not aware of. She leans forward.

Good God, it's Isaac.

It can't be Isaac but the way he holds the cigarette, the way he looks, the way he carries himself while he walks towards the house . . .

He's early and he's not supposed to be meeting her here. She can see him now. He's wearing his uniform. He looks exactly the way he did the moment she last saw him at the train station, before she lost him to the crowd. How is it him? How is he here? As he arrives on the lawn, stopping and looking up, he looks into her eyes and smiles and she cries with relief that he is here. How she will explain his arrival here to her parents is beyond her but right now she can think of nothing but him.

He raises his hand in greeting. In the other is his cigarette. He smiles at her and stands so still, his gaze upturned in her direction. And then she can bear it no longer. She must get to him. She must get to him as fast as she can.

She turns away from the window, moves across the room, opens the door and runs along the corridor, not caring who hears her or sees her. She gallops down the stairs, two at a time and runs towards the library. He is here. He is here. She pulls open the curtains, fumbles with the key in the lock, flings open the door and runs barefoot across the terrace and down the stone steps towards the lawn where Isaac is standing.

Only he isn't.

He isn't standing there. She runs to the spot where he was only moments ago and looks around but he is not here. Cordelia stands in the cold December night and looks around, catching her breath and inhaling the faintest scent of cigarette smoke in the place where she saw Isaac standing.

But he isn't here.

CHAPTER 39

CORDELIA
26TH DECEMBER 1914

Cordelia is in a daze on the Cornish Riviera Express as the steam and coal smoke billows past and blurs together with countryside. After more hours than she can imagine sitting in one spot, she arrives at Paddington station, hails a hackney cab and is deposited at Brown's Hotel.

She plays the early hours of this morning over and over in her mind as she travels. She imagined the entire thing, surely. She imagined Isaac. Only she saw him. She did. As clear as anything. And the smoke. She smelled his cigarette smoke lingering long after the event. It was unmistakable, the same cigarettes she's been purchasing for him and Edwin and sending on to them.

Staying behind in Cornwall on the off chance he might turn up there after that felt like the wrong thing to do. She had to go to him. He had to be on his way to her. Conjuring him on the lawn, creating him in her mind . . . she could not work out what that meant. She was far too tired and after checking in to the decorative suite, only just remembering in time to call herself Mrs Isaac Leigh, she felt that continuing on with their own battle plan, was the right thing to do. But he had been there. He had. She had seen him.

She pays scant attention to the concierge's instructions regarding breakfast time and simply waits for him to finish speaking before she asks, 'Is there a message for me?'

There's nothing. Nothing at all. Perhaps he could not find a way to telegram so last minute after all to confirm his departure.

Cordelia sleeps the sleep of the dead to compensate for the sleep she has lost. And when she wakes it is the next morning. And Isaac is still not here.

She asks the concierge if there is word from Lieutenant Leigh. But there is not and so after a breakfast of hot buttered toast and poached eggs that she can hardly eat, she bides her time, wandering with purpose through the streets of London. Whether or not she should be chaperoned enters her head far too late. Not that she would ever want it. But here she is Mrs Isaac Leigh and does not need a chaperone.

Posters for kit bags at Harrods, trench coats and officer's kits at Gamages and the ever-present pointed stare of Lord Kitchener glare down from the end of buildings and from omnibuses as they drive determinedly along the streets, carting people to and fro. People with places to be, Cordelia thinks. She has nowhere to be, except here with Isaac and he isn't here. Not yet. Not yet.

Along with a hundred other advertisements a theatre playbill is glued crudely to a wall and Cordelia stops to look at it. The Royalty Theatre has just opened *The Man Who Stayed at Home* – a play about a man who doesn't go to war and instead stays behind, tasked with weeding out German spies at an English seaside resort. The concept raises a smile from Cordelia and she wonders if Isaac might like to go this week – he asked if the theatre was still on – or if plays about the war might not be at all what he wants to do. How wonderful to go to a theatre with Isaac, to do something relatively normal with the man she loves.

But what does *he* want to do? What does *she* want to do, really? She wants to stay in that heavenly room with Isaac and never leave, never let him leave, never let him go back to the front. But he must. She knows he must. But first he has to get to London. It dawns on her that he might be there by now and that she has wasted precious time gallivanting across London to stare in shop windows and devise theatre plans and she turns on the spot, walking with haste back to the hotel. It is as she is wandering through Berkeley Square, only a snip from the hotel, that she sees someone she knows. It's the mother of one of the young men she let kiss her at a ball in the summer. She can't picture his face though. Strange how the mother is more memorable than the boy, Cordelia thinks, pulling the brim of her hat down and walking even quicker to the hotel.

How stupid she was to have risked being seen alone in London. Of course there would be people she knew here, people her mother and father knew who then might mention in passing they'd seen Cordelia in London and *what was she doing unchaperoned?* What was she thinking? She should never have left the hotel and she hurries on eagerly, picturing Isaac in their hotel room, kit bag slung on the floor, uniformed jacket on the back of a chair as he paces the room, wondering where she is, waiting for her as desperately as she's been waiting for him.

But the now hateful words are spoken by the concierge: 'Still no message Madam.' Cordelia's shoulders slump and she stares up at the ceiling in despair.

'Is there anyone I could message for you?' the concierge offers kindly.

'No. No thank you,' Cordelia replies snapping out of her slump. 'But if there is a message—'

'I will be sure to have it relayed to you immediately.'

'Thank you,' she replies dejectedly and goes to her room, where she will continue to wait, although now it is with slightly less hope than she had previously harboured.

She spends another day in the hotel, clutching the newspaper so very tightly as she reads the casualty lists, looks for news in the front pages for any battle held over Christmas that Isaac may have been caught up in. She's never felt lonely in her own company but here, like this, she is very much *alone* without anyone to talk to, to talk her down when her internal dialogue runs away with her. Without her realising it, a bereft feeling has entered her soul. Something is not right. She knows that now. She just doesn't know what. Is Isaac's absence down to simple delay, a stormy boat crossing that never transpired or was his leave cancelled without notice and he's been unable to get word to her? She just needs to know. She just needs to *know*.

Should she continue to stay? Of course she should. She must wait for him. She's brought all her pin money.

She's been inadvertently saving it given she's had nowhere to spend it, nowhere to go. So she can pay for the room. It's not that which concerns her at all. But to avoid speculation in the hotel's dining room, perhaps she could go to her family's London house in Holland Park and wait it out there. Perhaps that might be best. Perhaps it would not be best. And besides, she can't. The house has been shut up for the duration. She's not even sure if there are staff there. She doesn't need staff but she does rather need someone to unlock the door to her own home.

The lack of sleep returns and an uneasy night follows those from before, each nightfall making her blearier than ever, unable to make clear decisions when she wakes.

She's supposed to be in the Lakes. She should go there, to Hawkshead where Tabitha is waiting patiently. She should formulate a plan, leave a letter here for Isaac in case she misses him and he arrives after she has gone. Because she has to go. She can't stay here. She'll run mad if she keeps hoping, waiting, here in this hotel room.

It's such a journey but she has to go, catch a train, before the last one to Windermere leaves. She must go to Tabitha, to a friend – a friend Cordelia desperately needs. She needs Isaac more. But he is not coming. He is not coming. Horrifyingly, she realises that now.

CHAPTER 40

CORDELIA
ROSE COTTAGE, HAWKSHEAD, THE LAKE DISTRICT
NEW YEAR'S EVE, 1914

Cordelia paces back and forth in the dimly lit sitting room of Rose Cottage as Tabitha pokes the fire, disturbing the logs that flicker brightly. There has been no word from Isaac and Cordelia fears the worst.

Tabitha places a loving hand on her friend's shoulder and leaves Cordelia staring at the fire but Cordelia cannot pace aimlessly any longer.

'I'm sorry,' Cordelia says, entering the kitchen where her friend is already gathering vegetables together at the scrubbed wooden table for dinner. 'I'm being a terrible friend. Absolutely useless.'

'Don't be silly,' Tabitha says. 'I only wish I could help. It's me who feels useless.' In the chilled larder, Ann, the maid of all work, is hanging up a pheasant.

Cordelia sits at the table and takes the knife to peel the carrots.

'Not like that,' Tabitha says. 'You'll take your finger clean off.'

'I've never done this before,' Cordelia confesses. 'Growing carrots is far easier than preparing them.'

'Ann sometimes prepares dinner but I've got her on pheasant duty today,' Tabitha says.

'I don't know how you work the field and work the house and cook dinner too,' Cordelia wonders. 'And with only Ann providing a few hours' service a day. We have a whole fleet of servants for everything. Although admittedly not since the war began.'

Tabitha gives Cordelia a knowing look. 'There are considerably more of you in Pencallick House. And it is twenty times the size of Rose Cottage. And Cordelia, what would I do if I didn't do all of this? I'd die. Of boredom and loneliness.'

Cordelia can understand this. She's having a taste of this herself and her heart aches for her friend, sent away from her family in her disgrace. 'Are you really that lonely? Why don't you advertise for a lodger? You've a spare room.'

'No,' Tabitha says after a while. 'I don't think I'd like that. Where would you sleep next time you visit if I've a lodger?'

'At the Queen's Head in the village.'

'Perhaps. But what if I had a lodger and we didn't get on?'

'Advertise for another one and politely ask the first to go?' Cordelia suggests.

Tabitha makes an exasperated noise. 'I just couldn't. I would . . .'

'Would what?' Cordelia queries.

'I did rather have a fancy of having a child, at one point. I think I should have liked to be a mother. Right the wrongs of my own mother. Give a little person my absolute everything.'

'You still could,' Cordelia says warmly, wrestling with the carrots. 'You'd make a good mother. You've mothered me very well these past few days.'

Tabitha laughs.

'But you'd need to be married and you don't like men,' Cordelia points out sagely. 'Could you suffer a man in order to have a child? I'm not sure which is the longer commitment.'

'Exactly.'

'Could you . . . I don't know. How would you do it if you didn't have a husband?'

Tabitha shrugs. 'Adopt? I'd considered it, you know.'

'Have you? Properly?'

Tabitha looks away, embarrassed. 'Yes. There are plenty of motherless children in orphanages and such. I don't suppose it would be too difficult. If I really wanted it that is.'

Cordelia pulls together the carrot peelings in her palms to carry out to the piggery and then looks up. 'And do you? Do you really want it?'

'Yes,' Tabitha says and looks back to her friend. 'Yes, I think I do.'

'It would be an awful lot of work, raising a child *and* looking after the house and the smallholding.'

'Ann is here a few hours each day.'

'Still,' Cordelia says. 'I admire you . . . All of this, I couldn't do it.'

'Of course you could,' Tabitha cries. 'If you had to, you would.'

'And your parents . . . they'd help, of course. A grandchild.'

'They ruined me. No wonder I rebelled. No wonder I am the way I am. No wonder I prefer to live in isolation than with my own family. And an adopted child wouldn't really be theirs, would it? They'd probably want nothing to do with it. Or worse, everything to do with it. Actually, I could probably get away with never telling them if I did such a thing, now I think about it. They've never visited here. I could continue the peace and quiet a bit longer if they never know. Still, might not happen. Need to sleep on it a bit longer perhaps. As you say, big commitment raising a child alone.'

'Is it really banishment from Bowes House?' Cordelia asks as Tabitha stirs supper on the range and Cordelia drops the carrots gently into a bubbling pot.

'As near as damn it.'

'I cannot believe it ended in such a way.' And then a thought strikes her. 'I didn't tell anyone, you know? About . . . the laundry cupboard and the housemaid.' Actually, that's not true. She told Isaac. She smiles, remembering his startled reaction in his letters.

'I know.'

'Do you?' Cordelia queries. 'I hope you do. I stumbled upon you but other than being rather shocked and a bit curious I did nothing else. It was none of my business.'

'I know. It wasn't your fault. It was mine. The housemaid wasn't even the reason I was banished. I was less than discreet on more than one delicious occasion.'

Cordelia laughs, turning to fill the water glasses from the jug and then laying the table.

'It's for the best I imagine,' Tabitha admits. 'I felt caged there, only I didn't realise it. I do now. I feel free now. Here.'

'Is there . . .' Cordelia starts delicately. 'Anyone else these days?'

'No. I'm too wary here. I've built a nice life and I feel the pressure of ruining it, starting again. Not sure I'd be able to go through all that again. And then there'd be all those looks and stares in the village and the gossip and the few invitations a single woman does receive . . .' Tabitha shrugs.

Cordelia looks at her friend. 'I understand. Although, times are slowly changing,' she states.

'Times aren't changing that much,' Tabitha snorts. 'Let's not worry about me for the time being. I rather think we should be concerned with you and your young man. Has Edwin written back yet?'

'It's too soon. He probably hasn't even received the letter yet.'

'We must try to find out what's happened,' Tabitha says. 'Who in God's name do we ask?'

'I can't think. I've written to Isaac. I've written to Edwin. I've even written to Isaac's brother. If there had been a change to his plans Isaac would have told someone. The hotel would have forwarded me any correspondence. I've now written to Mother and Father and among my greetings of "Happy New Year" is a note asking for news of the battalion. His name hasn't appeared in any of the casualty lists.' Cordelia knows this because she reads and re-reads them. But there is no Isaac Leigh. She doesn't know what she'll do if she sees his name. She'll never be the same again.

'I'm sure word will come soon,' Tabitha attempts to soothe.

Cordelia rubs between her eyes, defeated.

CHAPTER 41

CORDELIA
JANUARY 1915

Letter from Mother to Cordelia

Darling Cordelia,

Happiest of New Years to you also. I'm so pleased to hear of the piglets at Tabitha's livestock farm. I do hope you won't return to us with thoughts of opening a piggery. Let Home Farm continue in that vein and you stick to the fruit and vegetable efforts.

The battalion fares well. A bit of a cold Christmas so Edwin says. Bleak, was the word he used. But he is well. They've had a few casualties. The baker's son is one and they're an officer down at the moment and awaiting a new recruit from England, who Edwin says will be wet behind the ears with no idea what he's letting himself in for. No doubt he will be there by now.

Edwin does say how hard it is to be alongside

men he's known in the village his whole life and then tragedy befalls them all and they have to either bury someone known to them since childhood or send someone home with horrid injuries. Or send someone up to a medical unit or some such and know they won't even make it halfway there. He says in a way he wishes the men hadn't joined up together, but had all gone their separate ways, entered separate units. No attachments to anyone around them, no suffering when one of them dies. But they have to try and they have to carry on. Enough of that sadness.

It sounds as if Tabitha lives very simply, I cannot possibly imagine. You do not cook and clean, do you? She has only one maid? It sounds as if you do most of the work while you are there and I am not sure if I would be impressed or horrified.

I thought Tabitha and her maid would be enough respectable security for you but from what I gather your friend lives very wildly and I hope you are not getting similarly wild ideas. I wonder now if we should have sent Ada up with you to chaperone only she is proving very useful out in the gardens with Gilbert in your absence. Please do update me on the piglets and if names are chosen for them. With hopes that you are not bringing one home as a pet,

Mother

Cordelia holds the letter out and Tabitha takes it, reads it, smirks towards the end at reference to her and hands it back. 'An officer down?' she says. 'Do you know who?'

'Of course I know who,' Cordelia cries. 'I'm going

to write to Edwin and ask him directly now. I don't care what anyone thinks. I never truly did,' she says quickly, as she walks purposefully towards the bureau, pulling a pen and a sheet of paper towards her. 'It was always Isaac. Always he who said we should be secret for my reputation. Always he who thought he wasn't good enough. I never thought that,' she says, tears forming in her eyes. 'I didn't think he wasn't good enough.' The tears blur so she cannot see to write. 'He's dead, isn't he?' Cordelia cries, putting down her pen, ink spilling and pooling on the page. 'He's dead.'

And then, weeks later a reply from Edwin arrives on a day when the water pump has frozen and Tabitha is threatening to bring the pigs indoors to escape the weather.

Yes, Edwin writes. *Isaac Leigh was the first officer we lost . . . How did you guess that? A bullet from a sniper a few minutes after midnight on Boxing Day. There had been a wonderful truce of sorts. He'd buried the dead all afternoon with a few others and then joined them in death the next day. Was due home on leave as well. Awful timing . . .*

And as she reads it Cordelia cries against Tabitha, great heaving wracking sobs that last hours and hours until Cordelia can barely breathe. And Tabitha, wonderful Tabitha holds her until she is spent, falling into an exhausted sleep from which she hopes never to awaken.

PART FOUR

CHAPTER 42

A YEAR LATER
JANUARY 1916
LONDON

Letter from Tabitha to Cordelia

My darling Cordelia,

How you are missed. It feels so very long ago that you were last here but it has only been six months or so since you left us in the summer. I wish you could have stayed longer and although you stayed for nearly six heavenly months it didn't feel that long.

Your last letter arrived only yesterday but I always write back to you as soon as I can so you know we are well.

I have had word from Mother and Father. I have had a lot of words actually. The continuation of the war has made them reconsider their position with regard to me in a way that the death of my brother did not. I do not know why they wish to make contact now and, please forgive me for my mercenary plan, but I hope it is to lavish me with goods and money. It is the only way they are able to show some modicum of support or love and I find I am not too proud to pretend to love them back in order to take it. Heavens knows I will need it with two mouths to feed in this house.

I know, I sound awful. But the money will come in immensely useful and will enable me to buy new clothes, build a proper hen house, among other things. My low finances always need a bolster. (I blame it on purchasing the Singer Ten two-seater. But that motorcar is just so very zippy.) I am to visit them, butter them up, see what I can scavenge.

I will not have them here.

I wonder if you will come here while I am gone and keep an eye on things, be with little William? I'll coincide my time away with that of your arrival. Let me know when suits you in the next month or two. If you struggle to square it with your parents, I wonder if perhaps you could tell them you are joining one of those new horticultural colleges that's opened for women. We have one nearby, you know. Well, sort of nearby. You need not *pretend* you are joining a course – you could actually join one. I've taken the liberty of enclosing the advertisement I saw in the *Westmorland Gazette*. See what you think.

William thrives. So, so beautifully. I am so very proud of this little man. I cannot wait for you to see him again soon . . .

'Who is that from, darling?' Mrs Carr-Lyon says, interrupting Cordelia's reading.

'Tabitha,' Cordelia says, scanning the rest of her correspondence, talking about her adopted boy and how chubby he's growing on a diet of rural life.

'What does she have to say?'

'She's found a women's horticultural college nearby and wonders if it's something I might like to attend – brush up on my knowledge for a few months. Then I might be of use in someone else's garden given ours has now been requisitioned. It wouldn't be for long but it might all help with regard to specific knowledge I'm lacking in. All very useful for when we get Pencallick House back.

'Besides,' Cordelia continues. 'Tabitha asks if I'll help look after things at the cottage while she goes off to be reunited with her parents.'

Cordelia's father cuts in, sniffing gossip. 'Do we know why she was sent away in the first place?'

'I suspect it was by mutual agreement,' she replies vaguely. 'They are very different sorts of people.'

'I always thought she was a bit restless,' her father says, thoughtfully. 'Like some sort of animal that refused to be caged. But if you like her then that's enough for me.'

Her father is not often this astute and she wishes she could tell him the truth about her friend, about how strong and wonderful Tabitha is, how clever, how independent – something Cordelia knows she could never be.

'Will you go?' her mother asks.

'Yes. If you don't object to my going off and learning a new skill?'

Father shakes his head. Mother looks thoughtful but says nothing for the moment. Cordelia secretly relishes the idea of a visit again but also she owes it to her friend. Tabitha looked after Cordelia when she was at her worst, full of grief and fear, pain and distress. It took her so long to recover from the overwhelming heartache after finally learning the truth of Isaac's death from Edwin. 'I'll keep an eye on the cottage and the animals while she is away. Besides,' she says, standing from the table. 'As we have been thrown out of Pencallick House, it will be nice to breathe country air again, put my skills to use.'

'We have given up the house to the War Office, temporarily. We have not been *thrown out,*' Mother says.

'We *have* been thrown out,' Father says with a half-hearted smile. 'But it's the right thing to do. And also . . . we had no choice.'

'Yes,' Cordelia sighs, thinking of all the work she'd put into the garden, the orchards, the vegetables, the grazing and pastureland. 'The gun practice in the rose garden or whatever they've taken the house for I'm sure will make all the difference in defeating the Kaiser.' She puts her napkin down. 'I don't mean to be snappish,' she says resignedly. 'I know it's the right thing to do. And I know we had very little choice in it. But I miss it. I miss the garden. I miss being useful. I miss Gilbert, although he's enjoying his retirement, or so he writes to me. I miss all of it. And it ended so suddenly, after we had been given a whole host of demands from the agricultural lot. We did all that and then they requisitioned the house anyway. I miss it. I miss that time.' *I don't like this time*, she thinks. *I am barely keeping my senses together. I am barely putting one foot in front of the other. I am bored. I am lonely. I am devastated and grieving. And I cannot tell you.*

'You are being useful here though,' her mother says. 'You have been reading to the soldiers in the convalescent hospital. And perhaps, you might find an officer among them that suits you? You've been there for weeks now and nothing. So many men are being killed Cordelia, and there are hardly any social occasions for you to meet eligible young men. This is probably your only chance.'

'Perhaps I could get one to propose to me this afternoon while I am reading?' Cordelia suggests. 'In between chapters?'

'Oh, what a good idea,' Mother replies, missing Cordelia's tone. 'But mind you find one that is not too injured. Nor get one that will recover enough to be sent back to the front. There's no point marrying one for him to end up getting killed anyway.'

Cordelia's mouth drops. Her father lowers his newspaper and gives his wife a horrified look.

'I shall do my best,' Cordelia says acidly, leaving the dining room.

She opens her lock box to put Tabitha's recent note inside and pulls out the letter she received from Edwin in January last year. There have been many since but this is the one that hurts the most.

Isaac Leigh was the first officer we lost.

She tortures herself reading it so often that she should just leave the letter out instead of locking it away. If she locks it away then she locks away the facts, the pain. But it can't all be locked away. Not really. She knows that now. She has had a year to recover from Isaac's death. A year. But it still hurts as if reading it afresh. Her brother's letter is so matter-of-fact about the man Cordelia was so in love with – is still so in love with. It hurts just thinking about him. And Edwin, so unaware of all of it.

And then the piece of information that she had missed those first few times she'd read it but had come to appreciate the gravity of soon after. That his brother David had also died.

He was the second officer killed – only days later, Edwin had told her. *Not paying enough attention. Mind on the loss of his brother, I think. They always joked one could not survive without the other. Turned out it was true. They were good officers. Good men. Pity they have both gone.*

No embellishments, no drama to this story. Just Edwin stating facts, always so glib. The war had made him flippant about death. And still she had not told him. She had cried and cried and cried, heaving wracking sobs every day for weeks and weeks. And because it would do no good, she had not told any of them.

Only dear, dear Tabitha, to whom she had told everything.

Letter from Cordelia to Mother and Father

March 1916

Darling Mother and Father,

I'm so sorry I've stayed in the Lakes longer than planned. Tabitha has been away and returned, reconciled in part with her family, which I am so pleased about. As is she. It has been years and perhaps she will find a bit of peace now they are on speaking terms, if not affectionate terms just yet. If you don't mind, I might not return home immediately. I am so enjoying the horticultural course. You would approve thoroughly. Up here in the North things seem to grow on a sort of delayed schedule compared to Cornwall. It is so interesting to learn the differences in soil, chalk levels that kind of thing. It varies throughout Britain and affects what grows and how. When this course finishes I think I might stay on to complete the next level. I will receive a certificate at the end of each. My first certificate in anything.

You should see the view from Rose Cottage. If we thought the parkland at Pencallick House was beautiful, this is a thing of wonder. It's so green. I have missed it since I was last here but perhaps I wasn't paying attention enough the first time around. Rose Cottage is made of stone and sits within a low, dry stone wall. In front of the house the grass is a deep shade of green and if you walk along a manmade path you can reach the shores of Esthwaite Water. Behind the house are trees and to the side is the smallholding, the piggery, the hens and geese. We are very nearly self-sufficient here. The cottage is so incredibly cosy and although it's March we have the log fire burning all day and night to warm us through. The climate is different here too. It is almost always pullover weather.

There is so much to do here to keep me busy and I fall asleep immediately here, something I was never really able to do much before. Tabitha's adopted little boy, William, is about a year old and thrives and thrives and we have Ann to take him off our hands when he's boisterous or ready for a nap, freeing us up to race around the house tidying and preparing meals, laundering and tending to the garden, before I nip off to gardening school in Tabitha's little motorcar.

I shall be back to the London house soon enough to visit. (Mother's birthday is not too far away and I look forward to celebrating and you must send word when Edwin is due his next leave. I shall grow wings and fly home.) I've enclosed a list of things I'd like you to send on to me please when you have a moment. There's no hurry at all but it should be useful to have some of my gardening books and some additional clothes. It is far chillier here than it is in London.

With all my love, Cordelia

CHAPTER 43

APRIL 1916

Tabitha is resting on the settee while Cordelia returns from her course by way of the railway station to collect her trunk that Mother has sent up from London. As Cordelia enters the bumpy unmade track towards Rose Cottage, crunching the gears mercilessly – she'll never get the hang of driving – she pulls over onto the grass to let another car past, waving to acknowledge the man behind the wheel who she vaguely recognises as he motors past. She wonders who it could be and then all is forgotten as she crunches the gear again and curses herself. Mother and Father are right; Cordelia is in danger of growing heathen.

As she sits on the floor by the fire a few hours later, she says, 'Thank goodness I thought to rescue all of this from Pencallick before the War Office took the house.' The trunk is open in front of her as she sifts through the books and periodicals that have been sent up. Ann returned to her home hours ago and little

William has fallen asleep on the settee after having had a succession of stories read to him by both Tabitha and Cordelia one after the other.

'Thank goodness he sleeps so well,' Cordelia observes.

'*Now,*' Tabitha remarks. 'Didn't used to.'

'Has it been *very* exhausting this whole time?'

'It's been wonderful actually,' Tabitha says gazing fondly at the baby who is growing into his tiny personality. 'He's becoming a real character now, mutters and sings away to himself. Such lovely noises.'

'Like a babbling brook,' Cordelia says with a warm smile. 'He's such a little angel.'

'He is.' Tabitha smiles, breathes deeply, bends to tuck a blanket closer around William and then closes her eyes.

'Are you quite well?' Cordelia asks. 'You look a little peaky.'

'Just overdone it in the garden,' Tabitha volunteers.

'My course finishes soon,' Cordelia says. 'I'll be around a bit more to help.'

'I don't need you to,' Tabitha says. 'Did it all by myself before you arrived, remember.'

'I know. But there's William now. And the goats are being delivered this week aren't they? You can't be everywhere.'

'I'll be all right,' Tabitha says. 'A little rest, the doctor recommends.'

Cordelia's head shoots up. 'You've called the doctor?'

'Just a precaution. Don't fret.'

Cordelia thinks. 'Is that who I saw leaving just before I arrived?'

Tabitha nods but her eyes are closed and she's nodding off to sleep. 'Just a precaution,' Tabitha repeats drowsily.

Letter from Cordelia to Mother and Father

May 1916
Darling Mother and Father,

Thank you so much for sending on my trunk full of things. It has been such a joy to see my books, to be able to read delightful Gertrude Jekyll again.

Tabitha is unwell. She caught a chill a little while ago and the doctor believes it has gone to her lungs. She rests in front of the fire and catches up with her reading. I am glad to be here to help where it is most needed, especially now. In the cold of the night, when Tabitha rests in her bed and William finally sleeps soundly. Over the last few weeks he's gone from an angelic little sleeper to a restless soul. Ann says it was inevitable and that we'd all been too lucky so far. Why do little children struggle so much to sleep at night but fall asleep so inconveniently during the day? I hope he grows out of it and back to his old slumberous routine quickly.

While I am singing him to sleep I find myself thinking of fruit and vegetables. I have either gone completely mad or knowledge is finally settling itself into my brain.

I read in *The Times* that Lowestoft and Yarmouth on the east coast have been raided by German battle cruisers. Can you believe such a thing? Germans firing on British seaside towns. It is beyond belief. I can't imagine it happening at Pencallick. To be on the beach, in the cove, standing on the rock and looking out to sea and then coming face to face with a German cruiser who then begins shooting and bombing indiscriminately on citizens. In England! I pictured the war in foreign fields and I must admit I did read the account and wonder if this might form the start of an invasion. If we might witness Germans and hand-to-hand combat on this soil. Where will be the men to save us? We will have to save ourselves, I suppose. Shame Father packed all the guns away when Pencallick House was requisitioned.

Today I have been into Hawkshead to shop for those things we can't produce on the smallholding, taking William with me for company, and Ann has looked after Tabitha for me. William is such a delight, such an easy baby. Squawks away and wants to be lifted from his perambulator so he can be coo'd over by the shopkeepers. Hawkshead is a pretty village with low white cottages all nestled together on cobbled streets. In a way, it looks a little like Pencallick only it's surrounded by greenery and mountains and there's not a fisherman in sight. I think you would love it here. I love it here.

Yours, Cordelia

'The doctor called again today,' Ann tells Cordelia quietly when both women are in the kitchen preparing supper.

'Today?' Cordelia queries as she chops carrots. 'Tabitha hasn't said.'

'No,' Ann says thoughtfully.

'Why not?' Cordelia asks as if Ann is inside Tabitha's mind.

Ann shrugs and issues a thoughtful look as Cordelia hands William a large carrot stick for him to gum at.

William looks delighted until he tastes it and then makes to hand it back to Cordelia.

'Ha,' Cordelia laughs. 'You must try *some* savoury items, William,' she insists, knowing he does not fully understand her. She hands it back to him as he sits at the table in a high wooden chair carved by Ann's father. 'I'm sure children are not supposed to live solely on creamed porridge and fruit. What did the doctor say?' she turns back to Ann as William scowls at his carrot stick.

'I wasn't privy to that conversation,' Ann points out. 'But you can't have missed that cough developing.'

Cordelia hasn't missed it. Tabitha's cough and William's newfound night restlessness are the only two things that wake her from her blissful sleep gained only from wearing herself out during the day.

'Did he prescribe anything?' Cordelia asks.

'You'll have to ask her,' Ann retorts. 'I am but a humble servant,' she says with a smile and then issues the baby a firm command in her no-nonsense voice. 'William, try the carrot or no raspberry crumble later. You mark my words. No carrot. No crumble.'

'I think he *might* be a little bit too young to understand such an order,' Cordelia points out.

William puts the carrot in his mouth and gnaws at it purposefully.

'Oh,' says Cordelia.

CHAPTER 44

Letter from Millicent to Cordelia

June 1916
By now you will have heard that I have broken things off with Edwin. It pained me to do so but it is the right thing to do for both of us. I think of his smile and his charm and his easy manner and it makes me smile and wish him well. But I do not think I was in love with him. In fact, I know now that I am not. I have fallen in love with a soldier in my care. I did not mean to. Please believe me. But a rush of love hit me with all the force in the world that when it happened, I knew. I knew that's what it was when I had not known that with Edwin two years ago. Two years. Will this war ever end?

Cordelia, I have always respected our friendship and with things across Europe as precarious as ever I should like to think the hand of friendship would stretch between us as usual, and that you should not wish to forget me because I have let your brother down. I did it as kindly as possible and I hope he should want me to be happy, as I want him to be happy. I long for this war to be over, for so many reasons but so that your brother can return home and find a woman who is deserving of him and who will love him with the entirety of her heart.

I have been back in England for some time. I am at a convalescent hospital now. The soldiers' wounds are severe but they are chronic rather than immediate. The pace is slower but the work harder, I think but I do feel more achievement here. Each time someone leaves, to return home to be with their loved ones, I rejoice in a way I never really could at the clearing stations. There was, I realise now, so much death that it stopped being a shock. How horrible that the sight of a man leaving this world in front of my eyes neither shocked nor saddened me in the end. Not like it did at the start. I am not sure if that is a good thing or otherwise. Each time a man leaves here, well enough to return to the front I wonder if I should secretly break his foot in his sleep or thwack him hard about the knee so he could do no such thing, so he could return home marred at my hand, but safe. But this is the world in which we live. I only hope we do not have to endure this for much longer.

Please don't think ill of me for the Edwin situation. I wish him only the very best kind of love in the world and I think he would not have found that with me.

Your friend, always, if you'll have me – Millicent

Letter from Cordelia to Millicent

I cannot condemn you for falling out of love with someone and in love with another. As if I could blame you, lovely Millicent. And no, I had not heard. Edwin writes very rarely and I wonder if I should mention it first. I think I will wait for him to tell me. I would not want him to think we had been talking about him without his knowledge. Mother and Father passed your letter on to me so jovially that I presume they do not know either yet. I am staying with my friend Tabitha Bowes in the Lakes. She's quite unwell and doesn't seem to be rallying as quickly. I wonder if you remember her. She was at some house parties a few years before the war but not immediately before because . . . oh, it is a long story. I shall tell you sometime. Address is above if you want to reach me speedily although I am supposed to be returning home to the London house (from where your letter was forwarded on to me) next month for Mother's birthday. (Did you know Pencallick was taken by the War Office? We do not know what for. It's all very secretive.)

Tell me about your soldier. Soldier or officer? I suppose it does not matter now, does it, and knowing what you know about me and my beloved, late Isaac . . . I can barely write his name without crying . . . You'll hardly find me judgemental about rank and file.

Edwin will recover. Perhaps not immediately. I think fondly of him watching you eat cake at the soldiers' benevolent bazaar two summers ago. I could see love in his eyes. I'm sorry, I'm not helping here at all. He will recover. What is important is that you have found love, recognised it, acted upon it. I only wish I'd done that sooner with Isaac, even if only by a week. It might have made the world of difference.

Your friend, Cordelia

Letter from Millicent to Cordelia

July 1916

Oh Cordelia, you are a brick for understanding so easily. I knew you would. Thank you. I can't tell you what it means to have your support.

Samuel was a machine gunner in the Queen's Own Royal West Kents. So you see, not an officer. He used to be a staff writer at a local newspaper before the war started and I expect he will return to it once he is recovered better. He limps horribly and it hurts to stand at the moment so he is in a wheeled chair and I doubt very much they'll want him back on the front like that. I know Mother and Father will never forgive me for this. But my heart wants this. And so does his. And I will not give him up. We cannot be together for the moment, as he is recovering and I am still nursing although the powers that be are steadily turning a blind eye to discreet matrimony. So we will wait, happily, until it is our time. Whenever that may be. At least he is near me even if we are conducting the beginnings of our affair in secret. I will be sent away in disgrace if anyone finds out. And I do so enjoy my work.

I wish your friend Tabitha well. I do hope she gets well soon. I don't think I remember her, no,

I'm sorry but she must be a wonderful sort of person if you are nursing her better. I remember how you hated the very notion of nursing.

Your friend, Millicent

Cordelia does indeed hate the very notion of nursing but she finds, now the time has arrived and her friend truly needs her, that she can put her mind to it readily enough.

'Tabitha darling,' she whispers to her. Tabitha has been asleep for a day and a night. Whatever is happening to her it is not letting go. 'Will you have a little bit of soup? Just a little. I promise I did not make it,' she says, aiming for lightness. 'Ann made it so it will taste heavenly.'

Tabitha's eyes open.

'I'm sorry to wake you. I know you need rest but you also need sustenance, Dr Reynolds says, and you've not eaten properly in days. I'll let you go back to sleep after you've had a few spoonfuls.'

Tabitha nods and Cordelia puts the bowl down on the dressing table, helps lift her friend gently up against the pillows so she can eat. The doctor has been again today. But he would not – or has been told not to – inform Cordelia what the prognosis is.

'It's . . . just . . . prolonging . . . it,' Tabitha says raspily, looking at the soup Cordelia attempts to spoon-feed her.

'What do you mean?' Cordelia asks.

Tabitha looks stubbornly at the spoon. She looks as if she's going to refuse to eat but then at the last moment she opens her mouth.

'I feel . . . like a baby,' she says. She's speaking slower today than before.

'You're not well. Let me get you better. Then you can hold your own spoon when you rally.'

'I'm not going . . . to rally,' Tabitha says. 'Eating is prolonging . . . the eventual . . . outcome.'

'Don't say that,' Cordelia says.

Tabitha focuses her gaze on her friend. 'You have to take him,' she says slowly.

Cordelia, knowing she means William, gives Tabitha a stern look. 'It won't be necessary,' she says. 'You'll get better.' But as she says it she hears the catch in her voice. She knows those words aren't true. She knows it now. She just hasn't been able to believe it.

Tabitha issues a penetrating look. 'You have . . . to take him.'

She won't let a tear fall down her face in front of her friend. 'I will. Of course I will,' she says. 'Of course I will.'

Neither Tabitha nor Dr Reynolds will tell her what is happening but Cordelia can see if she doesn't feed her friend, make her drink sips of water, that she is going to fade away faster.

'I can't eat it,' Tabitha says after two spoonfuls.

'Ann has made a cake,' Cordelia offers. 'And there's fresh cream. I can—'

'I can't eat . . . anything,' Tabitha says, then she reaches out and takes Cordelia's hand in her own.

'Perhaps you could read to me . . . for a bit. I should like that.'

Cordelia protests, offering the soup again.

'Reading will feed me . . . more than that . . . will,' Tabitha says, turning her head to one side on the pillows and closing her eyes again.

'Shall I help you snuggle down a bit more?' Cordelia asks warily and she does so as Tabitha acquiesces. She stares at her friend's pale face. 'Would you like some more of those painkillers Dr Reynolds brought?'

But Tabitha doesn't reply. Her eyes have closed.

'What shall we read?' Cordelia says. 'I purchased the new H.G. Wells when I was in Kendal the other day. I've yet to start it.'

Tabitha nods, ever so slightly, her eyes still closed, her breathing shallow.

'All right,' Cordelia says brightly – too brightly. She reads until Tabitha's breathing convinces her she's sleeping, puts the book down and sits back in the chair, watching her friend as she rests. Over the next few hours Cordelia watches Tabitha closely and finds her mind wandering to the past. Thoughts fill her mind of Isaac, Cornwall, crabbing on the beach, cutting roses in the garden, laying in Isaac's arms in his bed, the men on the train going to war . . . The fog of the steam train winds itself around her mind and Cordelia wakes with a start at having found herself asleep. Outside dawn has broken, bringing with it the chorus of thrushes and blackbirds in the trees outside.

Cordelia leans forward in the chair, watching Tabitha closely, helplessly as she realises her friend is not drawing breath. Cordelia puts her hand to her mouth and feels warm tears fall silently down her own face. At some time between night and day, Tabitha – her darling friend – has let go of life and let the light fade from her.

Letter from Cordelia to her parents

Mother,

I am writing to tell you the most tragic news. Tabitha has died. My darling friend. I can hardly write for tears gathering.

She passed last night and the undertaker has been already, leaving William, Ann and me bereft. Her passing was not without significant warning but none of us, other than Tabitha, believed it would be the end quite so soon.

She had asked Dr Reynolds not to tell us but when he came to help and advise me today about what I should do, he told me about her heart and how it had been failing. Tabitha had known this for some time. She never told me. Perhaps to spare me? I do not know.

I am crying as I write this but I must write it. You will read the notice in *The Times* within days, I am sure, as I have sent a telegram to her parents to inform them this morning.

I expect their arrival shortly or word from them as to what they wish to do going forward. I have no experience in these matters and the doctor has been most kind advising me as to how I can help from here. But the rest falls to her parents to decide about funeral arrangements. I assume they will want to take her home to the church nearest Bowes House and bury her there. I am thinking out loud. I cannot stop crying.

I will stay on here and continue to care for William and the house and then after that, I do not know.

Grief affects us all in different ways and I do not know what to expect tomorrow. I only know how I feel today and that is bereft and devastated. She is gone. But I do not cry for me, I cry for the life she should have led and the one she ended up with. And I cry for what comes next. And for

William, because he is too young to understand why Tabitha is no longer here.

Your daughter, Cordelia

CHAPTER 45

Cordelia sees them as the Rolls Royce winds unevenly up the track towards the cottage. Tabitha's mother and father grip tightly as they are bumped heavily and then the motorcar stops.

'Mr and Mrs Bowes,' Cordelia greets them. She is wearing black, having hastily had the dressmaker in Hawkshead run something up. Mother and Father should be sending up suitably dark attire soon but for now there is this. 'I am so sorry for your loss.'

'Thank you,' Mrs Bowes replies. Tabitha's father says nothing.

'Will you come in?' Cordelia offers. 'Ann has made a pot of tea and a cake. You must be tired and hungry from such a long journey.'

The day is warm, the sun is high and they are all gently perspiring from the heat.

'Thank you,' Mrs Bowes repeats, fanning herself with her hand.

It is hard to share happy memories of Tabitha with

the two people who should have loved her the most but treated her so badly. Cordelia pours tea for a distraction, not quite knowing what to say or how to say it.

'You and my daughter were . . .?' Mr Bowes starts when he has looked around the room, taken in every detail, every book, every photograph on the mantle, every nature drawing still left out that Tabitha had sketched in her final weeks from her bed or tucked up under a blanket on the settee.

'We were friends,' Cordelia responds. 'I have known Tabitha for years.'

'Yes, I know that,' Mr Bowes snaps. 'I remember your parents but I wanted to check what your relationship with my daughter was,' he adds stiffly.

'I'm not entirely sure that it matters,' Cordelia braves and then stops herself. These are Tabitha's parents and they are grieving. 'But we were old friends,' she says in a lighter tone. And to remove all doubt, 'Tabitha looked after me when I lost the man I loved,' she clarifies, 'at the end of 1914. And we became even greater friends in the last year or so.'

'I understand,' Mrs Bowes says kindly, her eyes filling with tears. Cordelia senses an ally. 'No doubt you knew our daughter had previously been estranged from us.'

Cordelia nods, holds a teacup out to Mrs Bowes.

'It was my deepest regret we could not completely see eye to eye,' the woman says.

'I think Tabitha's too,' Cordelia offers, casting a side glance at Mr Bowes who offers no confirmation.

'We met with her, you know,' the father offers. 'But it did us no good. Not really.'

Cordelia thinks of all the times Tabitha spoke of her

parents. She was not fond of them and neither were they of her. Tabitha often wondered why she was the way she was, and alongside wondering why it mattered quite so much, she'd been raised in a hard manner, surrounded in luxury but devoid of all love, all care and attention. Tabitha's words, spoken when Cordelia first arrived at Rose Cottage, play in Cordelia's head. *They ruined me. No wonder I rebelled. No wonder I am the way I am. No wonder I prefer to live in isolation than with my own family.*

Perhaps Tabitha's parents were just a victim of their times. But then, she thought, wouldn't her own parents also be this way? They were born in the same era. Times would change eventually and it would probably be left to Cordelia's generation to adapt, or even William's. She often wondered how the world would be when he had grown into it. Would William have to fit into the world or would the world fit around him?

'There is a lot to organise,' Mrs Bowes says suddenly.

'Yes, and I am of course very happy to help in any way I can,' Cordelia offers.

Mr Bowes grumbles and shifts in his seat. Perspiration runs down his brow. Cordelia rises and lifts the sash window even higher.

'We have decided we will bury Tabitha here,' Mr Bowes offers.

'Here?' Cordelia asks, turning from the window. 'Not at the family crypt?'

Tabitha's mother casts a look at her husband. 'No. We have decided,' she reiterates.

'I understand,' Cordelia lies. Tabitha, outcast from her family in death as in life. But perhaps, that might be what her friend would have wanted: to be buried in the Lake District that she loved so much rather than far away in the family mausoleum.

'Then we will end the lease on the cottage and . . . I spied a lot of animals as we approached. Yours?' Tabitha's mother continues.

'No. Tabitha's but—'

'They'll need new homes or to be killed,' Mrs Bowes says. Cordelia is wrong. This woman is not an ally.

'Of course,' Cordelia whispers through her shock. She wants to say that she will stay here, she will look after the animals and—

'We understand there is a child,' Mrs Bowes says, casting her eyes around.

Cordelia freezes.

Mrs Bowes looks at Cordelia as if she is simple. 'Tabitha's child.'

Cordelia gives a slight shake of her head. 'He isn't Tabitha's child. He is her ward.'

'Regardless, the boy will legally come to us as her dependant.'

Cordelia stops breathing and then starts again, slowly. Of course William would go to them. Of course he would. This is what Tabitha had always feared, dreaded: her parents having anything to do with William – the past repeating itself.

'He's not here,' Cordelia says.

'We didn't even know about him,' Mr Bowes cuts in, angrily.

'She didn't tell us,' Mrs Bowes says. 'Didn't tell us she'd adopted a child.'

Cordelia doesn't know where to look or what to say, her mind whirs.

'We are staying at the Queen's Head. The landlord

expressed sorrow for our daughter's adopted son. We didn't know what he meant. It is yet another secret our daughter kept from us.'

Cordelia nods, her mind not working fast enough.

'Where is he?' Mrs Bowes asks.

'Not here, I'm afraid. He will return tonight. He is with Ann, Tabitha's maid. I thought, perhaps, not seen and not heard, at this painful time in a house as small as this . . .' She trails off.

'Quite right,' Mr Bowes says.

Cordelia smiles weakly and Mrs Bowes rises. 'May I see her bedroom? Her things? We may as well decide now what we take and what we leave. We won't make the journey again after.'

'Of course. Please follow me.' Cordelia rises. Tabitha's parents haven't even enquired where their daughter's remains lay, which undertaker Tabitha's body is with. Have they seen her? Do they *want* to see her? Cordelia takes Mrs Bowes upstairs so she can start collecting her daughter's jewellery and precious items. Cordelia will not offer to help. Tears spring afresh and she has no choice but to go downstairs, stand in the garden, cry silently outside the scullery room entrance and try to work out what she must do.

'So it is settled,' Mr Bowes confirms. 'We will return tomorrow to meet the boy.'

'William,' Cordelia repeats his name.

'And then we will bury my daughter tomorrow afternoon and close this cottage.'

'So soon? But funeral arrangements . . . Don't you need . . .?' Cordelia starts.

'There aren't any arrangements to make. The vicar

has agreed to hold a small private service and inter her tomorrow afternoon,' Mrs Bowes says.

Cordelia frowns, uncomprehending. 'She was very loved by those who knew her. She had made friends here. I believe there are those in the village who would like to attend. I think my parents would like to come too.'

'That will not be possible. We want to close this chapter of our lives and move on.'

Cordelia's mouth opens but she does not speak. 'I see. Will I . . . Will I be permitted to attend?'

Mr and Mrs Bowes look at each other and Mr Bowes nods. 'Yes. Fine.'

'Until tomorrow,' Tabitha's father says.

'Until tomorrow,' Cordelia replies.

When they are gone Cordelia sinks into the settee and stares out the window at everything Tabitha had worked so hard to maintain and that was now about to be broken down, piece by piece by her own family.

'I waited until they were gone before we came in,' Ann says. 'Thought it might be best. Didn't want to muddy the waters.'

Cordelia looks at the little boy, clutching Ann's hand, and smiles. She cannot send William to live with them. *They ruined me. They ruined me.*

'Thank you Ann, but it did no good. They know about him.'

'How?'

'They're staying in the village. Someone mentioned it.'

'Oh for God's sake,' Ann says indelicately.

'Quite,' Cordelia mutters. William detaches himself and toddles off towards the cupboard where his collection of toys are housed downstairs. He pulls out a wooden spinning top and a train.

'It was innocently done, I'm sure,' Cordelia says, watching the boy. 'But they intend to bury Tabitha tomorrow afternoon and take him with them when they leave.'

Ann gasps. 'Tomorrow? They're burying her tomorrow? And then going . . . with William?' They both look at William as he gives up on his toy, toddles over to the cake laid out for Tabitha's parents but untouched, and eyes it hungrily.

'Yes,' Cordelia replies. 'I can hardly believe it myself.'

Cordelia walks over, lifts William into her arms and sits with him at the table passing him a piece of cake while she thinks. He crumbles it up into smaller pieces before popping the pieces into his mouth one by one and nestling into her while chewing.

'What will you do?' Ann asks.

'I don't know,' Cordelia replies.

'Will you let them take him?' she probes. 'You can't . . . The stories she told about them. Cruel, they are.'

'I know. But like anyone I don't suppose they meant to be.'

'That's half the problem in my opinion. Those who don't know they're doing it won't know they need to stop.'

Cordelia chews on a piece of cake, breaks another small piece and watches as Tabitha's ward chews again. She can't let them take him, can she? What can she do? What can she suggest to halt them? The boy is so little, so gentle, so perfect. Would he survive the kind of regime Tabitha often described?

'They'll give him a good life but at what cost?' Ann

says. 'Money and riches and sadness forever. Privileged awfulness. But what kind of boy will he become? What kind of man. A miracle Miss Tabitha turned out the way she did.'

'Don't,' Cordelia says, burying her head into the boy's neck and kissing him, making him giggle. The sound cuts right to her heart. She can't send him away to live with them. Legally, did they have the right to take him? Is that how it formally works with a child that isn't technically of their blood? Her head swims. She isn't as brave as Tabitha. She isn't. She's never been brave – never had to be. But could she be as strong and independent as her friend had been? Does she have it within herself to save William from a life that so readily destroyed Tabitha? She needs time to think.

The only problem is, she doesn't have time.

CHAPTER 46

NOVEMBER 1918
TWO YEARS LATER
ALDEBURGH, SUFFOLK

Cordelia reads the headlines of the newspapers in the shop and clutches William's hand tightly.

Kaiser Abdicates
End of German Empire
Great War Ends

'Great War ends,' Cordelia reads aloud. 'My God. It's all over. It's finally over.'

She was finding it harder and harder to read the news these days, when it felt as if this long, hateful war would simply never end. Far from bringing respite from the horrors of war, this little patch of Suffolk coastline was bearing the brunt of German naval bombardments far more than Cordelia had thought possible. It had been difficult in the few short years she'd been in Aldeburgh not to feel for those families who believed their loved ones had been safe in the town. Fishermen, on whom the town was reliant had been gunned down out at sea: vessels and crew lost to German U-boat fire.

Zeppelin enemy airships had often chosen the Suffolk coast as a suitable point of entry and had been attacked by the Royal Flying Corps at Orfordness. This patch of sleepy coastline had proved to be in the line of fire on so many occasions that it quite shocked Cordelia. And yet, she'd chosen to stay. Because it was like this everywhere. Up and down Britain, the nation had stories of woe and now, of triumph.

'Can I have some Mackintosh's toffee?' William asks in his quiet little voice as he strains his neck to look at the glass jars on the confectioner's shelves.

'Yes,' Cordelia laughs with joy, reminding herself that today is a happy day – the happiest she's known in such a long time. The war is over. Edwin will come home. She has read the casualty lists in the newspapers, looking for his name and she'd never seen it. Not once. She tries to put out of her mind the fact she'd never seen Isaac's name either. Edwin has to have survived. He just has to have done.

'You're getting so tall. How are you growing so quickly? Is it all the toffee by any chance? We'll sit on the beach, despite the cold, and share a bag together.'

She purchases a newspaper. She will read it later. The end of the war – she thought it would never end. It has been four dreadful years. So much has happened to her, to this poor little man, she thinks as she pays for the items, chatting to the newsagent about how today is such a happy day, such an unexpected day – although it had to happen in the end – but how so many men went to war and won't return. Isaac, gone but not forgotten. Never forgotten. Cordelia thinks she'll never be able to move on from him. Nor does she want to.

She and William walk slowly towards the beach, climbing the mound of pebbles. She lays out her shawl for them both to sit on. She remembers the first time she visited the beach with William, disappointed in part to find pebbles instead of sand but that feeling had been far outweighed by total shock at being able to hear the boom of the guns on the Western Front.

'Flanders,' someone had casually told her as if they'd heard it more than once through the years. 'You don't hear it all the time. Only when the weather's right.'

But today it's different. The guns have stopped and won't start again, apparently, and all around her celebrations ring out. The seaside town is full of laughter and joy, happiness and merriment.

'One for you and one for me,' she says as she distributes the sweets in her lap and stares out at the vast expanse of deep grey winter sea.

'Thank you,' William says.

Cordelia smiles. She is raising William in safety but it has come at a cost. She has run away, essentially, from home. She's left behind everyone who loves her because they, surely, would have forced her to give William up to Tabitha's parents. And so she's cut herself off from her family. But it was the right thing to do, the safest thing, the best thing to do for him.

Her heart pangs for Tabitha. William was the only good thing to have emerged from this horrific war and taking him and raising him was the only good thing to have come from Tabitha's death. Cordelia's hand had been forced. Would William have been so happy if he'd gone with Tabitha's parents? No, he would have faced demons in later life the way Tabitha had done. Some people were not supposed to be parents.

Cordelia had toyed with the decision to take William to safety for so long that night – the night she took him and ran, catching the first train away from the Lakes and heading south. She had thought it was the wrong decision, she had thought it was the only decision. But two years later, the thought of having not done it makes her feel sick. She had no idea if Tabitha's parents had tried to find her and William or not. But imagine his life if he'd been with them. Ann had been correct when she'd said it was a miracle Tabitha had turned out the way she had. She'd been kind, sweet, clever, pragmatic: all things Cordelia had hoped William would turn out to be.

She looks at the boy as he sucks his sweet, toffee dribbling down his little chin before wiping it with his fist and giving her a grin. He picks up a pebble and lays it on top of another, waiting for her to place one on top also as they build a tower of pebbles and see who will be the one to bring the tower crashing down, his favourite thing to do here, other than splash in the sea. But November is hardly the weather for it, despite the bright winter sun.

'Will we see Mrs Delingpole today?' he asks.

'Not today, I don't think,' Cordelia says. 'The war has finished, William. Can you believe it? Mrs Delingpole might be too excited about the return of her son to entertain you while I work in the garden. But we'll go tomorrow afternoon. Tomorrow morning I'll be in Reverend Thorne's garden and Mrs Thorne always gives you a slice of sticky ginger cake, doesn't she?'

'Yes she does!' William says with glee.

She holds William closer to her as a noise starts up nearby. Cordelia looks around at the beach. Behind her church bells ring out in celebration as the town begins impromptu festivities to celebrate the Armistice. The end of the war. The end of fighting. The end of death. The end of all of it.

Since arriving in this part of Suffolk, Cordelia has been as no-nonsense as Tabitha once was. If Tabitha could set herself up on her own then so could Cordelia. And that is what she did. The absence of many gardeners – men who had gone to the front – meant that Cordelia found work relatively easily. Passing a large house at the top of Aldeburgh two days after arriving and realising her money wasn't going to get her far for long, she saw an elderly woman digging and grumbling to herself.

'Would you like a hand with your garden?' Cordelia offered as she leaned over the wall. 'I know how.'

And word had spread that a lady gardener was happy to help until their usual gardeners returned home from the front. It provides an income that keeps a roof over their heads, food in the pantry and coal in the grate. She lived this way with Tabitha and she is able and willing to do it now.

On the patch of green close by the Moot Hall someone has stuffed together an effigy of the Kaiser and a bonfire has started for him to burn upon. One day she'll be able to tell William what this war was all about. But not today. Today is not a day to mourn decisions made by old men to send young men to their deaths. Today is a day for celebration.

Cordelia looks to the sky as an aircraft flies overhead and fireworks sputter and burn in the sky even though it is broad daylight. Crowds gather and sing, dance and cheer. Cordelia greets people she's come to know as she and William head back home, clutching a bag of fish and chips as a special treat of a midday meal, although William probably won't eat anything given all the toffee he's consumed.

'Today, it doesn't matter,' she says as he tells her he's not hungry. 'Nothing matters today.'

As darkness descends, she lights the lamps and candles and sits down to read the newspaper. William pulls out his drawing paper and pencils at the kitchen table and tries to draw the plane he saw in the sky today so Cordelia has five minutes with a cup of tea before she is expected to pick up a dropped pencil or find a fresh sheet of paper for him. She doesn't mind. She would do anything for him.

Outside the window of their little cottage in the backstreets of Aldeburgh, cheers go up in the street again and there is a knock at her door. Cordelia steps the three or four paces in order to open it and her neighbour Margot, a kindly young woman whose husband is away still, greets her.

'I've had a letter,' says the young woman. 'He's alive. He's alive and he's coming home. He wrote it before the Armistice was signed but he was in a camp and not due back to the front until next week he says so he must be alive, mustn't he?'

'He must be, yes,' Cordelia says, clutching the hands of the woman in front of her. She has only known Margot a short while but has come to understand the power of friendship more these past few years than ever before.

'He'll come home to me. I can't tell you how happy I am,' Margot says.

'We're letting the heat out. Come in,' Cordelia says warmly, thoughts of five minutes' peace happily forgotten.

'We're all going out. Come with us. Both of you.' She looks to the back of the cottage and gives William a wave who waves joyfully back. 'Bring a lamp. There's a torchlight procession walking through the town. And wrap up warm. Then back to mine and we'll open that bottle of elderflower wine you made me for Christmas.'

Cordelia laughs, 'Haven't you opened it yet?'

'I was saving it for a special occasion. Wrap up warm and I'll be back in five minutes.'

'Yes let's. William, come on,' she says, closing the door and taking his coat from the hook by the door. 'We're going out to celebrate.'

'In the dark?' he asks seriously.

'In the dark,' she says conspiratorially.

The door knocks again and Cordelia cries out with laughter. 'It's not been five minutes yet.'

Cordelia throws open the door but on the other side is a man and not Margot. He takes off his hat. Down one side of his face runs a long scar. He smiles warmly. 'My name is Joseph Grey. I am a solicitor. Do I have the honour of addressing Miss Cordelia Carr-Lyon?'

Cordelia inhales her fear. Fear of being found. Fear of losing William to them. Fear of all of it. No one has called her that in two years. 'No. It is Mrs Cordelia Leigh,' she lies. 'Carr-Lyon as was.' Her story that she was widowed in 1914 has not been questioned once since her arrival and whoever this man is, he's not about to ruin it for her now.

The man glances about, almost a little nervously. 'I apologise,' he said. 'Mrs Leigh.'

A loud bang sounds from somewhere in the town and the sky fills with specks of silvery fireworks, glistening above them and then gone. The man jumps nervously and Cordelia detects that he has been to the front. She has seen many of them in the town since the injured started returning in fits and starts. Sons, husbands, fathers. Some shake. Some simply stare, their injuries hidden within. He glances back to her again. His injuries appear to be within and, she looks at the scar on his face, external too.

'Would you like to come in?' Cordelia asks softly.

Margot emerges from her cottage and gives Cordelia a quizzical look. 'You go on,' Cordelia says. 'We'll catch up.'

Margot nods and mouths, 'Everything all right?'

'Yes,' Cordelia mouths back as she lets Mr Grey past her and closes the door behind her. William is attempting to put his coat on by himself.

'Five minutes, William. We'll go in five minutes.'

'Mrs Leigh, you are a very hard woman to find,' Mr Grey says after he's finished looking quickly around the small sitting room that opens directly onto the front door.

'I would be if you were looking for Miss Carr-Lyon.'

He laughs. 'Yes. Quite. I've been looking for you for quite some time,' he says.

Cordelia stiffens. 'Why?'

'Please don't look nervous,' he says. 'I don't mean you any harm. Might I be permitted to sit?'

'Yes, of course.' Outside a series of fireworks and bangs reverberate in the street. He sits stiffly, breathes in and out and then composes himself.

'Would you like me to switch on the gramophone to drown out the noise?'

'Oh. No. Although that's very kind of you. Thank you. In among the strangeness of returning home, I shall have to get used to many things, including loud noises.' He carries with him a satchel and he places it next to him on the settee opening it. 'I promise you Mrs Leigh, I am not here to deliver bad news.'

'Really? Or does that depend on your definition of bad news and what my definition might be?'

He looks concerned. 'No. I assure you.' He pulls out a stack of papers. 'Now . . . how to begin?'

Cordelia throws more coal and wood onto the fire and pulls her shawl around her shoulders. 'At the beginning, perhaps?'

'Yes,' he says. 'Forgive me, I'm a little out of practice at this sort of thing. More used to shouting orders under a hail of bullets. Real life, again, is . . .' He stops. Starts again. 'To the beginning,' he collects himself. 'I suppose if I'm going back to the beginning . . . I am a solicitor, as was my father.'

We're going right back to the beginning, aren't we? she thinks. But she says, 'Where?'

'Ulverston.'

She narrows her eyes. It means nothing to her.

'In 1915 my father died, just at the moment I meant to join up. I am an only child, you see, and my mother didn't relish the prospect of losing me and being left alone so shortly after my father's death.'

'I can understand that,' Cordelia says.

'I meant to join up in 1914. I wanted to join up. But my mother begged and begged me not to and then when my father died, I felt my hands were tied somewhat, the choice removed. I stayed. I helped. I contacted his clients and took over the business. My father had a pension and life insurance so Mother would have been all right, but I felt I needed to carry on, for her. But then conscription came and being the only solicitor in the practice I could have appealed it, probably. But it felt wrong to do so. Women were handing out white feathers for cowardice. But regardless, I felt I had no choice then.'

Cordelia nodded. 'I know what having no choice is,' she says.

He smiles.

'Sorry, I interrupted, please continue,' she offers.

'I joined the army. And everything stopped at Father's business. My business, I suppose I should think of it. At the office . . . let's call it that. At the office, papers piled up. Post piled up. I went away and it was as if all the clocks at work stopped in my absence. I have been home from France for about eight months now. And when I opened the office door eight months ago, I cannot tell you how hard I had to push to move the letters that had been waiting for me. Around a year's worth of letters. Can you imagine that? I never saw so much paper in my life.'

Cordelia smiles as she pictures it, but fails to see how this affects her. 'Would you like some tea?' she asks while she has the chance to interject.

'Yes,' he smiles broadly. 'If you are making a pot for you, yes please.'

After she's made it, she brings it over and it sits brewing between them on the table. Cordelia is aware of the time now. William is at the kitchen table watching them, eager for them to finish so he can go out and join the night-time party.

'Where was I?' Mr Grey asks.

'A year's worth of letters,' she reminds him.

'Yes. Obviously I had written to our regular clients before I went to the front and instructed people to find another solicitor if they required urgent legal work but with such little time, there were always going to be some that slipped the net. Some I forgot. Subscriptions I forgot to cancel, that sort of thing.'

Cordelia nods, starts pouring tea. 'Milk?'

'Yes please, Miss Carr-Lyon.'

'Mrs Leigh,' Cordelia interjects.

'Of course, I am so sorry. Mrs Leigh, you must be wondering what this has to do with you?'

'I am wondering rather, yes.'

'It has taken me six months to find you,' he says.

She looks up from pouring the milk into their cups. 'Six months?'

'I felt the urgent need to find you, you see. When writing letters out to locate you and getting very little in return had exhausted itself, I took up the mantle in person. I started as soon as I was able to piece together what had happened.'

'What *has* happened?' she asks warily.

'Miss Tabitha Bowes was a client of my father's.'

Cordelia's mouth is suddenly dry at hearing her friend's name after all this time. And then she knows. He has lied to her. She has been duped. They have found her. The Bowes have found her and are coming for William. 'You're here to take him, aren't you?'

'No,' he says hurriedly. 'I assure you no, I am not. I am here for a very different reason entirely.'

'Which is what?' she asks, unsure if he is telling her the truth.

'Yours is one of the more interesting cases I am dealing

with since my return and I felt so much rested on prioritising yours once news reached me that Miss Bowes had passed away. She left a will with my father in 1915 before he died, along with a series of letters that should have been passed on in the event of her death. Please forgive me, my duty in being at the front meant those letters have sat in the office while I've been away for the last few years, along with the last will and testament.'

'Tabitha's will?'

'I believe her parents did not think she had a will as she had not used the family's usual solicitor. This is where the confusion lies.'

'You've spoken to her parents?' Cordelia asks. She cannot stop her hand from shaking as she sips her cup of tea.

'Ordinarily, as next of kin, her parents would be the very first port of call. However, the will and the letters shine a very different light on that subject and I find myself in front of you, instead.

'I have brought a copy of the will with me and in among the legality, quite simply, Miss Tabitha Bowes left the majority of her estate to you, Mrs Leigh, although she lists you here as Miss Cordelia Carr-Lyon of Pencallick House, Cornwall.'

'Oh,' Cordelia says in confusion. 'Tabitha has left . . .' She doesn't know what else to say.

'The majority of her estate to you, yes.'

Her friend had thought of her long before she'd passed. She thinks back to those days in Rose Cottage, among the saddest and happiest of her life. Isaac's loss. Her friend's rallying companionship. And how Tabitha saved Cordelia from collapsing into total grief. 'That was very thoughtful of her, Mr Grey,' Cordelia swallows tears back and aims for pragmatism with this man she does not know. 'But Tabitha didn't have an estate, you see. She had hardly any money, as far as I could tell, and she rented Rose Cottage.'

Mr Grey looks confused, opens his satchel and rifles through notes. 'Did she tell you she rented the cottage?' he queries.

Cordelia thinks. 'No. I don't think she told me anything really. I assumed she did. Her parents also assumed she did.'

'She did not rent Rose Cottage. She owned it. The cottage and the surrounding grounds are yours, entirely. The smallholding too, but any animals will need to be re-purchased if you wish to stock it again. I understand they were all gifted to a nearby farmer after her passing. And as for the money, I'll admit there isn't a king's ransom as most of her allowance went on purchasing the cottage in 1913 and also a motorcar but that has since been sold. But I think you'll find the sum that remains for you, paid in annuity as Miss Bowes stipulates in her will, should cover any sensible living expenses.'

'Good lord,' Cordelia sinks back against the settee and stares into the fire. 'This is madness. Wonderful madness. But madness all the same.'

'I understand this must be quite a shock, but as you say, it is a pleasant one, I hope. I will be happy to guide you every step of the way and no doubt this information will come thick and fast here so allow me to speak plainly now and then we can run through it all in finer detail as the weeks progress?'

'Yes, all right,' Cordelia says, confusion still coursing through her. Then she laughs and then claps a hand to her mouth. 'I'm so sorry, I'm a bit shocked.'

William walks over and joins Cordelia on the settee. She runs a hand through his hair and kisses him on the top of his head as he nestles against her. It is growing late. Soon he'll be tired.

'The cottage is in a bit of a sad state of repair,' Mr Grey starts.

'Have you been?'

'Yes, I thought it worth checking there was actually something there for you to inherit. Two harsh winters and a lot of overgrown brambles might make for heavy work.'

'I'm sure I can sort that,' Cordelia says.

'I'm sure you can,' he replies. 'Do you intend to live there or sell it?'

'I . . . I haven't had a chance to think. I suppose I . . . I think we might live there, if we can. I think that's what Tabitha must have wanted when she left it to me.'

Mr Grey is quiet and then, 'What do *you* want? Those who have left us cannot command us.'

'I know,' Cordelia says as she looks at the young man. 'I've made a good life here for us. But I adored Rose Cottage. And so did William. It's a little piece of Tabitha, waiting for us in a beautiful part of the world.'

'I am biased, because I live there, but you are right.' Mr Grey sits forward, takes a sip of his tea. 'I cannot tell you how pleased I am to be able to deliver such good news to you, finally. I have waited a long time for this day.' The man beams.

'Mr Grey, thank you.'

'You are very welcome.'

Something occurs to Cordelia. 'Mr Grey, can I ask, how *did* you find me?'

He looks a mix of sheepish and proud. 'The short answer is that I went to Hawkshead and I found Miss

Bowes' maid, Ann Davis, who was also listed in Miss Bowes' will and had also been left a sum of money. She refused to respond to my letters at the start, believing it to be a trick. Once we'd got past that particular hurdle I was able to convince her that my original letters to her, also asking if she knew your whereabouts, came with good intentions. I had to show her Miss Bowes' will, in actual fact. She was quite stubborn about that.'

Cordelia smothers a laugh. 'Yes. Yes, she can be quite forceful.'

'She is obviously an ally of yours and having loyal friends is something to rejoice in. I'm surprised you didn't receive a letter from her warning you of my arrival although I might have beaten her to it.'

'She doesn't know my address. I sent her a letter from the boarding house,' Cordelia says. 'The one we stayed in when we first arrived here, telling her William and I were safe and well. But after that . . . I wondered if it might be best to . . .'

'Sever connections . . .?' Mr Grey dares.

Cordelia looks up, wonders how much he knows.

He continues. 'Ann Davis was vague when she told me she thought you resided in Aldeburgh. I thought she was being purposefully vague but perhaps not. I made gentle enquiries at the newsagent earlier today and was guided here.'

'I should write to her again,' Cordelia says. She had just been far too paranoid that the letter might be noticed by the postmaster and awkward questions might ensue, unravelling Cordelia's plan. It had not been worth the risk.

'This brings me neatly to the letters, which I'd almost forgotten about,' Mr Grey says.

'The letters?' Cordelia asks.

'Miss Bowes wrote a series of letters to be posted in the event of her death. She foresaw a situation arising that would be to no one's benefit and took measures to avert it. One was to me, or rather, to my father as she believed him to be still living. One was to her parents and one was to you. I was instructed to read all of them, log their contents and to sign an affidavit if either party ever called upon me in a legal capacity. I was instructed to show you both letters so you knew the situation in its entirety,' Mr Grey says. 'I have already ensured the letter to her parents has been sent on. And this, in my own hand, is a copy of it purely for your reference.'

Cordelia feels her face drain of colour. William. Tabitha's parents. 'You've sent the letter on already?'

'Do not worry,' Mr Grey explains hastily. 'You are not to worry. It is all taken care of. Miss Bowes has explained this matter to me entirely posthumously. The law is very much on your side,' he says. And then he looks at her kindly. 'Your son is safe.'

'He's not my son,' Cordelia says quietly. 'He was Tabitha's ward.'

Cordelia looks at William, into his kind dark eyes, so very like his father's. Mr Grey's smile doesn't fade. He stretches forward and hands Cordelia the letter.

'You forget,' he says kindly, 'that I have read all the letters.'

CHAPTER 47

Letter from Tabitha to her parents

June 1915
Dear Mother and Father,

I hope you never have occasion to read this, filed away as it is with my last will and testament. But I can foresee events unravelling in an awful manner if the worst happens and I pass away unexpectedly having not reached old age. This thought has been creeping up on me over the past few months and I am growing nervous that I will be the main cause of ruining people's lives, simply because I did nothing to avert a crisis. So I am doing something. I am doing this and I hope it is not needed.

I will speak plainly. I have not told you about the little boy, William, my ward because I did not want you to know. The reasons for this are twofold.

I know I am different. I know I am not what you expected in a daughter and I am sorry for any hurt I caused you. But I could not help the way I felt, the way I was, the way I am.

On reflecting back over my childhood and the way I grew into a young woman, I find it hard to forgive your method of parenting. I'm sorry to say it but there it is. I should like to say this is the main reason why I did not want you to ever meet William. I should like to think my ward was kept in ignorance of what bigotry was. Here, with me, he knows only love and kindness and will, I am sure, grow into a happy young man. I only hope I am here to see it. And if I am not, this brings me on to the second reason why his presence here is kept from you.

Quite plainly, that reason is because he is not my son, adopted or otherwise. He is simply my ward.

I took him in for my friend Cordelia Carr-Lyon, whose son he really is.

This secret is not mine to tell, but I fear if I do not state this plainly to you, on my passing, that events may arise that might cause untold damage in the future. Heaven forbid you should ever try to claim him as your grandson in my absence. He is not yours to take, because he is not mine.

This letter has been filed with solicitors Messrs Grey and Grey, Barrow-in-Furness. In addition to sending a copy to you, they are instructed to hold a copy on file in the event of its necessity. They also have a copy of my last will and testament, which leaves almost everything I own to Cordelia.

Mother and Father, in the event I should pass away before you, I have just two requests to ask of you. This, in my death, I hope you will honour as I believe these are the only things I have ever asked of you.

One, that you do not try to claim William. He is not yours to take, as he was never mine.

Two, that you do not divulge the truth about William's parentage to anyone. It would ruin Cordelia's reputation and shame her parents, something which we have worked tirelessly, and made sacrifices, to protect. I ask you this in good faith and remind you that although I tell you this, it is not my secret to share and thus is not yours either.

Your daughter, Tabitha Isabelle Bowes

Letter from Tabitha to Cordelia

June 1915

Darling Cordelia,

I hope that I am a long way from death and in fact, as I write this you sit across from me at the kitchen table, attempting not to slice your finger off as you cut a pile of lettuces for our lunch.

Beautiful William, as you have decided to call him, is finally quiet after a nice bout of crying and rests in the evening shade in his perambulator just outside the scullery door. All is quiet and peaceful, in this house at any rate, while the war outside rages on.

I would like to think it does not touch us here. But of course it does. William is the most blessed proof of how the war has found us here.

I hope by the time you read this, I will be in my dotage and will have forgotten entirely to update my will and this letter will be utterly, blissfully redundant. But, just in case it should not be, and it is needed, here it is in black and white as an addendum, so to speak, to my will. I have written to Mr Grey, my solicitor from whom you might have been sent this letter, and you will find a copy of my will rests with him. I have instructed that another letter be sent to my parents and the contents of it noted in case there is a challenge for William. I do not anticipate there being a challenge. But Mother and Father are a funny sort, unpredictable. So we shall see. In any case I hope I have sorted it.

If you are reading this, then I have died and my final act is to have told them the truth. I have not told them details. But I have told them enough, I believe, so that should they try to raise William, believing him to be my child or even believing they have a right to him simply because he resided with me, they will not legally be entitled to do so.

You are his mother, Cordelia. You will always be his mother. And while he lives with me and I raise him in your absence as you return to your parents, please know I love him and that we both, in turn, love you. I hope one day he will be able to call you Mother. And I know you fervently wish for that too. But for now, I understand your position, unmarried and with a newborn baby. I am only pleased that I am in a position to help, that I was in the right place at the right time and that you were able to look to me for this help. I am always here for anything you need, Cordelia.

It is with this in mind that I offer you some safety. In the event of my death, Rose Cottage is yours. You will find peace and safety here and enough money to live on and to educate William. Should you wish to sell the property, I leave that choice to you. It is yours to do as you wish if ever your secret is discovered or you feel unable to reside with your parents if they discover the truth. Parents are a funny lot. One never quite knows what reaction they will give to any event.

I offer you every type of care and love there is and know that I have tried to keep your son safe and well, raised him to the best of my abilities and I hope he turns into a kind young man. If he is anything like his mother, I know he will grow into the best sort of person.

Now enough of this. The day is bright, William thrives and we are about to eat lunch, although I think you've given up chopping lettuces and are now looking at me curiously, no doubt wondering what I am up to, scribbling away so furiously.

You are very loved, Cordelia and I know that whatever happens to you, all will be well.

With all my love,

Tabitha

CHAPTER 48

Cordelia's eyes are full of tears and she folds the letters over and lays them in her lap. She cannot meet Mr Grey's gaze. 'You must think dreadfully of me,' she says.

'Of course not,' he replies softly. 'I am curious to understand what happened. But you do not need to tell me if you do not wish to.'

Cordelia glances up at him. 'I left him in her care. I didn't know what else to do. I expected my fiancé . . . well, he wasn't my fiancé, not really, but I expected him to return to me. He said he was going to propose to me and I know he would have done if he'd known about William. He would have done anyway. He died before I had the chance to tell him.'

Mr Grey looks at her kindly.

'I confess,' Cordelia continues, 'that I didn't know about William. Not until I was five months pregnant. I suppose it was naïve of me but there was so much going on around me, the war, the man I loved, the house and the garden to contend with and I didn't care too much for my own health or notice too many changes. I ate very well here with Tabitha, living off the land and what with all the cakes I was eating here . . . well . . . you understand my meaning. But then every time I went near the piggery I started throwing up. I put it down to it being . . . the piggery. But after a while, Tabitha deduced what was happening whereas I was not worldly wise enough and I did not.'

'You are not the first person, nor shall you be the last to fall in love and become with child,' Mr Grey says kindly.

Cordelia looks over at William, who has returned to the table and is scribbling furiously, his dark eyes intent on colouring in. Dark eyes, just like his father's. 'It was the happiest news and the worst news. Isaac, William's father, did not return from the front and I was alone. Only I wasn't. Because Tabitha was there. I didn't know what choices I had. I couldn't keep him, or rather I didn't think I could keep him. I investigated the local orphanage but I just couldn't send him there. I couldn't give him up forever and it would have been forever. And I couldn't have taken him back with me, back to Cornwall. I couldn't present my parents with a baby conceived in such a way. They would have taken him from me and put him in an orphanage anyway. They are good people, but even they couldn't embrace such shame. I couldn't expect them to. I couldn't inflict this on them. Either way, I was lost. I wanted my child and I didn't want to have to apologise for him every day.'

'I understand,' Mr Grey says. Although Cordelia knows he never could, not really.

'It took a long time for us to establish what was best and it was Tabitha who suggested it,' Cordelia says. 'In my hour of need she was there. She suggested she keep him, not as her own but as her ward, pretend he was of vague origin and spare my secret ever coming to light. I would have to give up being his mother in name but not because it was what Tabitha wanted – far from it – but because it was best for me, best for William as he grew up not to know the truth. I was his mother from a distance. It wasn't a perfect solution. It was a painful solution but it was the only achievable one that presented itself to us at the time.'

Mr Grey nods. 'And then Miss Bowes passed away.'

Cordelia gives a sad smile. 'Yes. And then she passed away. I do often sit and wonder what would have happened to William if she had passed away without my having been there, without me having been able to take him. They'd have him now, no doubt – her parents, I mean.'

'From what the maid, Ann Davis, tells me, yes they probably would.'

'And then I'd have had to go there, try to take my son back from them. I wonder if they would have believed me or if they'd have tried to keep him. I wonder if I'd have had the courage to tell them the truth, that he was mine. I just don't know now.'

Mr Grey smiles sadly. 'I think you probably would.'

'I think I probably would too. The outcome would have been the same. My reputation in ruins, not able to live among the people I thought of as my own. But that's what happened anyway. I wrote my family a note to explain I was going away but I didn't tell them where or why. I couldn't lie. I didn't know what lie to tell. In a way, perhaps this has done me a favour. I have employment and a roof, food for us and a life and more importantly I have my son and I am able to call him my own, here in this place where they all believe I am widowed.'

'Or at Rose Cottage if you want it,' Mr Grey points out.

'Yes . . . or at Rose Cottage,' Cordelia says with a smile.

'A widowed woman, a small child. You can maintain the same story in another location, you know. I shan't be the one to tell. I should consider it a privilege to be able to offer any help I can.'

Cordelia falls silent and the fire crackles and flickers beside her. 'Yes,' she says thoughtfully. And then, 'Would you like to join us for supper Mr Grey?'

Mr Grey beams in return. 'I would like that very much.'

CHAPTER 49

THE LAKE DISTRICT
MARCH 1919

Cordelia and Joseph Grey stand in front of Rose Cottage. Her cottage now.

'It's very weather-beaten,' Joseph confesses. 'The brambles are . . . well . . . you can see.'

She adjusts a sleeping William in her arms. He is just shy of four years old and tired from their travels, although they ended their long journey north at Joseph's home before travelling on.

Together they assess the damage. How the passing of time can do so much. The lower windows and front door are covered in brambles. An upper windowpane has bowed and the gusts of cold wind that must have rolled through the countryside and into the house through such a small entry point have probably done untold damage within. She doesn't want to look inside but she knows she must. It will break her heart and eat into a lot of the money Tabitha left her for the next few months in order to put it right. But put it right she must. This is her home now. Hers and William's. Tabitha gave it to them and she'll be damned if a bit of weather will keep her from the cottage.

'Shall we try the scullery room door?' Cordelia asks, walking round.

'Would you mind?' She gestures to William. She has found an unexpected friend in Joseph and the solicitor heaves the little boy into his arms. Fighting her way through the weeds and brambles, lifting her skirts so as to entirely embarrass her already-quite-nervous friend and pushing up the sleeves of her knitted silk cardigan, Cordelia stamps on the brambles with her practical laced boots to squash them down. She reaches for the handle and pulls and then bends, looking through the keyhole. The key is in the lock on the other side and the door firmly locked.

'Blast,' Cordelia exclaims.

She still holds the key to the overgrown front door in her hand. 'Well, there's only one thing for it. I suppose the first thing to do is find an axe and start hacking away.'

Half an hour later when Joseph has finally chopped and pushed aside the old brambles, kicking them to the side of what used to be the path, he steps aside and Cordelia walks forward, pushes the key into the stiff lock, turning it with full force and with great effort pushes open the warped front door.

Behind her, William has found some old trowels and spades and has taken up digging in a patch of weeds, proud of himself that he is doing what he's watched his mother do since he was a baby. She wonders if he remembers this place, the first year or so of his life being spent here. Of course he doesn't. How can he?

Cordelia glances inside the dim cottage, the windows covered in thick layers of dust and grime on the inside and mostly overgrown bushes and brambles on the other.

'What's happened to this place?' She steps inside and Joseph follows her in.

'Pity we didn't think to bring any lamps,' he says. The bright winter sunlight doesn't quite penetrate the room. 'I'm not sure what I was expecting,' he admits. 'But I didn't expect for all the furniture to still be here.'

'Neither did I,' Cordelia exclaims as she sees the room laid out in exactly the same way it had been the night she'd left with William in one arm and a carpet bag of clothes for both of them in the other. She steps across the threshold, over a pile of letters and a newspaper subscription that had piled up until the newsagent had probably realised there was no one there to pay his bill and stopped delivering. Cordelia flicks through the top few letters, all addressed to Tabitha.

'Did her parents not inform anyone she'd passed away? Did they not make an announcement?' she asks.

'I don't know,' he replies. 'I'm sorry. I was in France at the time.'

'Of course you were,' she says, remembering too late. Tabitha's parents hadn't told anyone, judging by the amount of mail for her deceased friend. They hadn't announced their daughter's passing. They hadn't done anything with this house or Tabitha's worldly possessions. It was as if they'd simply forgotten she had been here at all. Cordelia walks to the table by the fireplace, where her gardening book still lies. She'd put it there the day of Tabitha's passing. She picks up the book, blows the dust off it to see the words on the page and then puts it down.

'It's just so sad,' she announces. 'It's just so incredibly sad.'

'No,' he says, walking towards her and placing a friendly hand on her shoulder. 'It's not. It's a new beginning.'

CHAPTER 50

Over the next week, Cordelia works tirelessly by day in the cottage. The grounds will have to wait. Her priority is to make the interior habitable. On paying a visit to Ann, the two women fall into each other's arms, crying and laughing and sharing their experiences of the last few years. Ann can't believe how tall William has grown and they reminisce about their time together and about Tabitha, about how Ann's older brother died at the Somme and how Cordelia wrote to Edwin in recent weeks to congratulate him when she read he was receiving a medal for bravery, having carried one of his men across No Man's Land and back to the trenches. But as she'd left no returning address, Edwin was unable to write back to her.

'You should write to him again. Tell him where you live. Let him decide if he wants to be associated with you or not. Don't you decide for him,' Ann says.

Cordelia laughs. 'I've missed you.'

'Don't be daft,' is her forthright reply.

In the last year, Ann has taken a job as housekeeper to the vicar, which means she can't return to Rose Cottage but her younger sister Daisy, who turns twenty-four in a week, is available a few hours each day.

And so Cordelia and Daisy work inside the cottage by day with William playing outside. And then in the evenings Cordelia and William return to Joseph's house that he shares with his mother, both of whom are kind and hospitable. Joseph had preceded Cordelia's arrival by informing his mother she too is a widow. It bonded the two women instantly, although it comes with a trickle of guilt on Cordelia's part. But it is the story Cordelia knows she'll have to continue with if she and William are to remain respectable. And she needs it. She needs it for him.

She and Joseph have formed an honest friendship and Cordelia finds it sad that this young man has returned from the war nervous and unsure of himself. She wonders if he was like that before he went. She believes not. What has the war done to him? She thinks of Isaac: *the things I have seen.*

She wonders if Joseph Grey has seen those same things and if that is why he jumps at loud noises, why his hands shake every now and again when he butters his toast.

But Cordelia's spirits soar when she catches Joseph looking even more nervous than usual upon meeting Daisy on the day William and Cordelia move back in to Rose Cottage. Daisy has baked a cake and decorated it with berries in celebration as he enters clutching a copy of the will Cordelia asked him to draw up for her.

'Hello,' he says and smiles, appearing unable to move or speak much after that.

'Hello,' Daisy says quietly in return, her eyes meeting his.

Cordelia smiles knowingly and insists he stay for cake with them, leaving them alone, disappearing to attend to William even though he very obviously doesn't need attending to.

Later, as he is leaving, Cordelia corners Joseph at the door. 'Did you ask her out for tea or for luncheon?'

He shakes his head mournfully. 'No. Should I have done?'

Cordelia hisses, 'Yes!'

'Really? I was a bit nervous to.'

'Mr Joseph Grey,' she whispers. 'You stood in front of whole battalions of German soldiers and avoided sniper fire. I'm sure you can ask a woman to tea.'

He glances into the kitchen where Daisy is moving dishes towards the scullery sink. 'Actually, I think I'd rather face the Germans again,' he whispers. 'I'll do it next time I'm here.'

'No you won't,' she commands. 'Life is fleeting. You'll do it now.'

'Oh good lord, what are you doing?' he asks as Cordelia gives him a shove towards the kitchen and then makes herself scarce in the spring sunshine at the end of the overgrown garden. But she can't help noticing Joseph's triumphant smile as he walks down the path towards his motorcar a few minutes later.

CHAPTER 51

APRIL 1919

Cordelia's world is perfect. Or as near to perfect as she is ever going to get it and she smiles happily as she works in the garden on what is the first warm day she's seen this year. She discards her coat as she toils, turning up soil turned hard and cutting down grass turned to seed. The garden is almost a blank canvas once again. All Tabitha's hard work has been done away with in such a short space of time. How swiftly the years have worn the house and garden to dullness. It needs brightening up again. It's so sad, Cordelia thinks. Just so sad-looking. And then she's reminded of Mr Grey's buoyant words. 'It's a new beginning.' And it *will* be that. It *is* already that. It is a new beginning.

She's enjoying rejuvenating the small kitchen garden and teaching William that the food that sits on his plate each evening for supper, comes mostly from the view outside the window. New hens have been installed but the piggery is in such a state of disrepair Cordelia wonders if she'll be able to keep pigs again. There's a lot to think about. She will need to earn money. Mr Grey was correct. There isn't a king's ransom bequeathed to her. But what there is will stretch if Cordelia is careful and if they become a little more self-sufficient. Tabitha's books about running a smallholding have been dusted and read. They will be read again. There is much Cordelia needs to learn and she wants to so very much.

The first Sunday after they fully return to Hawkshead, Cordelia and William are greeted warmly by the vicar and parishioners after the church service. The vicar speaks warmly of Tabitha and then shows Cordelia where her friend's grave lies.

Tabitha Isabelle Bowes, the headstone reads with her date of birth and date of death and nothing else. It was placed by the stonemason only recently, so the vicar says, as if Tabitha's parents had forgotten to carry out this final act for their daughter until only a few months ago.

Cordelia wonders if she can hire the same stonemason to return and carve into the large space on the stone an epitaph that is simple but that says all it needs: *Beloved friend.*

But before that she makes a plan to plant wildflowers around the grave. Although her friend was not wild. Not in the least. Simply unconventional. But wildflowers around her grave, a riot of pinks and purples, blues and yellows might give Tabitha something to smile down from the heavens about. Cordelia hopes Tabitha is smiling down on her and William, now they reside in the house Tabitha left in her will.

Her friend had been correct when she'd written in her letter, *Whatever happens to you, all will be well.*

All will be well, Cordelia feels it. But not only that,

she knows it. And then she holds William's hand and as William skips his way back to the cottage, Cordelia lifts her skirts a fraction, pays no attention to see if anyone is looking and skips her way down the lane with him.

Yes, she thinks as she tucks him up in bed that night. *We can be happy here again. We are happy here already.* She is settled and so is William.

But there is one thing niggling at her that she knows she must triumph over. That is her relationship with her parents. She must inform her family of her whereabouts. And her situation.

There is no hiding it from those she loves. There is no need. Not anymore. And if they don't take her as they find her, then her position here in Tabitha's cottage, isn't too dissimilar from what Tabitha's situation was. This place was Tabitha's refuge, her sanctuary. And it is Cordelia's now. Nothing can take that away.

At the end of the day when she has quite made up her mind, bravery makes her stupid. Or stupidity makes her brave. She doesn't know which. But she takes a sheet of writing paper and begins.

Darling Mother and Father, Edwin and Clive,

Please forgive my absence and my silence over the last few years. I hope you will forgive me but I suspect when I tell you the reasons for my departure, you might not. But I want you to know what has happened and so I shall lay it out for you here.

I am a mother. I have a beautiful four-year-old son named William. This week it was his birthday. I gave birth to him in April 1915 after I fell pregnant the summer before. I will not tell you who the father is. It doesn't matter now. He is no longer here but he intended to marry me when he was due home on leave at the end of 1914 . . .

Cordelia tells her family everything that has happened to her in the intervening years, how much she misses her parents, Clive and Edwin. How she whooped with pride when she read Edwin's name in a list of medal recipients for bravery after the war had finished. She longs to be part of their lives again, and to have them in hers and William's.

You have a grandson, she concludes. *And Edwin, Clive – you have a nephew. He is the most precious and wonderful thing in my life and I should like you to know him. Please write to me at the above address if you could accept me as I am now, the person I have become and the beautiful child that is my everything. With love, your daughter, Cordelia*

And then she does something strange, even by her own standards. She's never kept a diary but there have been things she wanted to write down. But instead of writing her feelings in a diary, she writes them to Isaac. The Isaac from five years ago who she loved, who she still loves, whose dark, thoughtful eyes mirrored his son's, who sleeps soundly upstairs, loved and cared for.

Dear Isaac,

My darling. Can you sense that you are a father? Did you have an inkling before you died that you had given me such a precious gift that night? Do you look down on us and think wonderful things? Your son is a marvel. Just like you. He is kind and pure-hearted, full of joy. And charm. He works his charm on me the way you did. I am forever buying him toffees.

I wish you could be here to see him. I wish so many things. I wish we had acted on our impulses earlier than we did so that we'd had more time. I wish you had not joined up with your brother. You would have been conscripted eventually but might that lateness have saved you? I will never know. My heart aches for you and the man you would have been. There are so many things I wish had been different.

I cannot imagine anyone else comparing to you. I would not want them to. So please, wherever you are, I hope you are at peace. I hope you look down on us and know you are loved. You always will be.

Your Cordelia

And then when she finishes, she kisses it, gently placing it in the fire, watching it flicker and char, crackle and burn, its embers floating up the chimney, towards the heavens for him to find.

CHAPTER 52

The Cordelia in 1919 has different wants and needs to the Cordelia from five years ago. She thinks of Isaac so frequently and regrets never having thought to ask for a photograph of him before he went to the front. Everything happened so fast, that week in August. She'd never thought that glimpse of him at the station in August 1914 would be her last. If she had, how differently she'd have done things.

Rose Cottage is in order, finally, although there are still Tabitha's things to work through and decide what to do with. Mr and Mrs Bowes had taken jewellery and precious possessions – of course they had. But so many things remain. So many drawers unopened, so many clothes in cupboards. So much to do now the house is neat and clean.

Cordelia has care for William, which enables her to make inroads into her letters of application as a gardener nearby, which she intends to do tomorrow. She's seen a notice in the regional newspaper for a gardener to help the owner a couple of hours three days a week at a nearby estate in lieu of the fact almost their entire team of gardeners have not returned from the front. A couple of hours three days a week will give Cordelia a bit of spare money.

That night William comes down the stairs long after she's put him to bed. 'I can't sleep. It's still too new a bed. Too new a room.' She doesn't remind him he used to live here, sleep here. He won't remember.

'Come and have a cuddle in front of the fire with me then,' she says instead.

'Will you tell me a story?'

'Which one?' she asks.

'The one about the gardener at the big house and the girl who lived there,' he requests as he climbs onto the settee and into her lap.

'Again?' she asks with a smile.

'Again. It's my favourite.'

'Mine too,' she confesses.

'But this time,' William asks sleepily. 'When you tell the story . . . can there be dragons?'

After William has gone to bed, Cordelia goes through the motions of shutting up the house. She locks the door and puts the key on the shelf in easy reach, where she has piled up all of Tabitha's mail and the newspapers from the war that had been delivered. She flicks through the bundle as she walks around, looking at the headlines from the war and deciding she can't relive all that again so soon. Or ever again probably. Too much death, too much tragedy. And for what? Young men dying for old men. She puts the newspapers into the kindling basket, throwing one onto the fire to keep it going just long enough while she looks through the mail. She will open the letters tomorrow, write back to each sender individually and inform them of the passing of her friend in 1916. What an awful job, but it had to be done.

Just as she decides to give up the task of looking through the enormous pile of post, something catches her eye. It is an envelope addressed to her, postmarked August 1916. She looks at the return address and sender.

VAD M Trevelyan,
St Dunstan's,
Regent's Park
London

And under that, dated a fortnight later, another one. And then underneath that, there is a third and final note from what Cordelia can see as she hurries through the rest of the pile.

She opens the first one. It was sent so long ago. In a bid to keep William's parentage from the world, Cordelia had not dared write to Millicent, dared not tell her where she was living. There was always a chance the letter might fall into her parents' hands, given both sets of parents were good friends. It just hadn't been worth the risk. Cutting off everyone had been the only way. But Millicent had tried to get in touch with Cordelia three times over the years.

It had been hard, severing that friendship but it had been the right thing to do for her and William. She wonders if she can rekindle it now. Then she reads the words in the first letter and finds they do not make sense. Nothing makes sense.

Cordelia.

Isaac Leigh is a patient at St Dunstan's.

Looking through his notes, he has been here for quite some time but I have just been transferred over from another St Dunstan's annex in Blackheath.

He is listed as Lieutenant I Leigh and it did not occur to me he was anything to do with you.

He has suffered extensive surgery and today while we conversed he asked me where I am from. I spoke about Cornwall and he told me how he was there before the war, how he used to be a garden landscaper. I think he used a different word, architect maybe? I forget, it was all such a blur because I think I must have stilled somewhat and he asked me why I was pausing. Then I asked him, 'Lieutenant Leigh, what does the I stand for? What is your Christian name?'

And he replied, 'Isaac' and I think I turned quite cold.

I admit I did not know what to do or to think. I must have seemed incredibly surly because so many questions ran through my mind that I was quite unable to talk after that and he seemed content in silence. Should I ask him about you? Should I ask him how he came to be here? Should I ask him why it is Edwin thought he had died? Should I ask him how it was that you came to think he had died? Should I ask him why he has allowed you to think he has died when he is here, alive? Because his faculties are completely intact so he can hardly have forgotten you.

As you can see, I don't know what to think first or what to ask first. There must be perfectly innocent explanations for all of it and I believe, sitting here writing this to you, that the simplest and most obvious explanation is probably this: that he was shot and he was moved up the line and has gone through the rigmarole and processing and eventually wound up here to be treated . . . and having been shot, Edwin believed he had in fact died right in front of his eyes. And that was an end to it. But if so, and this is the bit I can't understand, why has he not written to tell you he is alive?

I have not said who I am so he does not know our friendship. I am duping him. Until you write to me I will try delicately to find out as much as I can before he leaves, which I fear will be soon. Patients can stay on here, be taught new skills to help them adapt, but he doesn't seem the kind to volunteer to be taught anything.

He remembers everything, Cordelia. He has not lost his memory although he shakes a little from time to time. If a sash window closes too suddenly or a plate lands on a table at meal times a little too loudly, he jumps. As do most men in here. Please come as soon as you can. But I must prepare you. The shaking is not everything. He has wounds, Cordelia, and they are extensive.

In the last few years I have seen men forget their former lives, forget their own name but not him.

I am in bafflement and there is only one way to understand this and that is if you are to ask him. If he means to you now that which he did when he went to the front, you must come here.

I have written to you at Rose Cottage and I have sent a copy of this note to you at your London house in case I have missed you. I have no idea where you are so must try all routes. I hope I haven't hurt your brother and offended your parents by calling off our engagement, so I hope my letter there wasn't thrown in the fire to burn away, once they realised I was the sender.

Write immediately,

Millicent

Cordelia is freezing, despite the fire burning in the grate to ward off the evening chill. Every part of her has stiffened. This cannot be true and yet Millicent has no reason to lie. But he cannot be alive. He cannot. Edwin told her he'd died. *He was the first officer to leave us.*

Cordelia looks at the date again, 1916. So long ago. This letter is so old. She puts her hand to her mouth and finds her hand is shaking. Her mind is blank. What can she do? In 1916 Isaac had been alive. But his injuries had been extensive. What does that mean? He had been undergoing surgery. But had it worked? Has he since died? She hears a noise that sounds like a dying animal and then realises it's her. She tries to quiet herself so she doesn't wake William, sobbing quietly into her hands, trying to muffle the sound of her own crying.

And then, with shaking hands, she finds the next envelope from Millicent and wiping tears away so she can make out the words she reads the next letter, dated a fortnight later.

Darling Cordelia, have I scared you away by telling you about Isaac's injuries? Or did you not receive my last missive?

I could not blame you if you chose to remain as you are rather than with an invalid. I have not told him about you although I have dug a little deeper and discovered that he is certainly your Isaac. He was a lieutenant in the Duke of Cornwall's Light Infantry and Edwin was his commanding officer. I could not possibly tell him my relationship to Edwin and, thus, to you, for fear he would clam up. I worry he is easily unnerved. His brother died only a short while after Isaac left the front line but he does not know the circumstances of his death. He assumes shot, as most men were.

I want to ask him, 'Why haven't you told Cordelia you are here?' But instead I asked if there was anyone he would like me to write to on his behalf or if he would like some assistance writing letters? But every time I ask he replies, 'No thank you.' He says he has no one left to write letters to. I have asked, 'Is there no sweetheart who you should like to know your whereabouts? You are allowed visitors here.' And he shakes his head, 'No thank you.' I cannot get more out of him.

Darling Cordelia, I do not know what else to do. Shall I mention you to him? So far I have not. But I worry if that was the wrong thing to do now? Should I just tell him, 'I know Cordelia. She loves you and misses you. Please write to her and encourage her to come to you.' But is that the wrong thing to do? And why hasn't he already done this? Have you found someone else? Are you in love with someone else? I'm so sorry to pain you and ask you such a personal question but I cannot fathom why you are not writing back to me or visiting. I expected you this week. I am torn, I don't know what to do and I will await your instructions before proceeding further.

Please write, even if it is to tell me to keep out of your business, to detach myself from further enquiry and to put my efforts elsewhere.

With love, as always,

Millicent.

I could not blame you if you chose to remain as you are rather than with an invalid. Cordelia reads this line over and over. An invalid? My God, what has happened to him? Her Isaac. Of course she still loves him. She never stopped. This cannot be real. It cannot be real. He was shot. Where? Where – that has invalided him? She cannot imagine. An arm? A leg? What?

The third letter is dated in early 1917. So long after the first two. On tearing it open, Cordelia instantly understands why.

Cordelia, please excuse the delay in sending this letter to you. So many things have happened and I didn't want to keep sending letters to you when the first two went unanswered. I am sure you have your reasons as to why you have not replied. I do not know what those reasons are but I have come to respect them, whatever they may be.

So I will tell you this final piece of information. I don't know if you want to hear it but I can't just sit on it without having told you.

Isaac's surgery did not work and he left us two months ago. I cannot tell you what befell him after that. He refused any offer of help. I watched him from the uppermost window the day he discharged himself. He would not wait any longer for, as he called it, 'pointless help that does no good.' It may not have been pointless but I believe he had quite simply had enough of being here.

As he walked slowly towards the waiting car, I could not help but compare him to some sort of animal walking towards captivity rather than away from it. And then he was gone. And I turned away from the window after the car had left the drive and I went back to my duties. That is all I have to relay to you. I imagine you to be happy, settled and perhaps even married now to someone else who the war did not touch, or who it did but who fared much better than Isaac.

I am married now. Samuel was as good as his word and waited. I wanted to continue nursing but after witnessing such horror and suffering, I realised I could not put off my own happiness any longer. Who knows how long this war will last and as Samuel says, I cannot save everyone, and the time to focus on my own life has arrived.

And then soon, hopefully, there will be children.

I have enclosed my marital address, should you wish to hold on to it. Perhaps the day will come in a few years when you feel able to connect with an old friend again, one that has always wished you well.

Although I did not become your sister-in-law, I should like you to always know I am your friend. I sometimes think of those final days before the world changed, walking through the garden at night at Pencallick House with your brother and eating cake and playing games at the bazaar, the tennis parties you had the week your court was installed, swimming at the cove when we were children. I think of those days fondly as I hope you do too.

With all my love and affection, then and now,
Millicent Shawcross (Mrs)

At some point while reading this letter Cordelia has truly begun crying but shock numbs her now. He has been alive the entire time. He has been alive and he has not wanted to see her. Millicent, dear dear Millicent, trying her best for her friend and her patient. Cordelia cannot fathom what she would have done in such a situation. But it is not worth thinking about it now. No good can come of it. She cannot change what has happened. He has not wanted to see her. He has not written to her. He has been in England, the entire time. Four months at the front line and then the rest in hospitals. Until some time before Millicent's final letter.

And then where? Where did he go? And for how long? Isaac's surgery did not work. What does that mean? Was it life-saving surgery and it has not worked? Is he dead now? Did he go off to die somewhere? *I could not help but compare him to some sort of animal walking towards captivity.*

Cordelia cries his name over and over as she clutches Millicent's letters. Is he dead? He is, isn't he? She will grieve all over again for him, the way she did the first time. This is cruel. These letters, they are not helpful, waiting for her here. They are cruel. Although it is not Millicent's fault. She tried to help. But these letters now send her into a kind of despair she never thought she'd feel. Not again. This is even worse than the first time she grieved for him. There had been hope and it had been dashed. And it has happened again. Hope and then . . . nothing.

She must stay strong, she thinks, as she shakes in shock and then she goes to the cupboard and takes Tabitha's dusty bottle of whisky, spilling it over the Welsh dresser as she pours some into a glass and then drinks it stiffly before carrying out the procedure all over again. She leans against the dresser, the crockery shaking noisily behind her as she slumps against it and sips her second drink slowly.

Cordelia wishes these letters had never been here, waiting for her return. But the more she thinks about it the more confused she grows. And now she has even less idea what to do than ever before. Cordelia climbs the stairs, opens the door to William's room and looks at her sleeping son, so peaceful, so blissfully unaware of the fate of his father. But what was Isaac's fate? Cordelia doesn't know. She has been handed the opportunity to find out and so she has to, doesn't she? She has to find out, even if it's too late. Even if he has died. Isaac's surgery did not work.

She stifles fresh tears. But now she has to know.

CHAPTER 53

Three days later, Cordelia and William walk hand in hand through the mix of Georgian and Victorian architecture of Tunbridge Wells. The town is beautiful with its mix of tall, elegant white buildings and makes Cordelia realise that for all the beauty of Cornwall and the hedonistic pleasures of London (not that she lives that life anymore, thankfully), she really hasn't seen enough of her own country.

She wonders how Tunbridge Wells has fared throughout the war. How has Millicent faired since her arrival here to this genteel part of Kent? From such horrors on the Western Front, nursing and patching up wounded soldiers, to moving back to England to a hospital caring for men with severe injuries . . . Cordelia is grateful the fates have seen fit to make Millicent happy, married to someone she fell in love with and who loved her enough in return to wait for her while she nursed the sick rather than marry. Millicent, good, beautiful Millicent, who deserved everything she'd ever wanted, and more. *If nothing good comes of today, if all my hopes for Isaac are ruined,* Cordelia thinks, *then I had William, Edwin is alive and dear Millicent is married.*

At the end of a long row of tall terraces, Cordelia looks at the numbers to make sure she has the right one, walks along the black and white tiled pathway and climbs the front step, pulling on the bell cord.

Cordelia gives William an encouraging look as she holds his hand. She's still not sure if she should have brought her son or not. But she cannot be parted from him on this quest to find out the fate of his father. She cannot.

'Can I help you?' a young maid asks when the door is opened.

Cordelia stands on the doorstep and holds her carpet bag in one hand and William's hand in the other.

'Yes, I wonder if Mrs Millicent Shawcross is at home?'

'Who may I ask is visiting?' The young woman looks at William who smiles, and then looks at Cordelia.

'Mrs Cordelia Leigh.' She has long resigned herself to this name. The explanation of a child without being Mrs Leigh has never been worth the risk.

'Please wait here a moment.'

Behind the maid, Cordelia hears the loud bang of a door as it slams back against a wall, having been yanked open so quickly. And then Millicent appears, at speed, in the corridor and looks towards her in shock.

'I thought I heard your voice. It's really you.'

'Yes,' Cordelia says and she cannot help it when tears form in her eyes.

The housemaid makes herself scarce and Millicent runs towards her friend, embracing her tightly on the doorstep.

Then Millicent steps back, her hands on her friend's shoulders, holding her, examining her. She smiles as happy tears form in her eyes.

'I'm so sorry it took me so long,' Cordelia says at the same time Millicent announces, 'Well, it's about time.'

Millicent pours tea and glances at William as he eats a cake.

'Is that nice?' she says. 'Would your mummy let you have another, do you think?'

William looks at Cordelia hopefully, his little face covered in cake crumbs.

'Just one more,' Cordelia says. 'There are not enough sweet things in the world for William.'

'Perhaps you'd like to wrap it in a napkin and take it to the garden to play?' Millicent suggests.

William nods and Millicent rings for her maid and instructs her to show William where the cricket things are kept. 'Will you keep him busy for a few moments? We'll join you shortly.'

On the sideboard are pictures of Millicent and Samuel Shawcross on their wedding day and a small photograph of a baby. 'Yours?' Cordelia asks, standing to look.

'Yes,' Millicent confirms proudly. 'Jeremy. He's asleep upstairs with Nanny.'

'Oh Millicent, congratulations.'

'Thank you,' she says, blushing. 'I would have invited you to the christening only I didn't know where you were or what had happened to you. No one did. Father says your parents have been worried sick. They went to Hawkshead, you know, to look for you.'

'I didn't know that,' Cordelia replies.

'I didn't know it until recently either,' Millicent says.

'If I'd known you'd gone away from Hawkshead I'd have stopped writing to you there too.'

'I've written to my parents now everything has worked itself out,' Cordelia says. 'But I had to give myself some space in order to understand what was best. I kept thinking, it'll be all right soon. I'll contact them soon and it'll all be all right. But in the end . . . I had so many complicated reasons to stay away.'

Millicent looks thoughtful and then asks, 'How old is he?' She nods her head in the direction of the door through which William has just departed.

Clever Millicent knows William is the reason I cut family ties, Cordelia thinks and then replies, 'Four.'

'When was he born?' Millicent asks with a sad smile.

'April 1915.'

Millicent works back in her mind, eyes narrowed, counting back on her fingers. She nods slowly. 'Oh Cordelia, you poor poor thing.' She rushes to her friend and holds her in an embrace, which Cordelia returns heartily.

'Not really,' Cordelia says. 'Maybe then, but not now. I thought everything was as it should be and then I returned to the cottage for the first time in so long and I found all your letters waiting for me.'

'Oh gosh,' Millicent says. 'Is that what happened? You didn't get them? I wondered every single day if you'd write back and then when you didn't, I had no idea if you'd ignored them or if you genuinely hadn't received them.'

And with that Cordelia has no choice but to explain to Millicent where she has been and why.

'But the empty cottage in the Lakes was yours the whole time you were away?'

Cordelia nods. 'I just had to wait to find out.'

'Waiting,' Millicent ponders aloud. Then she says with a long sigh, 'I feel that I have spent the last few years simply waiting. Waiting to be able to be a nurse and then once I was one, waiting to be able to marry.'

'Do you think,' Cordelia says thoughtfully as they move to the settee, 'that there is a single woman in England who hasn't spent the last few years simply waiting?'

'Probably not,' Millicent laughs. 'It sounds as if you've spent time waiting to see if your son could stay with you, waiting to feel truly safe, waiting for a proper home with him?'

'Yes,' Cordelia says thoughtfully. 'Yes, I think I was. I didn't know it though. I spent a lot of that time petrified about being discovered, Tabitha's parents taking him from me and me having to explain in a courtroom how I had given birth to him while being unmarried, in order to keep him. I was petrified I would shame myself and they'd take him from me anyway. I was so worried what people would say, what my mother would say, worried that I'd be disowned, which I probably will now I've written to them to tell them. Because I have told them. And I'm not ashamed of William. He's everything to me. I would never give him up.'

Millicent smiles and holds her friend's hand. 'Besides,' she says, 'you are Mrs Leigh, remember.'

'Yes. But not really.'

'No one needs to know that.'

'No, I know,' Cordelia says sadly.

'Now you just need to know what's happened to his father,' Millicent replies.

'Yes,' Cordelia replies, her gaze meeting Millicent's.

'He doesn't look at all like you,' Millicent says softly, which makes Cordelia smile.

'That's because he's a tiny replica of Isaac,' Cordelia says wistfully, proudly. Because she is proud of her son.

The room falls silent. She doesn't know how to ask this next question. But she just has to ask it. 'Millicent, do you think he's dead?'

'I don't know,' she says.

'You said his surgery hadn't worked.'

'No, it hadn't. I'm so sorry.'

'What happened? You were quite vague in your letter.'

'I was *purposefully* vague in my letter. I didn't want to shock you in my first letter and then of course you didn't write back and it didn't feel right to lay it all out for you to read after that. I thought it would discourage you further rather than encourage you.'

'I don't think anything you could say would have stopped me from coming to see him, if I'd have known.' She pauses. 'He was shot, wasn't he?'

'Yes,' Millicent replies. 'Or rather, no. He was hit by shrapnel. In the head.'

'Oh God.' Cordelia puts her hand to her mouth.

'He wasn't wearing his helmet. He'd been doing something to the side of the trenches. I'm not sure what. It was on Christmas Day or rather it was on the first few moments of 26th December. There had been some sort of truce along some sections of the line.'

'I'd read about it,' Cordelia says faintly from behind her hand.

'Well, their section had laid down their weapons, played football, shared food, buried their dead.'

Hateful tears enter Cordelia's eyes as she thinks of Isaac doing all of this.

'Some sections continued their truce for days, refusing to shoot each other until aerial bombardment put a stop to it days later. But Isaac and Edwin's battalion was subject to a sniper attack. From what I have ascertained from Isaac himself, it was perhaps just one sniper who disagreed with having held the truce in the first place. Something about a bullet ricocheting rather than a direct shot. But who knows if that is the truth or not. The facts are more garbled and diluted the longer after the event takes place. I don't suppose it really matters who or why or how now. The fact is it happened and Isaac received a terrible head injury.'

Cordelia can't think. 'I don't know what I expected but it wasn't that.'

'I'm so sorry to be the one to tell you this.'

'I'd rather you than anyone else if I'm honest. Do you know,' Cordelia says quietly after a moment, 'I saw him. In the grounds of Pencallick House. I saw him, in his uniform, walking towards me. Boxing Day morning. And then he was gone. But he wasn't there. Not really. I knew it at the time. I just didn't know what it meant.'

'He might have been there,' Millicent replies comfortingly. 'But not in the way you think. He was being taken down the line by stretcher bearers presumably.'

He'd been there. Cordelia had seen him. She'd thought at the time he was really there and then when she came to understand that he hadn't been, she'd assumed it was because he'd come to say goodbye. Perhaps that's exactly what he had been doing.

'Instead of finding his way to me, he found his way to you,' Cordelia thinks aloud.

'Eventually, yes. I can't even remember what I wrote in that letter to you now, I scribbled it so hastily. It wasn't working – the surgery, I mean. He didn't want to go through it anymore.'

'Do you think he was right to refuse any more surgery?'

Millicent takes a deep breath. 'Yes, I think he probably was. The shrapnel had almost all been removed and what remained . . . I don't think it would have made a difference.'

'A difference? Will it kill him? Has it killed him?'

'Cordelia. I honestly don't know. I felt sorry for so many of those men. If it wasn't shock and issues with their faculties, then it was severe physical injury instead. Those that were in such heavy shock couldn't talk and those that could talk . . . wouldn't. And then finding a way after all of it to carry on living . . . I can't imagine how so many have just gone back to their lives.'

Cordelia thinks of Joseph Grey, how his hands shake when he holds the newspaper, how he puts them in his lap until he's finished so no one can see, how he drops his knife when he cuts his food, how his writing judders when he holds a pen. What he must think about when he goes to sleep, what he tries not to think about when he goes to work. 'I don't think they ever just return to normal.'

'And then of course,' Millicent continues, 'you can be like Isaac. You can walk and talk, you can think and have all your limbs but other things are taken away, senses are removed. I'm not sure what's more cruel.'

'Senses?' Cordelia questions. 'What do you mean, senses?'

'Isaac can't see,' Millicent says in surprise. 'I thought you understood that.'

'What? He can't see? Why would I understand that?'

'Because St Dunstan's is a hospital for the blind,' Millicent replies. 'I thought everyone knew that. It's famous.'

Cordelia stiffens on the settee, her mouth drops open.

'It's why I had to offer to write letters for him,' Millicent continues. 'Why the surgery to remove shrapnel, while giving him a bit less pain in the long run, was never really going to reverse the process – never really going to work. I thought you understood what I was saying this whole time.'

'No,' Cordelia protests. 'I didn't understand that at all.'

'He's blind.' Millicent confirms to a startled Cordelia. 'When he left St Dunstan's Hospital . . . oh Cordelia, he is completely blind.'

CHAPTER 54

Cordelia watches William playing cricket in the garden with Millicent's husband, in a daze. Millicent's husband waves and encourages William to down tools while they wander over. Cordelia notices his limp immediately.

'Hello,' he says warmly, his sandy hair falling down as he attempts to smooth it. 'I just popped back for a sandwich before I head back to work. The door was closed and I could hear voices. I didn't like to disturb.'

'Samuel, this is my old friend Cordelia.'

'Hello,' he says again, holding out his hand to shake. 'Pleasure to meet you. I've heard lovely things.'

'Likewise.'

'Your son is a fine young cricketer,' Samuel says.

William beams with delight at the compliment as behind them Nanny emerges from the house, carrying baby Jeremy, awake and crying for both affection and milk.

While the baby feeds from a bottle and Samuel goes inside to eat his lunch, they settle themselves in the garden. Cordelia touches her friend's hand. 'You have made a beautiful family.'

'Thank you,' Millicent says. 'I am happy. I only hope you can be too. What will you do?'

'I'm going to try to find him,' Cordelia says. 'As if I could do anything else? If he doesn't want me then I will understand. Maybe. But he needs to know he has a son. He needs to know he's a father. He needs to know I still love him. I can understand why he didn't want to meet with me, or tell me he was alive. Just about. But I have to go to him.'

'I'm glad you said that,' Millicent says as the baby sucks on the bottle noisily.

'How do I find him? Will the hospital give me his address – do they have it still do you think? It's been so long.'

'Yes they will have it. But they might not give it to you.'

Cordelia groans at another hurdle and looks to the skies.

'Which is why I took his file and copied it down after he left,' Millicent says proudly.

Cordelia looks at her friend in awe. 'You stole it?'

'Of course I did,' she says. 'Despite the fact you weren't returning my letters, I did rather hope this day might come. Eventually. I didn't think it would take quite this long though.'

'Oh Millicent. You are marvellous.'

'I know,' she sighs showily as Nanny comes over to take the baby. Then Millicent goes inside to fetch the address.

'Cordelia, please bear in mind he might not be there,' she says on her return. 'Bear in mind this address might be a total fabrication. He did rather look the sort to lie about his whereabouts in the end. Stubborn. Just wanted to be gone. He'd had enough of doctors prodding and poking him.'

'I'll try not to get my hopes up.' But her hopes have already risen. She can't help it.

'I regret it now, not telling him about you,' Millicent says. 'That day he walked out of the hospital, pushing the stick out in front of him as he tried to find the motorcar, refusing help from the porters . . . I wish now I'd run to him, told him, encouraged him to find you. I'll always regret not doing it.'

Cordelia holds out her hand and clasps Millicent's. 'Don't regret it. It sounds as if he's a different man now and I don't think there was anything more you could have done to bring us together.'

CHAPTER 55

Cordelia and William accept the invitation to stay overnight with Millicent and Samuel and set off early the next morning. By the time they enter the village of Fen Byron in Cambridgeshire the day is growing late, the sun threatening to set, casting an orange halo across the fens. The village is idyllic, the shop, the pub, the Tudor buildings and the church. They walk past it all, drawing interested glances from the few passers-by they meet. She's had to stop and ask for directions from the railway station more than once.

At the end of the lane on the far side of the village she finds what she's looking for. The house Isaac described to her is here. The house he grew up in, until his parents died and his uncle sent he and David to school. Isaac had last told her it had been let to tenants, that he'd like to move back here one day in his retirement and work in his own garden. But this is the address listed as his residence, the address Millicent copied from his patient record.

The Georgian house sits far removed from all the others but in front is a low wall, within which is housed a verdant, lush front garden with rose bushes not yet in bloom and a magnolia, the branches from which birds sing as if they haven't a care in the world.

It is peaceful here. She hopes if he is here, that he has at last found some peace.

The front door is already propped open with a doorstop and from within, someone whistles. A woman. Another thought strikes Cordelia now; one she hadn't previously considered. What if Isaac has met someone else since, has come to rely on them, need them, is *in love* with them? But she forces this thought away as William's hand squeezes hers for attention. He whispers up to her, 'Are we allowed to be here?'

Although she had taken him with her to Millicent's, here, in Cambridgeshire, today it feels different. She pauses, feeling her confidence leave her. She hasn't been clear with William why they are here. She has been awake all night once again, wondering how much damage it would do to the little boy to tell him they are seeking his father, only to find he may have passed away from his injuries in the intervening years. She doesn't know if she is braced for this eventuality. But she has to consider it. Not to consider it would be obtuse, setting her and William up for the most awful and painful fall.

Either way, she just has to know. She has to hope for the best but must be prepared that the worst has already happened.

Cordelia knocks on the large open door but no one comes. The whistling moves further away and Cordelia looks into the entrance hall, pushing the door wide open gently to reveal a long corridor that stretches towards a scullery style kitchen at the back. A kitchen door at the back is open onto a garden she can't quite see and without realising it Cordelia has entered the front door and is crossing the entrance hall.

William's hand is still in hers and they move through the house looking for the woman whistling. Is this Isaac's wife? Has he married? Is it a housemaid? A nurse? Is this even Isaac's house still? Her heart races and she exhales, inhales, exhales, inhales until she follows the sound into the garden.

The woman is in a housemaid's uniform, whistling merrily as if she hasn't a care in the world, pegging laundry onto a long washing line, her back to Cordelia and William.

Cordelia wants to speak, wants to ask this woman who she works for here. Wants to say Isaac's name, to find out if he still lives here, to find out if he still lives at all.

But she can't speak. Now she is here, after all this time, she dare not hope. Around her the garden is quiet, only the breeze gently ruffling the leaves of the sycamore trees towards the end of the long garden. Has Isaac done all of this? Has he encouraged this garden to flourish? She has to know. But the woman has turned around and is facing her.

'Can I help you?' she asks, an expression on her face of shock that someone has entered the house, entered the garden without announcing themselves.

'We did knock,' Cordelia immediately defends herself, although she knows she shouldn't have walked through the house so brazenly. But her feet guided her through, guided her here. 'My name is Cordelia . . .' She pauses. She does not give her real name, does not give the one she's been using. She's torn in two directions.

'I'm looking for Isaac Leigh,' Cordelia dares. *Please God, let him be here, let him still live here, let him still live.*

'I'm afraid he is not at home at the moment.'

So he is here. He is alive and he is here. Cordelia could weep with relief but she gasps with happiness, making William smile up at his mother – sharing in her joy – although he's obviously not quite sure why this is a happy occasion.

'Do you know how long he might be?' she says. 'I need to see him. It's been a very long time.'

'Is he expecting you?' the maid asks, giving her an uncertain smile.

'No. I don't think he is.'

'Well . . . if you'd like to wait for him there's a table in the shade over there,' she says pointing to the long garden where the end gives way to trees dotted around. 'He's gone for a walk down to the lake. I don't imagine he'll be too long.'

He is here. Isaac is here. And he can take himself off for a walk unaided. There is hope here. There is so much hope here.

'I've a freshly made jug of lemon barley water and some teacakes. Would you like some?' the maid asks them.

'Yes please,' William says immediately.

'William, you're going to explode if you eat any more today,' Cordelia says half-heartedly, her eyes on the tree line for any sight of Isaac. *My God, he's here. The man I love is here*, she thinks.

The maid walks inside the house to the kitchen and then returns with the tray of teacakes, lemon barley water and two glasses, placing them on the table to which

Cordelia and William have been invited to sit. On the table there is various writing paper and pencils with a glass weight on them to hold them down. And a contraption Cordelia has never seen before, that looks handmade. It is a wooden board with strings that run horizontally into which paper can be inserted. Does Isaac use this to write, the strings guiding him to write neatly?

While the maid pours, Cordelia looks around the spring garden. Bright yellow daffodils and tiny purple muscari sit together in a cornucopia of colour, while narcissus and tulips vie for attention and bluebells have grown in the grasses beyond. The garden is beautiful, wild. There is not a hint of formal landscaping. Instead if feels . . . pure, as if flowers just grew by accident. She doesn't know where to look first.

'Does he do all this?' she asks in awe.

'The garden?' the maid asks, puzzled.

'Yes. Does he tend to it?'

'No. There's a gardener comes once a week. Bit of a job to keep up with the weeds. I help a bit. No idea about plants and the like but I know a weed.' The garden stretches on and on, past rows of trees from what Cordelia can tell.

Cordelia's eyes never leave that space. 'I didn't even know what a weed was when I started out.'

She thinks of Gilbert educating her, and Isaac, his shirt sleeves rolled up, spade in hand. The day he taught her about roses, that last day in the fountain together as they planned their final meeting in his cottage, the urgency of it, the end of it.

'Is he married or engaged?' Cordelia asks quietly. She can't wait any longer. If he's either of those things she has to leave. She has to leave now.

'No.' The puzzled look turns to sympathy. 'He keeps himself to himself. A daily walk down there to the lake and that's it, really.'

Cordelia nods, glancing in the direction the maid has pointed, towards the end of the long garden. If there is a pond or lake past that she cannot see it.

'It's only small, Fen Byron lake,' the maid continues. Then she pauses as she looks at William, properly. William who looks so much like his father.

The maid's mouth forms an 'O' shape as she pieces it all together. She looks at Cordelia with a curious expression. 'He won't be too long, I'm sure,' she says turning back towards the laundry line. If Isaac is going to be a while Cordelia will go and help the maid peg the laundry out. There appears to be only the maid here and it will give Cordelia something to do, a task to focus on, to calm her nerves.

William eats his teacake and grins at his mother, simply happy to sit and wait for 'Mummy's old friend' to return.

'You're such a good boy,' Cordelia says to her son. 'I'm so very lucky.'

'Me too,' he says, smiling at her as he reaches for his barley water with both hands, spilling a little onto the stack of envelopes.

'Oh,' Cordelia leaps up, grabbing them and wiping them with one of the linen napkins that the maid has brought.

'I'm sorry, Mummy, I didn't mean to. It was an accident.'

'I know, it's all right. Don't worry.'

'Do you think your friend will be angry?'

She remembers Isaac's easy-going manner, that smile,

those eyes. It hurts. It hurts to think of him, knowing he's going to reject her. She can already feel it coming.

'No, I don't think he'll be angry.' And then she glances at the address on the envelope properly.

Miss Cordelia Carr-Lyon,

Pencallick House, Pencallick, Bodmin, Cornwall.

She stares at it as if it can't be real. She stares at it for too long. Has he just written this? She glances at the tree line. Still no sign of him. And then she rips open the letter. As she tears the envelope open she glances down at the one directly underneath; it's addressed to a solicitor in Cambridge.

She stares at the letter in her hand, attempting to control the trembling. Her mouth is dry as she reads the words, shaky and uneven.

Cordelia,

There is so much I want to say and I think I have left it too long. There was so much I wanted to tell you before I left. And so much I wanted to tell you in my letters home though I didn't want you to share in the things I saw, the things I did. And there was so much I wanted to tell you when I came home on leave. But it never happened.

And now I am in danger of pouring everything out to you here. But this is the only time I will do it, so give a man you used to love five minutes of your time in reading this and then never think of him again.

I don't know how to tell you what has happened to me. I was stupid. It was my fault. I did the very thing I told the men not to do. I stood up to my full height. A momentary lapse of concentration.

A simple thing that has ended everything for me. But it did not need to end everything for you. That is the decision I took on your behalf. And now, I stand by this and hope you have gone on to love and be loved in return by someone worthy of you – a man who is not useless, a man who will not be a burden to you when he used to be so able, a man who can look after you the way you deserve to be looked after, who can be with you in every way possible. Not this shell of a man.

I think of you so often, I think of those last few days with you more than I should. I think of you in my arms, I think of you in the garden of Pencallick House that night I was in danger of kissing you, I think of you in the lake that first time we spoke. I think of you in order to remember, in order to comfort, in order to survive. But I think it's simply driving me to madness. I have been driven to madness by thoughts of you. Because each morning, when the night has passed, the darkness still remains.

I hope you can forgive me. I often wondered, over the years, if I listened hard enough if I'd hear you approach one day and if my resolve would crumble. Because I was resolved, my darling Cordelia. I was resolved not to come home to you when I'd realised the damage to my eyes was permanent. I lived in such false hope for so long. And although I wanted so desperately to know you were near, I am glad you did not come to me. I'm glad, all this time later that you did not find me in a hospital, did not stand over me quietly while I slept and saw the bandages around my eyes, my head. I don't think I could have coped with knowing you had been and left, or knowing you had been and stayed. I am glad you did not come.

In the hospital a kindly nurse asked me if I had a sweetheart and despite there being you, I said, 'no.' I think I had decided already to spare you. It may not have mattered to you how I am now. I will never know. But it matters to me.

I am not the man you once loved. I am not the man you once knew. I do not know if I have made peace with that. But let me tell you this, I love you now as I loved you then. And it kills me. It kills me in a way that sniper never did and I cannot go on like this. I know that now.

I am going to close this self-indulgent ramble now and tell you goodbye. I should have said goodbye to you years ago. Perhaps you had already left. Only now I need to leave also.

I know you will forgive me. I did not want to leave without having said goodbye, without having told you how much I loved you, one final time. I hope you know.

I hope you will forgive me for any pain I have caused you.

It means everything to me that you do.

Isaac.

It is as if her heart has stopped, her mind has stopped and she is uncertain what all of this means. She looks at her son who has climbed down from the table and is making daisy chains on the grass and then she looks back at the letter.

He is letting her go; after all this time he is letting her go. But what does this mean: I cannot go on like this . . . I could not leave without having said goodbye. Leave where? Where is he going?

Isaac can explain himself when he is back from his walk and she will tell him she loves him and that she's never stopped. She will introduce William to him and he will know her secret and they can be together, finally.

And then it's as if a veil has lifted – and she knows.

She knows what it means but she cannot bring herself to believe it. She won't believe it.

'Isaac,' she whispers and then she drops the sheet of paper to the ground as she understands what his goodbye means. She looks towards the end of the garden where it disappears out of sight behind the sycamore trees, towards the lake. And then she knows. He is not coming back.

'How long has he been gone?' Cordelia asks, walking without realising she's doing so.

'Perhaps since a few minutes before you arrived?' the maid says. 'Would you like some more barley water?'

'No. Thank you. Will you keep an eye on William? I'm just going to . . .' but she does not finish. She is already running.

CHAPTER 56

ISAAC

He stands at the edge of the lake, feeling the water lap around his shoes. He bends down, trying to maintain his balance as he takes each shoe off, removes each sock and lets the water flow gently over his feet. He inches in slowly, shivering from the cold. He stood for a while first to check he can't hear anyone in the water. It wouldn't do to kill oneself while there are day-trippers picnicking or swimming.

His cane is behind him. He let go of it some way back, heard it clatter to the ground, discarded when he felt the gravel change underfoot, when he knew he was within reach of the water and there were no more logs or rocks to stumble across. He is here. He has reached the water's edge.

Is this cowardice or something else entirely? He doesn't need to know. He is past needing to know. He only knows this is what he is going to do. He has been thinking of it for weeks, trying to find something to live for; wishing each morning he woke up that his vision had returned, wishing each morning he woke up that he hadn't.

But this morning he awoke and knew the only way to escape it all was to bring about his own escape. He wonders if placing rocks in his pocket might be best in order to aid his escape. He's heard people do that kind of thing. But he needs no encouragement to sink. The things he's seen. Ironic really, considering he'll never see again.

He remembers back to the way it started with her, Cordelia. As she ran towards the water, entering it so readily.

He too is about to do the same now. This is how it's supposed to be.

It is fitting that it will all end the way it began.

'I'm sorry,' he says as he walks into the water. If it is cold he cannot feel it. He can't feel anything anymore.

CHAPTER 57

CORDELIA

The water ripples as she reaches it, as if there has recently been movement here. She has already run past a walking stick, shoes, socks scattered as if they'd never be needed again. If he has gone under that is the only trace of him.

She is determined. She has not come this far to have him die. She has lost him once already. She will not do it again. She pulls off her shoes and hat and throws them behind her and then runs into the cold water until it is waist height. Then she lifts her feet and dives under.

Seconds pass. She does not know how many and she surfaces for air. Despair fills her mind and tears cover her face along with the fresh water in which she swims. Cordelia goes under again. And again. And again and then through the depths she sees him, perfectly still as if he were a moment captured in time.

She reaches out and pulls him, drags him towards her and when she resurfaces she turns his body over, his dark hair made even darker by the water and covering his eyes.

'Isaac?' she cries when she has managed to drag him to the water's edge. She can't pull him any further and water laps around them both. All her strength has failed her now. She shakes him. Her hair covers her face and she screams in frustration, pulling her hair back. 'Isaac!'

No. No. Please, no.

'Isaac!' she screams.

But there is nothing. He has been under for so long. He's dead. She stares at him. 'Please Isaac,' she says desperately. 'Please.' She doesn't know what to do now. She's come this far and he has left her.

Her mind races back five years, back to how they found each other, because although this is the end, every end must have a beginning. *'What would you have done if Clive had drowned? Or I?'*

'I'd have tried to save you.'

'How?' she'd asked.

'It was in a newspaper a few years ago. An advertisement for a contraption that covers your nose and mouth, pumps air into the lungs. A Pulmotor, although I'm not sure who would ever purchase such a thing . . .'

'Do you have one?'

'No.'

'Well then,' she'd said.'It's rather the end, isn't it?'

'I was going to go on to say . . . I suppose you just do the same thing, cover the nose and breathe into the mouth.'

'Yes, I suppose you could.'

She doesn't know if it's too late. She doesn't even know if what she's about to do will work but she has nothing left. She has found him. After five years she is here, and so is he. And back at the house, so is their son.

Cordelia moves quickly, scrambling up, kneels over him, holds his nose, puts her mouth on his.

And breathes.

CHAPTER 58

CORDELIA
ROSE COTTAGE, THE LAKE DISTRICT
TWO YEARS LATER
1921

The baby is in Isaac's arms as he sits up in bed next to Cordelia. A girl. Tabitha Mary named after a friend who gave so much, and after Isaac's mother. She is four weeks old and just as fierce as her namesake, wailing for milk at every given opportunity. Isaac's knuckle is in her mouth, buying Cordelia some time.

'Are you ready and pretending not to be so as to have a little rest?' he asks playfully. 'You've earned it, you know. I can get Daisy to fix a bottle?' He starts to move.

'No, I'm ready,' she says exhaustedly for what must be the tenth time today. Isaac withdraws his knuckle from baby Tabitha's mouth and carefully passes Cordelia their baby. 'I thought William was a hungry child but this is ridiculous,' she says.

'Is my knuckle red?' He lifts it to show her. 'It feels red?' he asks when the baby is settled.

Cordelia kisses him unexpectedly, whispers, 'Yes,' and when the baby is steadfastly suckling, she takes his hand and puts it to Tabitha's face so he can feel her feeding. He runs his hand down the baby's soft chin and to her neck and feels her swallowing. He smiles, feeling his baby's drinking motion.

'Oh,' he says in wonder. 'You clever thing, you.'

'Which of us are you talking to?' Cordelia asks.

His smile is still bright, his hand still on Tabitha. 'Both of you.'

'Daddy?' A six-year-old William knocks on the open bedroom door.

'Yes.' Isaac holds out his arms and William climbs in next to him, shuffling into a gap.

'If I read you my geography work will you tell me if I've got it wrong? It's about water erosion.'

'Of course,' he says.

Cordelia listens as William reads about soil and rocks, watches Isaac as his brow furrows, nodding seriously, listening intently to every word. And she glances down at their daughter, sucking furiously, her eyes closed in a state of bliss.

Isaac too closes his eyes as he listens. They are paler than they used to be. It has been two years since that day at the lake and his eyesight has not returned, will never return. But he has accepted it now and lives completely and fully, helping with the animals in the smallholding, declaring them easier than gardening when a man cannot see. 'Animals, unlike plants, are very vocal in telling you what they want.' The hens especially love him and gather around him as he's in charge of freeing them from the hen house every morning. (They loathe Cordelia as it's her job to round them up and pen them each evening.)

Clive visits in his school holidays and enjoys helping with the pigs. Mother and Father wrote in pure desperate happiness, on immediate receipt of Cordelia's letter, relieved that their only daughter was actually still alive. Any concerns about William's birth were replaced with adoration and love when they saw their first grandchild and discovered Cordelia and Isaac had married in the interim. They spoil William and baby Tabitha rotten. A continual stream of toys, books and toffees are forever arriving in the post from Cornwall.

And Edwin is due to visit soon with his wife, a Scottish nurse who asked Edwin for directions on a railway platform, both of them getting on the wrong train together, and falling for him far too much to return home after her training.

Cordelia is surrounded by love and endeavours to give as much love out in return as possible. If Isaac ever catches himself in a still, thoughtful moment it is rare and wanted, because he is too tired – after playing with William after school or being woken by baby Tabitha – to do anything else.

They have spoken just once about the day he tried to leave this world. When he woke and expelled water from his lungs, coughing and coughing and begging for forgiveness, they held each other and cried. She told him everything by the water's edge. And when they stopped crying and shivering, they picked up his discarded shoes, socks and stick and returned to the house, and to their son, holding each other and not letting go.

Standing in the spring sunshine, their clothes wet, Isaac answered William's question as to why they were soaked. 'Because I've been for a swim and forgot to take my clothes off first.'

'That was silly,' William laughed and Isaac managed a low chuckle. 'Yes it was rather, wasn't it?'

Isaac squeezed Cordelia's hand tightly and then reached out to feel his son's face. 'But everything's all right now. Because your mother has rescued me. And so have you.'

And later, that first night, after Isaac told William a bedtime story with funny voices and knights and dragons and tucked his son in for the first time, he came down the stairs, felt his way along the corridor and entered the sitting room.

Cordelia didn't re-read the letter he'd written her that day. There was no need. It was immaterial and she tore it into tiny pieces and watched as the fragments of Isaac's despair burned to dust in the fire, replaced now with love and joy.

'Cordelia?' he asked, checking where she was, as she watched the final pieces char, disappearing into the flames.

'I'm here,' she said, walking towards him, taking his hands in hers.

'I thought I had nothing to live for and now I know I have everything,' he said in a choked voice. 'I promise faithfully that it will never ever happen again.'

Then he held on to her hands, got down on one knee and proposed.

And now, as their noisy children surround them in the beauty of Rose Cottage, she is here and so is he – exactly where they are supposed to be.

ACKNOWLEDGEMENTS

Firstly, thanks to my brilliant editor Cara Chimirri who always knows the right way to tweak a novel and offers brilliant suggestions with huge levels of enthusiasm and always with a bright smile on her face. Cara, you are such a pleasure to work with. And to all at Avon involved in design, sales, marketing, copy editing. Thank you all!

Mega thanks to the mega agent that is Becky Ritchie: the first line of defence for all the ideas that may or may not eventually become novels! Thanks for talking me up, talking me down (from the ledge) and for everything else in between.

Becky's ace foreign rights team at A.M. Heath deserve huge thanks as they continue to sell my books around the world. I cannot tell you the joy I get from an email from Tabatha, Prema or Alexandra. You are all goddesses. Likewise, massive recognition to the marvellous Jack Sargeant who holds my hand over all issues relating to foreign rights admin. Jack, you make tax forms just that little bit more bearable.

To the man of my dreams, Steve. Thank you for everything, always. And to Emily, Alice, Mum, Dad,

Luke, Cassie, Natalie, Sarah and Nicky. The love and support is very much noticed.

Thanks to the Write Clubbers. Monthly meets for cake and critique is the best.

And to you, lovely reader, thank you for buying *The Hidden Letters*, or borrowing it from your library. Nothing means as much to me in this wacky process as when I get an email from a reader sharing their own family history stories or telling me you've enjoyed one of my books on holiday, at home, on the commute . . . So get in touch and say hi and share your own family history! I love it and will always reply. Likewise, if you have a moment to leave a review on Amazon or Goodreads (or both!) it makes my day and helps readers find new books to read.

Join me on social media where I share pics and musings about forgotten history, books I think you might like, cakes I've baked badly and wine I've drunk well. And sign up to my newsletter via my website to win books and stay informed about what's coming next from me.

Lorna xx

http://www.lornacookauthor.com
www.lornacookauthor.com
/LornaCookWriter
/LornaCookAuthor
/LornaCookAuthor

FURTHER READING

Last Post: The Final Word From our First World War Soldiers
Max Arthur, Weidenfeld & Nicolson, 2005

Harry's War: The Great War Diary of Harry Drinkwater
Edited by Jon Cooksey and David Griffiths, Ebury Press, 2013

Letters from a Lost Generation: First World War Letters of Vera Brittain and Four Friends
Edited by Alan Bishop and Mark Bostridge, Virago Press, 2008

Staring at God: Britain in the Great War
Simon Heffer, Random House, 2019

The Edwardian Country House
Juliet Gardiner, Channel 4 Books, 2002

Royal Horticultural Society Gardening through the Year
Ian Spence, DK, 2018

Edwardian Fashion
Daniel Milford-Cottam, Shire Publications, 2014

London Society Fashion 1905–1925: The Wardrobe of Heather Firbank
V&A Publishing, 2014

The Fateful Year, England 1914
Mark Bostridge, Viking, 2014

Cornwall in the First World War
Pete London, Truran, 2013

Cornwall's Fallen: The Road to the Somme
Nick Thornicroft, The History Press, 2008

Cornwall and the Great War
Edited by Garry Tregida and Thomas Fidler, ICS Associates, 2018

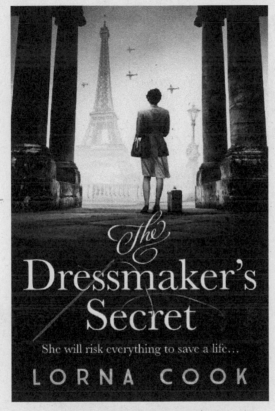

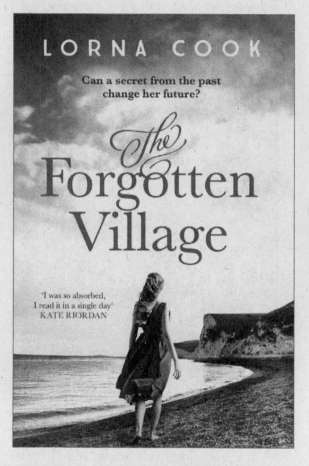

Can one promise change the fate
of two women decades apart?

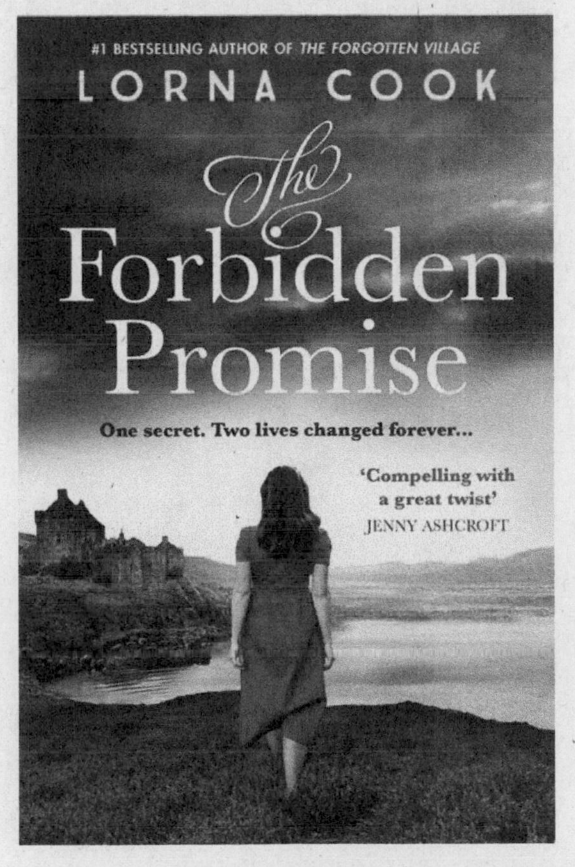

A sweeping wartime tale of love and secrets that
will have you hooked from the very first page.

Available now.

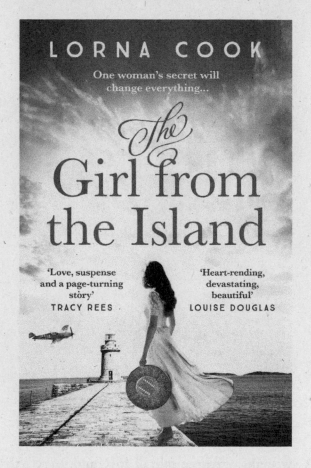